Dark Voyage
of the
MITTIE STEPHENS

*Also by Johnny D. Boggs
in Large Print:*

The Lonesome Chisholm Trail
Once They Wore the Gray
Law of the Land
The Big Fifty
Spark on the Prairie:
    The Trial of the Kiowa Chiefs

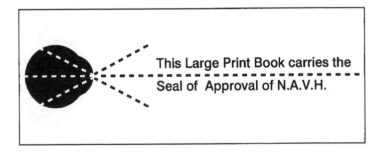

This Large Print Book carries the
Seal of Approval of N.A.V.H.

Dark Voyage
of the
MITTIE STEPHENS

A Western Story

JOHNNY D. BOGGS

Thorndike Press • Waterville, Maine

Published in 2005 by arrangement with
Golden West Literary Agency.

Thorndike Press® Large Print Western.

The tree indicium is a trademark of Thorndike Press.

The text of this Large Print edition is unabridged.
Other aspects of the book may vary from the original edition.

Set in 16 pt. Plantin by Liana M. Walker.

Printed in the United States on permanent paper.

Library of Congress Cataloging-in-Publication Data

Boggs, Johnny D.
    Dark voyage of the Mittie Stephens : a western story /
    by Johnny D. Boggs.
       p. cm. — (Thorndike Press large print western)
    ISBN 0-7862-7805-6 (lg. print : hc : alk. paper)
       1. Caddo Lake (La. and Tex.) — Fiction.
  2. Steamboat disasters — Fiction. 3. Steamboats — Fiction.
  4. Gamblers — Fiction. 5. Amnesia — Fiction.
  6. Large type books. I. Title. II. Thorndike Press large
  print Western series.
  PS3552.O4375D37 2005
  813′.54—dc22   2005009991

For two Western writers
who pointed me down the trail:
Bruce H. Thorstad and Fred Grove . . .
mentors, colleagues, pals.

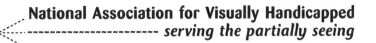

National Association for Visually Handicapped
------------------------- serving the partially seeing

As the Founder/CEO of NAVH, the only national health agency solely devoted to those who, although not totally blind, have an eye disease which could lead to serious visual impairment, I am pleased to recognize Thorndike Press★ as one of the leading publishers in the large print field.

Founded in 1954 in San Francisco to prepare large print textbooks for partially seeing children, NAVH became the pioneer and standard setting agency in the preparation of large type.

Today, those publishers who meet our standards carry the prestigious "Seal of Approval" indicating high quality large print. We are delighted that Thorndike Press is one of the publishers whose titles meet these standards. We are also pleased to recognize the significant contribution Thorndike Press is making in this important and growing field.

Lorraine H. Marchi, L.H.D.
Founder/CEO
NAVH

★ Thorndike Press encompasses the following imprints: Thorndike, Wheeler, Walker and Large Print Press.

Chapter One

Creeping clouds blanketed the bright moon like a shroud, covering the City of the Dead in darkness. The deep blackness came as an answer to Bobby Randow's prayer as he squeezed between two tombs, one granite, the other marble, and tried to catch his breath, afraid the men trying to kill him would hear his heart pounding. Gripping the butt of the Dance revolver in his right hand, Randow listened, chancing a quick glance skyward, knowing the clouds would soon pass, and the cemetery would be bathed in moonlight.

He'd die here in this century-old, above-ground graveyard, die in the midnight fog, die violently and alone, and no monument would note his passing, no newspaper would publish his obituary. No one would know he was dead, not even his mother, except his killers — and the catfish feeding on his remains after his murderers disemboweled him, filled his insides with stones, and sank his corpse into the Mississippi or Pontchartrain.

Well, it was his own fault. No one else to blame. He had tossed in his ante in a crooked game because of greed, decided to become a criminal instead of a wandering gambler, justified it with claims that the Yankees owed him plenty for four years of suffering, for the deaths of his father and brother. $100,000 in gold had lured him, but some deep-seated honesty, or the quiet Episcopal morality inherited from his father, had broken its spell, and he had tried to back out of this deal. Randow could have left New Orleans, simply slithered out of the city like a serpent, and would have been sitting in the saloon on a stern-wheeler heading upriver now, dealing draw poker, but he had decided to face his comrades, tell them why he wasn't going through with the plan. Southern pride. Texas stubborn streak. Lunacy. Whatever the reason, it had likely gotten him killed.

He had known that was coming, too. That's why he had cleaned and loaded the revolver before leaving his hotel, why he had placed six percussion caps on the Dance. Most men, scared of blowing off a toe, kept the nipple underneath a revolver's hammer naked. The memory caused him to check the pistol by feel, for the night remained black. His thumb rested on the cocked hammer, finger twitching inside the trigger guard. He had fired three rounds, put two bullets in Victor Desiderio's stomach when the shooting commenced, sent another shot chasing three other killers. Or had he pulled the trigger four times? He bit his bottom lip, tried to concentrate. His memory kept fading. He. . . .

Hushed voices. Moments later, footsteps tapped the stones lining the cemetery's path near Randow's sanctuary. Then silence.

Randow lifted the .44 and waited. The clouds cleared, and the moon, just a couple of days past full, soaked the thickening fog and cold, damp houses of the dead. He pressed his body against the granite tomb, and pushed wet bangs off his forehead. Somewhere along the way, he had lost his hat.

"There he is!" A bullet's whine followed the shout. Randow crouched, pivoted, and answered the shot, firing blindly. Two rounds left.

"There!"

"I saw it."

Too late he realized his error. They

hadn't seen him, couldn't have, until he panicked, and they spotted the muzzle flash. It had been a bluff, not even a good one if he had played his hand smart, shown a fip's worth of patience. Rifles cracked repeatedly, lead chipping the marble tomb, ricocheting off it and the granite over his head, behind him, in front of him, peppering the cramped quarters, and a fear swallowed him that he had not felt since 1862, when he had been caught in the federal enfilade at Corinth. Death had hovered near him that day, and again this night. Instinctively Randow covered his face with his arms, although only the grace of God could protect him now.

He had chosen poorly for a hiding place. The cannonade sounded like the Yankee musketry during his baptism in battle at Elkhorn Tavern, and later during the savagery of Franklin. Those Henry rifles — "Yanks load 'em on Sunday, then shoot all week." — the boys in the 9th Texas Cavalry had often joked — never let up. Bouncing bullets inched closer to him, causing his eardrums to peal, while another shrieking whine almost deafened him. Eventually the gunshots stopped, the echoes faded, but the whine continued until he recognized the sound.

He was screaming.

Randow clamped his mouth shut, amazed to be alive. He reached for his pewter cross, only it wasn't there. Hadn't been hanging from his neck for a month, when he had traded it for a cup of soup up in Jefferson, Texas, after his luck had gone south. His fortune tonight held, though. None of the ricochets had struck him; at least he didn't think he had been hit. The ringing in his ears faded, and he heard the men cursing, yelling.

"I'm empty!"

"Jammed!"

"Don't let him get away!"

He had to run. For a moment, he prayed the assault would bring a squad of city policemen. After all, this wasn't Waco or Fort Smith. New Orleans Parish boasted a population encroaching 200,000. Citizens would hear the gunfire and send the law to investigate. That would be his salvation. The thought was forlorn, fleeting. No one would save him, not in this part of town, not in a cemetery. Only voodoo practitioners ventured here after dark. That's why Jeff Slade had chosen it as a final meeting place to plan the robbery.

Randow sprang to his feet, squeezed the trigger only to groan at a sickening metallic *click*. Misfire, or he was empty, had miscounted his shots. In either case, the way sounds carried, Slade and his men would have heard and would charge him to finish the job. So he backed out of the tombs to the next pathway, and ran, holding the Dance tightly, dipping between another set of crypts, across another stone path, finally sliding to a stop in front of a tall whitewashed wall, honeycombed with the graves of the poor — "ovens" they were called — unlike the wealthy and landed gentry resting in the fancy sepulchers behind him.

Clouds hid the moon again, and a chilling mist cooled his face. He heard more shouts, footfalls on stone, and finally nothing except a distant horn moaning somewhere along the Levee. He pushed back the shell jacket he still wore, almost four years since he had taken the oath of allegiance, and holstered the .44. Randow mopped his face, ran fingers through tangled hair. Moonlight sifted through the clouds. The fog thickened.

He had to get out of the graveyard. Just follow this towering wall of ovens. No, no good. Slade, no fool, had posted a sentry at each gate, while he and the remaining two cutthroats searched the City of the Dead.

Randow thought back, fighting his memory, placing the voices. Three men, including Slade, one of Nathan Bedford Forrest's butchers, slayer of members of the Freedmen's Bureau in Arkansas, unreconstructed Rebel, robber, thief, murderer, Satan's right hand. What fine company Bobby Randow had been keeping; his mother would be proud. He spat out the sarcasm. *Concentrate. Think!*

Slade carried a revolver; the two others had repeating rifles, but one had jammed. Had it been repaired? It didn't matter. Even if the Henry was beyond repair, its owner packed at least one six-shooter, and the third man had undoubtedly reloaded his weapon. Nor could Randow in all likelihood get past Slade's guards at the gates. Could he hide, wait until dawn? Slade wouldn't continue his search with the coming of light, when policemen were sure to investigate. He would want to get rid of Victor Desiderio's body, if the Spanish blackheart were dead, and he most likely was by now, with two bullets in his gut, or soon would be. Slade wouldn't wait for Desiderio to recover, couldn't risk leaving the man alive to save his neck by revealing Slade's plan to authorities. His throat would be slit, and next his stomach cut

13

open, guts yanked out to feed the Swamp's rats and feral cats, his body weighted down with stones, and sunk into the water.

Or maybe not. If Slade gave up hope of finding and killing Randow in this sprawling maze of marble and granite, he might leave the corpse, bribe some Cajun waif to fetch the law, and the police would comb the cemetery come morning and find Randow. He'd have to answer for Desiderio, explain the bullets in the dead man's stomach, his empty revolver, tell what had brought him to a cemetery at midnight and forced him to kill a local gambler. In Texas or Arkansas, Randow would have felt pretty good about his chances — the bullets hadn't been in Desiderio's back, and the cardsharp, with a reputation that smelled like stagnant water, had been armed — but not here in New Orleans with its Reconstruction government and Yankee rule. With no friends in this city, Randow liked his odds neither with the law nor Slade.

So, he had to escape the City of the Dead.

He looked up at the whitewashed wall, made out grass and weeds sprouting on top, ten, maybe twelve, feet high. Walls of ovens served as fences for New Orleans's

Cities of the Dead. Beyond it lay freedom, a chance at life. He touched the cold stone, the depressions marking the crypts, reached up, fingering the edges, tried to pull himself up only to slip, his boot heels clapping the stone pathway, too loud for comfort. He bit his lip tighter.

Randow needed a ladder. Around All Saints Day, families of these departed souls flocked to cemeteries, decorating tombs, crypts, and mausoleums with chrysanthemums, bunting, memorials, brightening the gloomy fields, and Randow might have held out hope of finding a ladder left behind. This, however, was early February. No ladder, barring a miracle, would be around, and Randow figured he was fresh out of miracles. He had used his up this evening. That's why he still lived.

Moonlight brightened, and he made out the massive tomb across the pathway. He crept urgently toward it, reached up, jumped, and gripped the cold cross, pulled himself on top, and stood, tentatively, using his shaking arms to maintain his balance, boots slipping on wet marble.

He laughed dryly, inaudibly. Randow had gambled a lot in his life — cards and horses had provided his occupation the past four years — taken some wild bets, but this seemed pure folly: run ten feet across the arched top of a tomb slick with rain and scum, leap across a path three feet wide, and grab hold of the top of the wall of graves, pull himself up, and survive.

Well, baby brother Zack had always told him he had legs like a frog, could jump higher, swim farther, and run faster than anyone in Grayson County. During the war, even Colonel William B. Sims had proclaimed, before half the regiment, that Captain Randow's legs could be used as springals if the 9th ran out of powder and shot. Yet this was crazy. He'd break his leg, or his neck, and save Slade the trouble of killing him. He was about to climb off the precarious perch, to find some other way out. . . .

No shout warned him this time, only a crack to his right and buzzing past his ear. He almost lost his balance and crashed to the ground. Another bullet followed, and he knew they saw him. He righted himself, and ran, springing forward at the last instant, hurdling through empty space as the moonlight vanished and heaven's floodgates opened, unleashing wind and rain. He crashed against the leviathan graves, a sharp pain tearing through his ribs, fingers clawing frantically, digging into the sod, feet searching for a foothold, hearing curses — his own and Slade's men's. The toes of his boots found a secure spot, but it wasn't enough. He started slipping, sliding, hands groping blindly. A bullet spanged off the wall near his holster. Randow yelled, reached desperately in the darkness, and his right hand grasped something hard, cold, but solid. A piece of metal, biting into his palm. His left hand followed, gripped the narrow pole, and he pulled himself up, swinging his legs up behind him as a bullet tore through his jacket and another whistled past his ear. But he was up, atop the wall, almost burying himself in the sod-covered roof.

"He's up there!"

Slade swore vilely, and snapped another shot, fired more in anger, desperation, than at a target. The rain fell harder, and Randow rolled over, away from the gunmen, away from the wrought-iron cross someone had pounded into the crypts, a cross that had saved his life. He looked down the far edge of the towering wall, took a deep breath, and jumped, landing on wet grass, sliding, slipping, rolling, tumbling onto a cobblestone street. He pulled himself up and ran, darting down an alley, wind and rain pounding his face, numbing him, running, until a new fear, strange but palpable, stronger, stung him. His eyes widened as frightful questions shot through his brain.

What am I doing?

What day is it?

Where am I going?

Why am I running?

Bobby Randow had no answers.

Chapter Two

The deluge ended as the hack stopped.

Laura Kelley heard the driver set the brake, leap onto the street, and hurriedly open the door. Despite the driver's India-rubber poncho, the poor Creole must have been soaked to the skin. He looked miserable as he stood there, his mouth twisting as he tried to think of something to say. She expected him to offer his hand, help her out of the carriage, but one hand remained glued to the hack's door, the other hidden inside the black poncho.

Finally the man spoke: *"Mademoiselle,* this is no place for you. Please, permit me to take you to a proper place, a hotel, anywhere but this, this . . . *égorgeoir."*

She looked past him at the deserted streets, heard rain water gushing through gutters beside the *banquettes.* The Swamp, the wickedest part of New Orleans, which itself had often been likened to Gomorrah, seemed dead for a Wednesday night, or, rather, a Thursday morning. No street lamps shown in this part of town, and few windows revealed flickering candlelight or flaring lanterns. Only the moon, barely peeking through the clouds, illuminated the Swamp. Most of the whores and whoremongers must have turned in early, or perhaps the weather had scared them off. Laura wondered if she would have to wake up a certain proprietress at a certain notorious brothel.

In French, she said — "I will be fine." — before informing the proud, dark-haired man than she was *madame,* not *mademoiselle*. Actually she was a widow, had been one for almost six years although she no longer dressed in black, but didn't care to reveal that information in case the Creole was playing the part of a gentleman but in reality was a *coureur de veuves*. Still, she gave the shivering driver a reassuring smile.

He didn't appear convinced of her safety, so, clutching her handbag, she started to climb out of the hack. If she didn't take charge, the chivalrous Creole would catch his death. He remembered his manners, and helped her out of the cab. The chill caught her off guard, or perhaps it was the smell of the Swamp and the look of its buildings, forbidding like the cities Charles Dickens had described. Back in Alexandria, back when she and Apolline Rainier played together, she never would have dreamed that her best friend, a beautiful redhead with beaux outnumbering her father's cotton plants, would have wound up in such a place. Then, again, that was a long time ago, before a war.

The Creole's voice echoed off the drab buildings. "*Mademoiselle,* ah, *madame,* I beg of you. This place is full of the unholy, of *putains,* of . . . criminals."

Of which I am one . . . now.

That thought made her shudder, and the driver stepped toward her, but she backed away, reaching into her change purse to pay him off and be rid of him. He realized he had overstepped his bounds, and stopped short, swallowing an apology, although he couldn't resist a final argument.

"But, *madame* has no luggage. *Juste ciel,* I beg of you for the last time, please, do not stay in such a place."

She handed him a coin, and he took it, staring at it. "It is too much." He, too, spoke in French.

"Take it," she said. "You are a gentleman, and I thank you." Another smile.

"Few hacks would take me here at this time of night," Laura said, switching to English. "Few would be waiting at the Levee. You are worth more, my friend."

"*Merci bien.*" With a bow, he slid the coin into a trouser pocket, and climbed back into the carriage's boot, released the brake, and muttered something to his horse as they disappeared into the darkness. Laura stood there, listening to the clatter of hoofs on the cobblestones until she could no longer hear anything but the water and a distant roll of thunder. She swallowed and got out of the street, walking to the dreary building.

When she reached the door and started to knock, clouds hid the moon again, and a horrifying screech down an alley caused her to scream. She turned, dropped her handbag, almost bolted down the street, fought the urge to run sobbing after the young Creole and his carriage, to beg him and accept his generosity, but sanity returned, and she understood the sound had been a couple of tomcats scuffling over a morsel of food, or maybe a dry place to spend the night.

If anyone heard her scream, they didn't respond. No one cared in this part of New Orleans. She laughed at herself, her cowardice, as she picked up her bag and wiped off the moisture, then faced the door again, noticing light shining through a crack. The door was slightly ajar. She tapped on it.

Do people knock before entering a bordello?

She sniggered again, more to calm her nerves than anything else. No reply, so she tried again, harder this time, then heard the clatter of hoofs again on the street. It wouldn't be the hack, which had gone off in the other direction, but it might be a policeman or some rogue. Laura had no interest in seeing or being seen by either, so she pushed open the door and stepped inside. "Apolline?" She shut the door and repeated the name, so loud the haunting echo startled her. Exhausted, Laura closed her eyes and sank into a gaudy chair. Her nerves had been exposed for the past week. She waited until her heartbeat lessened. When her eyes opened, she smiled.

She had never been inside such a place. The chair she sat in, while comfortable, was a monstrosity, and the brightly wallpapered lobby clashed with the colors of the other furniture — a sharp contrast to the dismal gray exterior of this house. Apolline Rainier had much better taste than this, at least she had years ago in Alexandria.

23

The Creole-style house itself was nondescript, a long, one-story building of peeling gray paint, most of the wooden planks warped from years of coastal Louisiana weather. Stains and years-old mud, maybe even ancient blood, dotted the threadbare Oriental rug in the parlor, which had been painted a hideous yellow. Two love seats, one draped in blue, the other ripped leather, rested catty-corner from each other, and a lantern sat flickering on an end table. Beside the lantern rested a folded copy of *The Daily Picayune* and an envelope. Laura placed her handbag on the table, reached over, and picked up the paper to see the date. February 2nd — two days ago. She would have to pick up a copy of today's paper, sometime, to see if news of her crime had reached New Orleans.

She tossed the paper on top of the envelope, and let out a sigh. Her legs felt stronger, so she rose and started down the hall only to stop herself. She didn't want to intrude, to wake up some sleeping prostitute, but she needed to find Apolline. Laura made herself walk to the first door on the left, and knocked timidly, then louder, finally turning the knob and opening the door. The bedroom was empty. She found the next room also vacant. The third wasn't even furnished, and she began to doubt herself. Did she have the right address? Or had her best friend moved? She hadn't heard from Apolline in six months.

It had been folly to flee Alexandria to New Orleans. She felt like an idiot. No one was here, and she had never heard of an empty bordello. Suddenly she remembered the envelope on the end table, and hurried back to the parlor, tossed the newspaper aside, and lifted the letter. That made her feel better. It was addressed to Apolline Rainier, postmarked in Jefferson, Texas two weeks ago. Her eyes fell on the lantern as she laid down the envelope. Someone had been here. Someone planned on returning.

She'd sit and wait, surprise her friend when she returned. Laura was about to sit back down in the hideous chair when the door slammed open. She had been so preoccupied she hadn't heard the sound of boot heels clopping along the *banquette* and stone street.

A man, sopping wet, almost slipped on the floor as he slammed the door. He turned quickly, blue eyes wild, his face a mask, rain water streaming off his long, dark locks. He wore a Confederate shell jacket, a gun belt, wool trousers tucked into stovepipe boots. Laura choked back a cry and stepped behind the chair as he stepped toward her, his eyes finally focusing, his lips trembling. If he reached for the pistol, if he took another step closer, she'd push the chair over to trip him, and run outside before he could recover. Her eyes fell on her handbag; inside were a few hundred dollars, some coins, handkerchief, and a small Derringer, capped and loaded. Could she reach it in time? She had already committed one crime — *but killing a man?* Could she do it?

"What's happening to me?" the man practically screamed.

Laura stepped back, confused.

"What am I doing here? Who are you? What's going on?" The questions came like gunshots, and then the man — a captain of cavalry during the late war, if the soaked coat he wore indeed belonged to him — buried his face in his hands, shaking his head violently, squeezing his temples with his fingers. When he looked up again, his eyes appeared red, as if he had been crying.

"I . . . can't . . . remember!" the man yelled. He collapsed in the blue love seat.

Her knees buckling, Laura grabbed the back of the chair for support. She made herself move in front of the chair and slowly sat down, staring at him. His sobs stopped as quickly as they had began, and he looked up at her. Neither spoke. The only sound came from their heavy breathing, and that, too, finally, slowly died.

"I am. . . ." She wondered if she should tell him her name. Perhaps an alias would be in order. Laura almost laughed at that notion. Some outlaw she'd make. "Laura Kelley."

He blinked.

"Bobby Randow." The words came out slowly, softly, as if he were testing them.

That made her feel better, and she smiled. He had not lost his memory.

"Do I know you?" he asked.

She shook her head.

"What am I doing here? What is this place?"

Laura's smile faded. No, his memory had not been restored. She tried to think of an answer. "Why would I come here?" he asked, and she focused on his knuckles, his fingers digging into the cushions of the seat until the knuckles turned white. At last, he released the love seat from this

27

death grip and pounded his thighs. "I've got to remember. . . ."

"You know your name," she said.

That calmed him instantly.

"Where are you from?" she asked.

"Sherman, Texas," he answered almost immediately. "At least, that's where I was born and grew up." He leaned back in the love seat, staring at her, and tilted forward again.

"What's your name?"

She told him for the second time.

"Do I know you?"

"No. I don't think so."

He looked around the parlor. "I hope I don't live here," he said with a chuckle, but it held little mirth.

"You don't." She didn't know why she told him that. For all she knew, Captain Bobby Randow could be one of Apolline's helpers, a cook, even a procurer, but neither fit. Or maybe she was acting silly, a romantic, maybe she just wanted him to be a gentleman. The gray, shell jacket with the French braid and yellow trim, the haunting eyes and dark hair — all reminding her of Major Theodore Wilson Kelley, her husband, the love of her life, who fell in the late war during the siege of Vicksburg, who rotted away to disease, a slow, agonizing death without glory, without the mercy of Minié ball.

"What do you remember?" she probed gently. "What's the last thing you remember?"

His lips twisted as he considered the question, but, before he could answer, the door opened again, and Randow and Laura looked up at Apolline Rainier as she removed her cloak and bonnet, her eyes also dancing in confusion as she stared first at Randow, then at Laura. She closed the door.

"Bobby . . . ," she began, before turning. "Laura . . . what on earth . . . ?"

Laura did all the explaining. Randow simply asked Apolline the same questions he had asked Laura. Neither woman spoke much after the story, until Randow coughed, and Laura suggested they get him out of those wet clothes. They helped him take off his jacket and unbuckle the gun belt, tossing both onto the opposite love seat before helping him to his feet and guiding him down the hall to Apolline's office, where they settled Randow into a chair near the stove. Apolline found a kettle, mugs, and tea bags while Laura stoked the fire after depositing her handbag on an end table near the confused, exhausted cavalry veteran.

"That explains him," Apolline said. "What are you doing here?"

She blurted out the answer as if at confession. "I burned down Green Haven!"

"Laura!"

Laura replaced the poker before facing her friend.

Apolline's eyes registered disbelief. "How could you?" Apolline asked in horror.

"It was easy. Gallons of coal oil and a few matches. I burned it all, the house, the barns, guest house, the old slave quarters, even the ga. . . ." She couldn't finish. Theodore Wilson Kelley had proposed to her on the gazebo. Laura swallowed, fought back a tear, and continued, offering an explanation to her stunned friend. "What was I to do, Apolline? Let carpetbaggers take it?" Her voice grew stronger as she straightened, shaking her head adamantly. "Let those thieves sleep and dine where Mother and Father worked so hard, gave so much? No, that I would not abide. Yankees and their ill lot took everything else from me . . . Mother, Father, Theodore. I would not let them have Green Haven. So I burned it. All of it."

"By yourself?"

"Yes. Then I bought passage on the *Frolic* and steamed down here as fast as I could."

"They'll know it was you, Laura, especially with your leaving Alexandria. You'll be charged with arson, I don't know what else."

Was she an arsonist? She had owned Green Haven. Can't a person burn her own property? Well, the carpetbaggers wouldn't see it that way, would they, especially in light of those taxes she owed?

"That's why I came here," Laura said.

Apolline closed her green eyes. "You shouldn't have, Laura."

"I thought I could hide out for a day or two. I have some money. I went to the bank in Alexandria before I burned down my home. I. . . ."

She realized her stupidity: withdrawing cash from the bank, buying a ticket in her name on the *Frolic*. Laura thought she had planned everything so carefully, but she had done nothing but make mistakes. She hadn't even brought along a change of clothes. Everyone in Alexandria would know who had burned down the old cotton plantation overlooking the Red River, and more than a few could tell the constables where to look, especially once

31

they realized she had gone downriver to New Orleans. They would all point to Apolline Rainier's bordello as the first place to look.

She buried her face in her hands. "I'm so sorry, Apolline. I wasn't thinking. I never should have come here. They'll know where to find me. It'll bring more trouble to you."

"It's not that," Apolline shot back. "I'd let you stay as long as you wanted." She knelt in front of Laura, placed her hands on Laura's knees. "But I'm leaving . . . tomorrow, or rather this afternoon. I'm going to Jefferson, to start over, have already bought my ticket on the *Mittie Stephens*."

Laura looked up, struck dumb. She mouthed the word: *Jefferson?*

"Yes. The taxes are too high in New Orleans for my business, not to mention the bribes I have to pay policemen, and, like you, I have grown weary of carpetbaggers, the clientele of the Swamp. You can't stay here, Laura, because I've sold this place to a Negress madam who, well . . . let's put it this way. You wouldn't want to be here come tomorrow night."

The teakettle whistled, and Randow began to stir. Both women had forgotten about him.

Chapter Three

"Do you remember me?" Apolline asked after he had finished a second cup of green tea.

Randow shook his head. "I'm sorry. You know me?"

Apolline gave the former Rebel officer one of those smiles that had charmed every boy in Alexandria, and Laura felt a familiar pang of jealousy. Since their teen-age years, Apolline had won the heart of every Rapides Parish boy Laura had a crush on, until finally she moved to Baton Rouge and later New Orleans at the war's outbreak, turning her charm into a profitable business venture — if frowned-upon by Alexandria's wealthy and Baptists. Sometimes Laura wondered if Apolline had stayed in Alexandria, who would have smitten Theodore Wilson Kelley? Would Apolline have been his widow and Laura an old maid? She was practically what

Louisiana blue bloods considered past being an old maid — twenty-six — when she had married Theodore.

"We were lovers," Apolline told Randow, returning Laura's attention to the present. "For a while, at least. But you had another love, a stronger one than me. Do you remember, Bobby?" His head slowly moved from side to side. "The cards. Poker. You're a gambler, and I couldn't hold you." She let out a soft laugh. "I don't think any woman could hold you, *amant*. But that's all right. We remain friends."

He stared at her blankly. "Do I miss you?"

Laura couldn't hold back the laughter, and Apolline joined her. Their raucous explosion rattled the teacups, and even the dazed Randow smiled, although Laura assumed he didn't quite understand the joke.

"I should hope so," replied Apolline, dabbing her eyes with the hem of her skirt. Laura had laughed so hard — it felt good, too — she had to wipe away her own tears with a handkerchief she fetched from her handbag.

When the laughter subsided, Randow shook his head. "Poker," he said, testing the word like wine at a fancy restaurant.

His head bobbed. "Poker. I left a hotel. . . ."

"Which hotel?" Laura asked excitedly.

"The Saint Louis."

Laura blinked away astonishment. The opulent St. Louis Hotel catered to the richest river boatmen and merchants. From his appearances, she would have expected Randow to have hung his hat in one of the driftwood shacks in the Swamp, or some lice-filled, repugnant establishment on Gallatin Street, closer to the dismal gambling dens.

"Are you sure?" The question came from Apolline.

Randow nodded before setting the empty cup on an end table. "I dealt draw poker at Number Eighteen Royal Street, came here." His head bobbed again, confirming his own memory. "You weren't here."

"What time was it?" Apolline asked. "I was probably buying my ticket. . . ." She stopped suddenly, but Laura finished the sentence for her, although she was guessing: "On the *Mittie Stephens*?"

Apolline shot her a warning, which Laura didn't understand, then both women looked at Randow. From the expression on Randow's face, the name of the steamboat meant nothing to the young cavalry captain. He rested his chin in his palms while massaging his eyes, shaking his head, trying to finish his memory. "It was night. I. . . ." He let out a sigh in defeat and lifted his head. "That's all. Everything goes black."

"Let's try something different," Laura suggested. "Instead of last night, yesterday . . . let's go back farther. Your name is Bobby Randow, right?"

The head bobbed once.

"How old are you?"

"Thirty-seven."

The same age Theodore would be had he lived. Laura pushed that into the recesses of her mind to continue her interrogation. "Any family? Parents? Siblings? Wife?"

This time Randow's head shook. "No wife," he said softly. "Papa died at Shiloh. Zack, my younger brother, fell to yellow fever at Vicksburg during the siege."

She shivered at another similarity between this stranger and her late husband. Laura couldn't continue, but Apolline picked up where she left off.

"And your mother? Sisters?"

"Mama lives in Shreveport. No sisters. There was just my folks and Zack." He wet his lips. "Well, there was a sister, but she

lived only three or four days. I don't remember her, was only a button then myself."

"You served in the Confederate cavalry?"
Apolline asked.

"Ninth Texas. Gambled after the surrender." He looked up at the red-headed
beauty. "You're right. I play poker for a
living. I had two pair, jacks and eights,
called a monkey's bluff, and cashed in."

A "monkey" was an out-of-work sailor.
Laura felt excited for Randow, felt a sense
of hope.

Apolline gave him another bewitching
smile, cocking her head, and then shaking
it. "But you don't remember me, *amant?*"

Randow's head dropped. "No," he said
softly. "I'm sorry."

"What year did the Alamo fall?" Laura
asked. She felt a need to continue her part
of the interview, although the reason es-
caped her.

Randow eyed her curiously before answering correctly. He knew the month and
year of the Confederate loss at Shiloh,
knew his mother's name — Leigh Powell,
who had remarried four years ago — as
well as her birthday, and knew the name of
the gambling establishment at 18 Royal
Street, The Merchants' Exchange, where

he had played cards before heading to Apolline's brothel. He even knew the sixth President of the United States — John Quincy Adams. At least, Laura thought he had answered correctly. Actually she wasn't entirely certain herself, and, when she looked at Apolline for confirmation, her friend shrugged and tried, but failed, to stifle a girlish giggle.

"My turn," Apolline said. "What's my name?"

Randow slumped again. "I. . . ." His head shook in dismal defeat. "I'm sorry, ma'am. I can't recollect."

Laura thought she saw the traces of a smile on her friend's face. "And hers?" Apolline gestured to Laura, whose heart sank when Randow's head shook sadly again.

"What street is this?" Apolline asked. "What's the name and number?"

He answered with an oath and a shout: "I don't know!"

"Then how did you know where to look for me?"

The answer exploded, the curse harsher: "I don't know!"

Apolline ended her assault, and she knelt by Randow, cooing him with soothing hushes, lifting his right hand, and pressing the back against her lips. She spoke to him in hushed French, telling him everything would be all right, until he lifted his head and stared vacantly at the whitewashed ceiling. Finally Randow closed his eyes.

"I've never seen anything like it," Apolline told Laura as they made more tea while Randow slept.

Laura agreed. "I've never heard of anything like it. Who is he?"

Her friend smiled while the tea bags steeped. "A gambler, like we said. Texas-born, or that's what he told me, and the accent tells me that part's true. He dealt cards in Arkansas, Texas, and came through New Orleans a few times a year. You know how gamblers are, Laura. Well, I guess you don't. I met him when I was running my place on Gallatin Street, before I moved here, met him at a gambling parlor. He's quite handsome, don't you think?"

Laura shrugged. In a rugged sort of way, maybe Bobby Randow could be called handsome, maybe if he shed the fraying clothes, shaved, combed his hair. She couldn't ignore those blue eyes, though, almost blue-gray, like an infant's eyes, beautiful, penetrating, wholesome. The eyes didn't match the face. The eyes reminded her of Theodore. She closed her own eyes, hard, trying to forget about him. She no longer wore black, so why did she always think of him after all these years? Why hadn't she allowed some other man to court her? Alexandria, and its sister town on the south side of the Red River, Pineville, were filled with eligible gentlemen, and most war widows quickly remarried.

She looked back at her friend when Apolline announced gleefully: "I never charged him, you know." Numbly Laura took the cup Apolline offered.

"I'll take care of Bobby," Apolline announced after they had let the tea cool. "But what are we going to do about you?"

Laura hadn't forgotten about her own plight, but she felt more concerned with the sleeping man who had lost his recent memory. *Playing nurse again,* she told herself. She wondered how Apolline planned on taking care of him when she had bought a ticket on a steamboat for a trip to Texas, especially considering that she was leaving New Orleans this afternoon. Laura felt like arguing with her. She had money and a friend in town who might be able to offer Randow some hope: Dr. Charles

LeBreton. They hadn't seen each other in years, but LeBreton would not turn her away. He could help Randow, and maybe help Laura escape the law's grasp. She would visit him, leave Randow in his care, and escape. To Mississippi or Texas or Arkansas, or even farther — California, the Western territories. She hadn't any real plans.

"I. . . ." She stopped immediately.

The front door slammed. At first, Laura thought it had been blown open by the wind, but then came the voices, angry, almost violent, and Apolline spilled her tea as she turned and hurried. "Stay here!" she warned, and was gone.

Through the closed doors, Laura heard the voices, but only a few words could she make out, Apolline's adamant *no*s and a few bits of profanity in English, Spanish, and French that once would have made the two women blush. She couldn't understand what they were talking about, and, while part of her told her to relax, that Apolline could fend for herself and arguments had to be common in a place such as this, she also felt fear gnawing in her stomach. *The police have come looking to arrest me, arsonist Laura Kelley! No, not that*

41

soon. Men were after Bobby Randow. Now, why would I think that?

Randow had wakened, but seemed oblivious to the argument in the room behind him. She thought of his jacket and shirt piled on the table in the parlor, and Laura remembered the russet gun belt, the walnut butt of a revolver, and her eyes fell on her handbag on the end table between Randow's chair and the stove. *My Derringer!* When the voices stopped, she started to reach for it, although she didn't know why. No one shouted any more. Apolline would have screamed a warning if Laura were in trouble. *Wouldn't she?*

The door opened and closed behind Apolline and a man in a black poncho and black Spanish-style hat, water still dripping off the flat brim. Wire spectacles pinched his bulbous nose. His hair was reddish, graying, with an unkempt mustache and beard. Blue kersey trousers told her the man had once, or still was, part of the Federal Army, and ugly globs of mud and wet grass stuck to black cavalry boots. The man smiled, all the while grasping a thin cherry-wood cane with a gold handle in his left hand, and an ungentlemanly boot pistol in the right. The barrel of the single-shot cannon remained trained at the base of Randow's skull.

"This is Major Julius Siegel," Apolline announced. "A provost marshal from . . . ?" She glanced at the beaming man.

"Chicago." Siegel rounded the furniture and stared at Randow.

"Do I know you?" Randow asked, and Siegel gently lowered the hammer of his pistol. Randow hadn't even noticed the .50-caliber weapon pointed at his head.

"Nor do I know you, sir," Siegel said. He laid the pistol beside Laura's handbag. *Odd,* Laura thought, and pursed her lips. Immediately Siegel turned his back to Randow and removed his hat, bowing slightly to Laura.

"My apologies, ma'am. My associates and I are on our way to Jefferson, and are looking for Army deserters. I thought this might be one of them, but he's not. I'm sorry to have frightened you, miss, sorry to come barging in here with gun in hand, but in this city, at this time of the night, in this section of town. . . ." He left the rest unsaid.

In fact, Julius Siegel left a lot else unsaid, and Laura decided she did not care much for this man. Firstly he was admittedly a Yankee, undeniable with that nasal, uppity whine. Secondly he didn't say what had

43

brought him to Apolline's. He didn't say much to her after his apology, either, but abruptly showed her the back of his wet poncho and pulled on his hat while facing Randow.

"I'd like to ask your name, sir," Siegel said.

Randow underwent another interrogation. Laura felt sorry for him as the minutes ticked by. When Siegel had finished, he muttered a simple — "Amazing." — and picked up his pistol, shoving it inside one of the high cavalry boots.

"Excuse me," Siegel said, and went out the room.

Laura heard voices again. Siegel had left his friends in the parlor.

"Who is he?" she demanded.

"Provost marshal," Apolline said.

"And?" There had to be more than that.

"He pays for me, Laura," Apolline blurted out. "He bought my passage to Jefferson. I'm accompanying him on the *Mittie Stephens.*" Laura felt ashamed. Tears welled in her friend's eyes as Apolline turned to Randow. "Bobby . . . I. . . ."

Randow, staring at the ceiling but likely not seeing a thing, certainly displayed no jealousy, and that must have hurt Apolline more. Even prostitutes have feelings, Laura realized, as Apolline bit her lip and recovered, holding back tears. The room turned quiet. Siegel and his companions had lowered their voices, or perhaps quit talking. Maybe they had even taken their leave.

"What was that gent's name?" Randow's soft question broke the silence.

When the door opened again, another man followed Major Siegel. The provost marshal had removed his poncho, revealing a star pinned on the lapel of his yellow brocade vest, and revolver, butt-forward in a military-issue holster on his left hip, flap unfastened. Another peculiarity about Siegel, Laura thought, was that he dressed like a Yankee soldier waist-down, and riverboat gambler waist-up. Her attention, however, was drawn to the second man, who towered over the provost marshal. He was well dressed except for the mud and grass caked to his boots and staining his gray trousers. He sported a silk hat, tailored coat with velvet-trimmed collar, narrow tie loosened like a hangman's noose, no gun that Laura could see. His eyes were sky blue, penetrating, his face clean-shaven and handsome, his hair dark black, although, when he stepped closer after introductions and took Laura's hand to kiss it, she thought she smelled boot

45

polish, and wondered if he darkened his hair that way.

"Hugh Valdez." She repeated his name. Part Spanish, she guessed, and dismissed the suggestion that this gentleman dyed his hair with black shoe polish. His accent revealed no Spanish, though, perhaps a trace of Virginia or points east. Laura liked him almost immediately, even if she disliked his traveling companion. He had a dignity in his gait and humor in his eyes. More importantly, nothing about Hugh Valdez reminded her of Theodore Wilson Kelley.

"Do I know you?" Randow asked.

Still smiling, Valdez whirled. "This is the man?" he asked Siegel.

The provost marshal, gripping his cane in both hands, answered a dry yes.

Randow repeated the question.

"Not only do you know me, old chum," Valdez answered in a jocular voice, "you owe me five thousand dollars."

Chapter Four

To a former slave, born on a cotton plantation near McCarmel in Covington County,
Mississippi, the Levee was a city itself, the
strangest, biggest, scariest one Obadiah
Denton had seen in a long time. Two years
since his last visit, Denton had forgotten the
sprawling size of New Orleans, and thanked
the Lord he didn't have to take his family
through that disconcerting puzzle of streets
and buildings. He squeezed his wife's hand
and kept glancing over his shoulder to make
sure his sons, Emanuel and Matthew, hadn't
gotten separated while weaving through the
sea of people. Some wailed for charity,
others lounged about thousands of barrels,
hogsheads, hay bales, and cotton bales, and
many worked, bringing cargo on or off a
fleet of ships lining the wharf, pairs of black
smokestacks — more than Denton could
count — reaching into the morning sky.

Somewhere in the multitude of chatter, a

woman asked a question. So confused, lost, and nervous was Denton, however, that he didn't recognize his wife's voice until a half minute later when she repeated the question, although he still couldn't hear her clearly.

"You say somethin', Zoë?" He released his grip on her and adjusted the muslin sack he toted in his other hand.

"Said why don't you ask somebody is all," came her reply.

Denton shook his head adamantly. "Uhn-uh. Don't know nobody here. I'll find it, all right. You jus' make sure the boys stay close."

He couldn't trust any of these loafers. Grandpa George — grandfather to him, anyway, for he had never known his own father, sold up the river when Denton was two years old, let alone any real grand-parents — had told him to watch himself on the Levee, warned him that thieves and cutthroats lined the wharves looking for the careless and stupid to rob or murder. He'd find the ship . . . he hoped.

"What about them?" his older boy Emanuel asked. "They's soldiers like you was."

Denton stopped and whirled, following the ten-year-old's outstretched finger until

48

his eyes locked on a handful of black men nestled between stacks of cotton bales, on their knees, laughing and cussing as they rolled lead dice. Sure enough, they wore ill-fitting woolen trousers and slouch hats of the 9th Cavalry, although few had kept their Army-issue blouses or patent leather boots.

"They ain't soldiers, no more, Son," Denton said, "and I don't know 'em. Likely been mustered out."

"Most likely deserters," Zoë added with contempt.

Denton threw the sack over his shoulder, clutched his wife's hand, and hurried his family from the men until they reached a clearing of sorts. His mouth hung open as he stared at the side-wheeler before him. It looked twice the size of the transport that had carried a bunch of sick, colored soldiers soon to be sicker, including Trooper Obadiah Denton, from the Louisiana coast to Indianola, Texas in the spring of 1867. He couldn't remember much about that voyage, or even the one he had just taken on a far from seaworthy flatboat from Convent, Louisiana where Grandpa George called home these days, to a short distance from the Levee.

"Is that it?" Matthew asked.

Obadiah released his wife again and blinked, watching in amazement at the activity: men — black, white, and other colors somewhere between, strapping, not rail-thin like Obadiah Denton — walked up and down planks, loading the ship's lower deck with sugar-packed hogsheads. Denton's throat had turned raw, the way it often did back in dust-caked West Texas, and he longed for a drink of water. *Can I go through with this?* he thought.

Matthew repeated his question.

"Don't know," he told the seven-year-old in a hushed voice.

The next sound he detected was a familiar guttural grunt from Zoë, which — per her custom — she followed with a sigh of exasperation before asking: "Pardon me, mister, but is that there the *Mittie Stephens*?"

With a mixture of embarrassment and fright, Denton looked at the man his wife had addressed: a sun-blasted fellow with a long brown beard, stained overalls, rubber boots, and a woolen cap, his gums securing a pipe stem in his mouth, for he had few teeth. The man removed the pipe with contempt and shot out a reply: "No, it's the *Laurel Hill*."

"Thank you," Zoë told him anyway.

"You darkies can thank me an' yerself by learnin' to read. Her name's written on the blasted wheelhouse." The pipe returned, and the man disappeared behind a mule-drawn wagon laden with boxes of fruit.

Denton waited until his wife looked his way. "I tol' you," he started to say, but Zoë's iron face warned him to remain quiet. Sighing, he looked down the Levee one way, then another, trying to pick a direction.

"Don't pay that monkey no mind," a voice carried above the racket. "You-all looking for the *Mittie Stephens*?"

Denton turned to face an elderly, balding black man in a sailor's cap and jacket, sitting on the ground a few yards away, his back resting against a rotting hay bale, and an ancient blanket covering his lower body. A few coins, two plugs of tobacco, a stick of candy, one half-eaten apple, and several burned matches lay strewn across the blanket's top.

"The *Laurel* looks a lot like the *Mittie Stephens*," said the man, still smiling, motioning Denton and his family to come closer. Cautiously Denton complied.

"How you boys doing?" the man asked. Denton's glance discovered his sons hiding behind their plump mother's skirt.

The man laughed before looking up at Denton. "You'll find the *Mittie Stephens* twenty-two ships up from here, boss, likely being loaded with hay. She's a three-boiler, her master's a good river man. Supposed to steam up to Jefferson today."

"She ain't left yet?" Zoë asked.

"No, ma'am. Ships don't generally leave till four or five in the afternoon. You'll know when they're getting ready to steam, ma'am. It'll be blacker than midnight, the sky will."

Denton studied the man with some suspicion. "You sail on the *Mittie Stephens*?"

"No, boss."

"You sure know a lot about her."

The man looked past Denton at his family, and spoke to them. "Boys, I don't bite none. Can't." He opened his mouth wide to reveal fewer teeth than the rude monkey his wife had asked moments earlier.

Emanuel snickered at the display, but both boys stayed behind the protection of Zoë's skirt.

Shaking his head, the man faced Denton again. "I know about everything that happens on the Levee, boss. Know every ship . . . about every sailor. Been here every day rain or shine since 'Thirty-

Seven. I'd take you to the *Mittie Stephens* myself, but. . . ." He ripped off the blanket, spilling the contents on the soft, wet ground at his side.

The boys gasped; Zoë started a prayer.

"Lost my legs when the *Ben Sherrod* caught fire on the river before your boys was born. Likely before *you* was born." He returned the blanket and began raking the coins and other items except the burned matches into a pile beside him. "Twenty-two ships up, a side-wheeler like the *Laurel Hill*, being loaded with hay," the man said without looking up. "Master is Captain Homer Kellogg. If you're looking for work, tell him that Big Joe Marbury sent you."

The cripple was right about the captain's name, or else Grandpa George was a liar, and the one person Denton would trust with his life, with the life of his family, was Grandpa George.

Denton thanked the man, nodded at his wife, and began walking up the river. Before leaving, though, before feeling the comfort of his wife's fleshy hand, he fished out a penny and tossed it on the old man's blanket.

"Much obliged," Denton said without looking down.

"Safe steaming," came the reply.

Captain Homer Kellogg pulled off his wire spectacles after reading the letter of introduction Obadiah Denton had handed him, rubbed his eyes, and returned the eyeglasses into a leather case that he slid into an inside coat pocket.

"How long have you known George Harrold?" the captain asked. He had a kindly voice, a stark contrast to his knotted brow, coarse beard, and cold brown eyes. Kellogg tapped his tobacco pipe with a forefinger and leaned back in his chair, as if expecting a long answer.

Denton tried to look the captain in his eyes — that's what Little George told him Kellogg expected in his crew — but he found it hard to do so. It wasn't because he was scared of this white man, wasn't because the overseer at Major Cove's plantation would whip any slave who dared meet his stare, but rather because they were in the pilot house, rising above the highest deck of the *Mittie Stephens*, and Denton had the urge to look out those windows. Why, a body could practically see clear to Covington County, Mississippi from this berth, or maybe even West Texas.

"Don't really know him," Denton answered. "I know his father, Grandpa George we called him in Mississippi. He took care of me durin' the . . . well before we was freed. I was visitin' Grandpa George . . . he lives up in Convent, on the east bank of the river . . . when his son come home for a visit, too." Denton wasn't used to talking so much, and the next part scared him, but he made himself finish. "That's when Little George took sick, and why he up and wrote me this note to give to you, sir."

The captain fired his pipe before glancing at the two other sailors in the pilot house; Denton did not look at them.

"So what is it that you want?" Kellogg asked.

"Like that note says, Capt'n. . . ." At least Denton hoped Little George's letter explained everything. He had never learned his letters, nor had his wife and sons. "I works for you. Don't want no pay, nothin' like that, jus' passage to Jefferson for me and my family."

"Your family being?" one of the officers asked.

"Wife and two boys. They's good boys, Capt'n. They'll work real hard, too, sir, iffen that's what it takes. My wife, she can clean and cook real fine. That's what she did for Major Cove."

"Why do you desire to steam to Texas?" Kellogg asked.

"I hear tell there's a fellow tryin' to get some of us freedmen to make us a home in Colorado Territory, sir. They leave from Jefferson on the First of March. I wants to be part of that, Capt'n. I'm tired of choppin' cotton, tired of soldierin', jus' wants a fresh start, a good home . . . for my wife and boys. I can build somethin' out West, maybe. I like buildin' things, Capt'n, like carpentry."

Homer Kellogg must have been smoking since childhood, for when the captain removed his pipe Denton saw a permanent crease in the man's lip left by the curved stem. Denton tried not to stare at the mark and, instead, found himself looking out the window, watching men load barrels onto the neighboring steamboat, a long stern-wheeler that dwarfed the *Mittie Stephens*.

"So tell me about yourself, Obadiah Denton," Kellogg said.

Denton blinked, feeling his throat turn raw again. "Don't that letter there tell you ever'thing, Capt'n?"

"It tells me what George Harrold thinks of you, or maybe what his father told him to write about you. I want to hear your story, from your mouth. I read here that you served with the colored troops out West." The pipe returned, and Denton drew in a deep breath before beginning.

He was born a slave in 1842; at least, that's what he had been told. He worked the cotton fields and carpenter shop in Covington County for as long as he remembered, married Zoë when he was sixteen, or thereabouts, and Zoë was two years older. The next year Emanuel was born. Three years later, after Major Cove had gone off to fight with General Van Dorn, came Matthew. And before he knew it, the war was over, the South had lost, Major Cove had died of something called dysentery in Tennessee, and Obadiah Denton and his wife and sons were free.

He had worked odd jobs as carpenter and field hand in Mississippi and northern Louisiana for a spell after the war, before enlisting, to serve with the 9th Cavalry of colored troops, in Greenville, Louisiana in October of 1866. He served a tad more than two years, mostly in West Texas, before coming home to see his family again. He met Grandpa George — Little George Harrold's father, that is — in Convent, and took a flatboat down the river to the Levee in hopes of obtaining passage to Jefferson.

"Did you see much action out West with the Ninth Horse?" Kellogg asked.

Denton shrugged, then voiced his answer. "Some." Needles pricked his nerves, and he tried to block out the bad memories, the nightmares that would come again tonight.

"Sioux or Cheyennes?" another officer asked.

This time Denton stared at the inquirer, a wiry fellow with burnside whiskers and a crooked nose. The man was trying to catch Denton in a lie.

"Comanches," Denton answered. "Some Kiowas and Lipan Apaches. Don't find no Sioux and Cheyennes as far south as we was."

Kellogg removed his pipe and smiled, the crease in his lip whitening as the captain's grin widened. "Never seen a Comanche or any wild Indian myself. What do you know about carpentry work?"

"When I wasn't workin' cotton, I had a hammer in my hand on Major Cove's plantation, sir. Held a hammer long before I could drag a cotton sack. Worked as a carpenter once I was freed, too, helpin' other freedmen build homes and such in Mississippi, Louisiana." He liked those memories. "Even hammered a few nails in the Army."

"So why did you enlist in the cavalry?" Kellogg continued.

"Don't rightly know, sir. I heard 'em tootin' that horn one evenin' in Greenville where they was signin' us up, and, well, sir, I always been partial to music. I jus' walked up and asked if I could try that horn, and the officer, he had some soldier fetch me one. Next thing I knowed, I had made my mark and. . . ." He shrugged before he said too much, and offered the captain a warm smile.

"You played a trumpet in the Army, Mister Denton, but, on the *Mittie Stephens*, our instrument is a calliope. Can you play one?"

"A what, Capt'n?"

"Calliope. A thirty-two note steam organ. Maurice had it installed in 'Sixty-Six."

"Oh, sure, Capt'n. Little George said you had a fancy pianer on this boat. I can play practically everything once I figure it out. Big George, he has a pianer in his place, and the church he goes to has a fine-soundin' organ. I reckon I can play a ca . . . , ca-li. . . . You jus' show it to me, Capt'n."

"Mister Lodwick," Captain Kellogg said, "see if you can find a copy of the march, and let's see how well he plays. We'll be at the calliope."

The thin man who had tested Denton's honesty rifled through a desk drawer while the captain and other officer led Denton out of the pilot house, across the top deck, and down the stairs. They walked to the back of the steamboat to the end of the cabins. Around the corner, Captain Kellogg showed Denton the strangest-looking piano he had ever seen, even wilder looking than the pipe organ the white-haired grandmother played at Grandpa George's church.

That wasn't all, either, for a minute later Mr. Lodwick handed a thin book to Denton, who stared at it, holding it as if it might break. The cover had writing on the top and bottom, with a woodcutting of a steamboat sailing up a river nestled between the words, a huge American flag flying from the mast at the back of the boat, and black smoke churning from the tops of the two stacks. The ship depicted on the book looked a lot like the *Mittie Stephens*. Unsure of himself, Denton opened the pages to see even stranger looking symbols. Closing it, he stared at Kellogg tentatively.

"What's this, Capt'n?"

" 'The *Mittie Stephens* March'. We play it on deck to announce when supper is served." Suspicion hardened the captain's eyes. "You don't read music?"

"No, sir. I don't read nothin'."

"Then how can you possibly replace George Harrold?" Kellogg demanded.

"Well, sir, if you'll jus' hum it to me, I can play it." He lowered the muslin sack he had been toting. He had hoped he'd be able to play this march on his horn. He sat behind the steam organ that he couldn't pronounce and wondered if he could figure out this contraption. "First, Capt'n, let me get a feel for this here pianer."

He pressed a key, and almost jumped at the whistle, tried another. Thirty-two notes, Captain Kellogg had said. Yeah, Good Lord willing, he'd be able to play this thing. It wasn't anything more than a strange-sounding organ.

The thin man, Lodwick, rolled his eyes, but Kellogg's smile returned, and he began humming a rollicking, catchy little tune. Denton listened intently before rolling his fingers across the keys.

He lost himself in his music, closing his eyes, matching, improving, and eventually drowning out Kellogg's hums. When he became aware of his surroundings, his eyes bolted open and he shot out of his seat, embarrassed, while quickly muttering an apology. His ears rang from the shrill notes.

Captain Kellogg stood transfixed, unmoving like the crease in his bottom lip.

"Amazing," Lodwick broke the silence.

"Mister Lodwick?" Kellogg asked at last.

"He can play a calliope, sir."

"Mister Swain?"

The other man spit out a mouthful of tobacco juice over the ship's side. "He's better'n George Harrold, Capt'n."

"I agree" — Kellogg smiled — "but Mister Denton is asking for one-way passage to Jefferson. We won't have anyone to play our calliope for our return voyage."

"That's not a bad thing, Capt'n," the tobacco chewer said. "I grow mighty sick of that tune. A respite would do me pealin' ears a world of good."

With a hearty laugh, Kellogg offered Obadiah Denton his hand. Denton couldn't recall the last time — if there had even been a first time — when a white man had initiated a handshake. "Very well, Mister Denton," Kellogg said, "you have the job. In exchange for deck passage to Jefferson, you will serve as ship's carpenter and musician. Your wife can work in the ship's galley, and your sons will help the crew in the boiler room. You can stow your gear in the cargo room, sleep wherever you might find a comfortable spot. We shove off at five o'clock this afternoon. Welcome aboard, sir."

Chapter Five

Hopelessness. That feeling kept overwhelming Bobby Randow.

The pretty but haggard-looking blonde and the radiant redhead would look after him. Randow sensed that, more than knew it, but that was all he truly comprehended. A tall, dark-haired man kept smiling, laughing, joking with him, perhaps hoping to make Randow feel better about himself, about his situation. Randow tried to place the man's face, only couldn't, and seldom remembered his name, no matter how many times he was told it. Still, Randow felt the need to ask questions, so he peppered the women and men around him, repeating his inquiries — even the ones he knew to be pointless — believing that somehow this repetition would give him strength.

More than scared about his plight, Randow felt ignorant. He had always considered himself a bright young fellow. As a boy, when he had not been helping his father and brother do chores, or swimming, hunting, or fishing, he had read constantly. The Bible . . . his father's collections of Shakespeare, Milton, Homer, Plato, and Cooper . . . whatever newspapers and magazines made it inside their cabin, mostly *Scientific American*, *Spirit of the Times*, and *Texas State Gazette*. His mother had taught him arithmetic at an early age, and the schoolmaster with the crooked nose at the subscription school had hailed Master Robert Randow as the best math student in all of Grayson County. Robert Randow! That galled him. His name was Bobby, not Robert, and Papa had written it down that way in Mama's Bible.

Yet that was all in the past, and it was his future that frightened him, for what kind of future could he have? How could a man make a living as a gambler when he couldn't remember what he held? He would keep looking at his hand and checking the cards like some novice or nervous gull betting more than he could afford to lose.

The pointlessness of his memories bothered him even more than his uncertain future. He knew his teacher back in

Sherman, Texas had sported a crooked nose, knew the man's name — Bass Ware — even remembered how the middle-aged, rawhide-thin fellow came to get that crooked nose — he had called Lucas Bledsoe's drunken dad a "brangler" during a church social; Hank Bledsoe had proved Mr. Ware's assessment correct. Closing his eyes, he could picture the first girl he kissed — Patty Houston of Gainesville — Parson Birnbaum serving up brimstone before supper at one of the 9th's encampments during the war, or the five gentlemen he had played poker with at the Riverfront Tavern in Fort Smith, Arkansas three months ago. His first horse had been a piebald mare named Gretchen. His favorite game was draw poker, although he fared better at five-card stud. In Georgia, back in the summer of 1864, he had won five Yankee dollars by swimming across the Tallapoosa River and back. His mother lived in Shreveport, married to a cadaverous bill-sticker overly fond of John Barleycorn.

He knew all of this, and yet for the life of him couldn't remember what he did last night, or how he knew these people roaming about the house, refreshing his coffee while asking him how he was doing, if he remembered anything, or encouraging him that everything would be all right.

His sleep had been dreamless — or had he dreamed and couldn't remember? Randow wanted to curse himself, pound his legs until they bruised. Despite the sleep, he remained exhausted, and he was the only one, it appeared, in this house who had gotten any sleep. *I should be helping,* he thought, *but what can I do?* So Randow simply sat there, watching the bustle around him, listening to animated voices but not really understanding what was being said.

The redhead approached him with a dazzling smile, holding out a stained, threadbare jacket. *My shell jacket, made by a seamstress Mama knew in Sherman. They mailed it to me after the promotion at Elkhorn Tavern, when General McCulloch died.* Randow even remembered that.

"Come on, *amant,*" she said softly. "It's time to go."

He drained the cold coffee from the cup he suddenly noticed in his right hand, set the china on a table top, and rose, letting the woman help him into the jacket. "It's a touch on the chilly side today," she told him.

"Where are we going?" he asked. Randow knew he had asked this question before.

"You're seeing me, Major Siegel, and his men off. Then you and Laura are going to see a doctor."

"A doctor?"

"Yes."

"Where are you going?"

"To Texas." When he turned to face her, she asked him: "Do you remember my name?"

He opened his mouth, but her name died on his lips, and he sighed heavily. Coffee roiled in his stomach.

"It's all right, *amant*," she assured him. "I'm Apolline. Apolline Rainier. You'll remember. Don't fret over this, at all."

"Lot of things I wish I could forget, chum," echoed another voice. "So enjoy it." Someone else laughed.

Randow ignored this and repeated her name as she led him by the hand. *A rider pulling a horse by the reins, the horse following obediently, knowing he would be cared for.* The tall man in the swallowtail coat opened a door, letting the blonde woman and a red-bearded man with a magnificent cane walk out first. Randow and his guide followed.

In the parlor, Randow discovered two other men sitting on a couch. One cleaned his fingernails with a pocket knife; the other read a newspaper. Both were leathery in appearance, the newspaper reader smaller, wearing an ill-fitting Union frock coat, the other man in gray broadcloth, with dead dark eyes, black hair, and waxed mustache. He didn't know these men, or did he?

"Do I . . . ?"

"Sidney Paige, the major's clerk," the tall man said, pointing to the newspaper reader. "The other is Jules Honoré. Gentlemen, allow me to present Captain Bobby Randow, late of the Confederate Army."

Randow studied the man doing the introductions. The man's smile widened. "I am Hugh Valdez. Remember? And you don't owe me five thousand dollars, Bobby."

"I don't?" He had no idea what Valdez was talking about.

"I was joking." His smile faded, as though he saw the angry look on the blonde's face, although he couldn't, not with her standing behind him. "I apologize, sir. I should not make light of your condition. My only excuse is that sometimes laughter helps, but, in your case . . . well, sir, I did not mean to sound insensitive."

The blonde's expression lightened with the apology, while Randow wondered if he would remember any of this, or if any of it mattered.

"Let's go," the cane toter said brusquely, and Newspaper Reader and Fingernail Cleaner stood, tossing the paper on the floor and folding and sliding the knife into a trouser pocket.

Outside, the air felt damp on Randow's face, and he filled his lungs with pungent oxygen. That was a mistake, for now he remembered: *New Orleans does not smell like chrysanthemums. No, that's wrong. Chrysanthemums . . . they don't smell. New Orleans stinks of swamps, decay, and gas, at least in late winter. Winter! It's winter, early February.* Only he couldn't recall the date. *Chrysanthemums? Why would I think of chrysanthemums?*

The streets remained wet from last night's rain. He looked around at the cold buildings, cobblestone streets, *banquettes,* and water running through the gutters. The city showed signs of life. People, horses, and carriages moved about the streets, horns sounded from the river, and church bells chimed in the distance, but Randow felt lost. His sense of direction had vanished. This was New Orleans. He knew that much. He had gambled here, had stayed in a fancy hotel, had. . . . Blackness again. Maybe if he didn't try so hard to remember. Maybe. . . .

A hand squeezed his shoulder. He thought it was the redhead's, but found the blonde at his side, offering him a timid smile. Black bags hung underneath her red-rimmed eyes. She started to say something, but the major started walking again, hailing a cab, and the blonde followed the group. Hugh Valdez and Newspaper Reader — Randow had already forgotten his name — motioned Randow to start walking.

Sighing, he obeyed, but before he had reached the lamppost, he stopped and turned, looking back at the gray building where he had spent the night.

"My revolver!" he said. The memory was the strongest he had experienced all day. He started back for the house, but Valdez put a firm hand on his chest and stopped him.

"Why?" Valdez grinned. "You want to get arrested?"

Randow blinked, uncomprehending.

"The police don't cotton to men carrying weapons in this city." Valdez lowered his arm. "Even I don't carry a pistol, and I'm the law, deputy provost marshal." Randow became aware of someone at his side, and out of the corner of his eye detected the blonde.

"Major's got a hack for us," said the other man.

"That's an old Dance you had, Bobby," Valdez continued. "Texas-made during the war, more likely to blow off your hand than kill a rat. Leave it. Besides . . ." — his grin returned — "I don't think you should be carrying a gun . . . even if it were legal . . . in your condition."

The impatient major yelled from the carriage, and Randow relented. Valdez was right. He didn't need a gun, wasn't even sure he could load it properly any more. He started to say something, stopped, and nodded instead, turning and heading to the waiting hack. Halfway there, the blonde spun around and raced back to the house.

"Laura!" the redhead shouted from the major's side. "Where are . . . ?"

"Your cloak!" she answered. "You left your cloak."

"But. . . ." Apolline finished with a sigh.

The man beside Valdez grumbled and cursed, while Valdez chuckled slightly, putting both hands on his lips. Randow repeated her name. If he kept repeating it, maybe he would remember. *Laura . . . Laura . . . Laura. . . .*

She came out quickly, holding up the cloak triumphantly.

"If you please," the major called out, "we have much to do before our vessel shoves off this afternoon!"

Apolline Rainier left them at the Levee as soon as they reached the *Mittie Stephens*, saying she had to bring the Negress madam the key to her bordello and finish up a few other business transactions before leaving New Orleans. Julius Siegel's clerk, Sidney Paige, had departed the group only moments before, whispering something to the major, who had nodded. Laura Kelley didn't know where Paige had gone, and she didn't really care, although she would have preferred Paige's company over swarthy Jules Honoré. In truth, though, she would be glad to be rid of the whole lot, except maybe Hugh Valdez.

"You sure you can find your way back here?" Major Siegel asked Apolline.

"Now that I know where it is." With a

sad smile, Apolline quickly swallowed Laura in a hug. "I loathe farewells," she said. "I miss you already."

"I miss you, too," Laura whispered.

"Write me when you are settled. General delivery, Jefferson, Texas. Are you sure this doctor can help you out?"

"Quite," Laura lied. "He's a dear friend." She quickly added: "But not as dear as you."

"I feel as though I've let you down."

"You haven't." Another lie. If their situations had been reversed, if it had been Apolline fleeing the law in hopes of finding shelter in Alexandria, Laura would have forgotten her plans, postponed her trip, would have done anything and everything in her power to help her oldest and dearest friend. Not that many years ago, Apolline would have done the same.

"Look after Bobby. You always enjoyed playing nurse."

"I'll let you know what Charles says."

"Get some sleep when you can and don't. . . ." With tears in her eyes, Apolline pulled away.

Laura started to open her handbag to offer her friend a handkerchief, but decided against it, wondering what would happen if Siegel's men saw the gun. Ever the gentleman, Hugh Valdez handed Apolline his handkerchief, and she thanked him before disappearing amid hogsheads of sugar and throngs of people working feverishly about the Levee.

"Let's find our staterooms," Siegel told Honoré, "and see if the saloon is open. And Hugh. . . ."

Valdez faced his boss, who gave him a wry grin. "I think it would be best if you looked after Miss Kelley and Captain Randow. I don't like leaving them alone in a place like this, with Captain Randow's condition." He tipped his hat at Laura. "I am a Yankee, ma'am, but I do have manners."

When Valdez looked past Siegel at the *Mittie Stephens*, being loaded by black workers with bales of hay, without answering, Siegel continued: "You can buy passage, pal, cabin or steerage on another vessel, and the government will reimburse you. This isn't the only steamboat bound for Jefferson. By jingo, the way I hear this old bucket floats, you could swim and beat us to Texas."

Still, Valdez did not answer, so Siegel tried another approach. "I would think you would enjoy Miss Kelley's company, a charming, beautiful woman. . . ."

"It's not that, Major." Laura felt thankful Valdez had found his voice and silenced Siegel in the middle of his lewd compliment. "It's. . . ."

"You'll know where to find us," Siegel continued. "I'd stay here myself, but the Army is the Army. I'd take it as a great favor if you would take care of the captain, here, and Miss Kelley."

The next words came from Honoré: "I'll stay. Be mighty glad to."

Laura shivered.

"No," Valdez said. "I'll stay here." His smile looked forced when he glanced back at Laura, but she gave him one in return anyway. "I look forward to more of their company."

"That's grand," Siegel said. "Let me know how Captain Randow fares." He tipped his hat again at Laura before heading toward the side-wheel steamboat, Honoré following like a hungry seagull.

"You don't have to stay," Laura told Valdez after Siegel and Honoré were out of earshot. She added: "Hugh."

"I know . . . Laura. It wasn't you, or Bobby here. I have family in Texas, not far from Jefferson, and I was looking forward to seeing them. It's been quite a spell since I've laid eyes on them, but what's another day or two? My brother's family can wait. They're not even expecting me. I was going to surprise them."

That only left Laura slightly reassured. Valdez didn't know Laura's plight, and she wondered if he would hand her over to authorities upon learning that she was an arsonist. He was charming enough, affable, and she had felt a girlish sense of joy when Valdez explained that this family he wanted to see in Texas did not include a wife and children, but Hugh Valdez worked for a provost marshal. True, his job was to catch deserters, but would duty compel him to help Louisiana's Reconstruction government? She wanted to trust him. She needed to trust somebody.

Another thought troubled her. How could she explain her situation to Charles LeBreton with Valdez in the same room? She would have to figure that out, soon.

Chapter Six

She's docked at the Levee, waiting, activity on every deck, coming to life in the early afternoon, gusts flapping a huge American flag on her stern and the pilot lights dangling from her twin black stacks that stretch into a clear blue sky. A pelican sits perched on a post nearby, watching the side-wheeler with a look of bored amusement. The Mittie Stephens *has changed a lot since last I saw her, but Captain Kellogg has kept her fit. I cannot wait to see the look on his face, or feel her hurricane deck below my feet.*

Lieutenant Constantine Ambroise let the passage flow through his mind again, editing as he went. He wanted to stop now, pull out his diary, and log the entry, but that would have to wait.

"So this is the ship that almost kept you out of this man's army, eh, sir?"

Ambroise chuckled as he glanced at

Nicholas Sloan, a stout man with graying black hair, mustache, and beard already white. "Not quite, Sergeant," Ambroise replied. The other two soldiers in his command, privates Efisio Silvia and Dutch Emmerich, looked about as uninterested in the *Mittie Stephens* as the brown pelican. "I sailed on her twice, during the Red River campaign in the late war. It was her captain who almost made a riverboat pilot of me."

"I see, sir," Sloan said, but he was just trying to be friendly, respectful.

Ambroise almost asked the sergeant if he had taken part in the Louisiana campaign. He often wondered if they had ever fought against each other. Sloan was a Southerner, had served with the Confederacy but enlisted in the Federal Army right after the surrender. He never admitted this, but Ambroise knew it, or merely sensed it, and yet Ambroise trusted this deep-voiced man with a chest shaped like a pickle barrel, no neck to speak of, muscular arms, and broad shoulders. The lieutenant could confide in him, although that was probably because neither Silvia nor Emmerich spoke passable English.

"She's a big boat," Sloan said.

Ambroise nodded, although many ships

along the Levee looked more impressive. A three-boiler side-wheeler, the *Mittie Stephens* weighed 312 tons and drew a tad more than four and a half feet. From bow to stern she stretched almost 169 feet, and close to thirty feet port to starboard. Those measurements were slightly different than when Brevet Major Constantine A. Ambroise had sailed on her during the spring and summer of 1864. The *Mittie Stephens* had been built in Madison, Indiana as a troop transport, but, after Union forces had been turned back at Mansfield, the ship had been sold to a civilian company, running on the Missouri River first, and later back down south from New Orleans to Bayou Sarah. After being rebuilt in 1865, she had been sold again the following year to Captain Maurice Langhorne as a packet for the New Orleans–Red River route.

"Well, she looks like she'll float, Lieutenant," Sloan said. "Reckon that's why the general picked her."

"She'll float," Ambroise agreed, although he knew the real reason the *Mittie Stephens* had been selected. "Let's go aboard and find Captain Kellogg."

The four soldiers walked up the wooden ramp to the right of the towering jackstaff and onto the main deck, already over-crowded with hay bales. Ambroise stepped aside to let four, leviathan black men pass, struggling with their cargo. He frowned when he read the big black letters stamped on the barrels: **BLACK POWDER**.

He couldn't do anything about the ship's civilian cargo, though, so he dismissed his worries and led his tiny command up the main staircase to the cabin deck. The sight of a man in an Army-blue frock coat, standing outside a cabin near the wheel-house, raised his curiosity, so he walked down that passage. As far as Ambroise knew, his was the only group of soldiers traveling on this civilian vessel. Once he got closer, however, he dismissed the man as a soldier, at least one now. The stranger, pale, balding, and squinting, leaned against the railing, smoking a cigar. His coat was from the Civil War, his trousers blue and white checked, his boots not military issue. Ambroise walked past him without acknowledging his presence, or his own being acknowledged, and went around the wheelhouse to the staircase beside the secured yawl. Another man exited the far berth, from which a woman's voice echoed, and Ambroise frowned.

Stern cabins were reserved for unmarried ladies, with men denied entrance without the captain's permission. Something about the look of the red-bearded man with the fancy cane told Ambroise that the lady's visitor had not obtained Homer Kellogg's permission.

It's none of my business, he told himself, and went upstairs to the hurricane deck.

He ran into a crew man almost immediately, and asked if Captain Kellogg were on board. "In the pilot house," he was informed, so Ambroise climbed the stairs to the texas, covering the length quickly as his excitement built and heart raced. He couldn't help but smile as he went up the final set of steps and entered the pilot house without knocking.

"Permission to come aboard, sir?" His voice expressed the enthusiasm of a child.

Silver pencil compass in hand, Homer Kellogg sat at his desk, staring intently at maps and charts. He grumbled an indeterminable answer before turning around, that omnipresent French briar bowl pipe hanging from his mouth, bent stem carved into his bottom lip. In that position, half turned from his desk, he froze while seconds ticked away. Ambroise couldn't think of anything to say, but his smile widened, and at last Kellogg set the compass atop a chart and slowly removed his pipe.

"Constantine . . . Constantine Ambroise, you look well . . . for a land lover."

"You look fit, too, Captain." Ambroise stepped inside, asking Sergeant Sloan to come with him, but ordering his two privates to wait outside. Before he could introduce Nicholas Sloan to the captain, Kellogg had risen from his desk, crossed the room, enveloped Ambroise in a crushing hug that lifted him off the floor, both men laughing. Ambroise joked that if the good captain didn't let up, he would have to explain Ambroise's broken ribs and bruised back to Captain Langhorne, the United States Army, and Mr. Alain Ambroise of Madison, Indiana.

Released from this friendly torture, Ambroise staggered back as Kellogg's pipe returned. Once both men caught their breath, Ambroise introduced the sergeant to the ship's master, who offered his hand.

"Has my former bound boy told any lies about me?" Kellogg asked.

"No, sir." Sloan grinned. "None that I'm aware of, Captain."

"Then I'll tell you the truth about him, Sergeant. In the spring of 'Fifty-Eight, when I was captain of the *Princess*, running between New Orleans and Vicksburg and up the Red to Shreveport, this young lad came to me and said he wanted to become a riverboat pilot. He brought a letter of introduction from his father and enough credit, I thought, to buy an apprenticeship, with my payment to be deducted from his first year's salary after he became a pilot. Has he told you who his father is?"

"No, sir, not that I recall."

Ambroise shook his head and found a chair. This might take a while.

"Alain Ambroise. Now, I doubt if that means anything to an Army lad, Sergeant, but on the Western rivers it means a great deal. Alain Ambroise happens to be one of the finest shipbuilders in these United States. He built this ship, or, at least, he helped build it when she was first launched in 'Sixty-Three. The *Mittie* was rebuilt a couple of years later." Kellogg shot a glance at Ambroise. "And how is your father, Constantine?"

"Well, sir, but retired now, building ships in bottles instead of ships for the rivers. He sends his regards."

"Aye. He's not the only one getting long in tooth, but back to my story. So I took on Mister Ambroise, thinking it would be the easiest five hundred dollars I ever earned. After all, I thought the rivers flowed through his veins, his father being a shipbuilder and all." Kellogg snorted. "This man was the worst cub pilot ever I saw. Never fayed in with any of my crew, never said anything but flapdoodle, and couldn't tell a flatboat from flood wood. He strained my faculties, I tell you, Sergeant. When I received a letter from his father, asking how his son was faring, I hastily replied that I might send him a bill. The *Princess* was fast, Sergeant, not like the *Mittie Stephens*, built to be swift, the envy of many captains, pilots, and clerks from New Orleans to northern Louisiana. But once your lieutenant became my cub pilot, well, we set records for being unpunctual. Crews started to call the *Princess* the *Laggard*. A hop toad could move faster than the *Princess*, son."

Kellogg's pipe had gone out, so he fished a match from a pocket on his waistcoat, struck it with a yellow thumbnail, and refired it. He leaned back, reflecting, puffing, and shaking his head. Ambroise enjoyed the smell of the tobacco smoke almost as much as he enjoyed hearing his old mentor's voice.

"Yet he proved his salt, Sergeant, showed clear grit the following February. Criminy, it's coming on ten years now, isn't it, Constantine?"

"Yes, sir. February Twenty-Seventh, a night I sha'n't forget."

"Nor me, lad."

Ambroise and Kellogg let out simultaneous sighs.

"What happened?" asked Sloan.

Kellogg removed the pipe. "Boiler exploded. She went up in flames and sank in minutes, not far from Baton Rouge. Lost most of my crew and several passengers. A ghastly sight it was, Sergeant. Still gives me the horrors. One more like that and I will swear off the river. All told, we lost seventy men, women, and children."

"It would have been worse, Captain, if not for you."

"Balderdash, Constantine. Everyone would have been called to glory if not for you. Even one of the newspapers compared him to Odysseus." His eyes turned to Sloan. "Constantine should have died himself, Sergeant. His back was badly burned, his coat a smoldering ruin, yet he found my second mate and what was left of my deck crew manning the yawl, loading it with our surviving lady passengers and children, flames nicking at them the whole while. Constantine said there wasn't time for the yawl, that the *Princess* would be under the Mississippi before they ever got

86

it loaded and lowered, and he was right. He practically pulled the screaming women and children from the yawl, tossed them into the river, ordering the crew into the water to save them, to pull them to shore, grab anything that would float. Why they took orders from him, I do not know, but they did. Saved many lives.

"Well, the *Princess* was an inferno by now, blown apart and sinking fast, yet Constantine climbed the stairs, heading for the pilot house, looking for survivors until he realized there was none, that he had to get off this ship, and fast. Somehow . . . the Lord's doing, I suppose . . . he heard a drowning man's desperate cries from below, so Constantine Ambroise, the worst cub pilot ever to steam up the Mississippi and Red, dived in the frigid waters and pulled two other men to shore, saved them from drowning. One of those men, Sergeant, was me."

"You would have done the same, Captain." Ambroise turned to Sergeant Sloan. "What Captain Kellogg isn't telling you, Sloan, is that he was pulling a badly burned passenger to the shore himself, but he was too tuckered out having been blown into the river from the texas deck when the boiler went up."

A silence fell across the pilot house, broken a full minute later by Sergeant Sloan: "Is that when you decided to give up a naval career, Lieutenant?"

"Yes, thanks to Captain Kellogg. He wrote a letter of commendation to my Congressman, and the following summer, having recovered from my burns . . . they were not as bad as Captain Kellogg says, by the way . . . I was at West Point."

"You've done well, too, in the Army," Kellogg said.

Ambroise shrugged. "Still a lieutenant, though."

"Aye, well promotions are hard to come by, on land or sea, especially with the Army cutting the size of the troops. Enough reminiscing. You're here with soldiers, Constantine. That means you are here on federal business."

"Yes, sir." From inside his blouse he pulled out his orders, which no one had seen except his commanding officer and Sergeant Sloan, and passed them to Kellogg.

The paper crinkled in the captain's big hand. Kellogg found his eyeglasses on his desk, put them on, and read in silence. When finished, Kellogg looked over the rims of his spectacles and said: "That's quite a load, Constantine."

"Yes, sir."

"More than I am comfortable with, in these times."

"I know, sir, but we have kept it a secret. No one knows about this but Sergeant Sloan, myself, Captain Langhorne, the paymaster, and General Bishop . . . and now you, sir."

Kellogg returned the paper with a chuckle. "You're smarter than that, lad. One hundred thousand dollars in gold coin? That's a sizable payroll, and the Army can't keep secrets. I bet the troops around Jefferson are already talking about it, planning on where they shall spend their money. Plus, the soldiers transporting the gold to New Orleans, they know about it. And if you think Maurice Langhorne can keep a secret. . . ." Kellogg's head shook, and he changed course. "I take it that you had something to do with the selection of my packet for the trip."

Ambroise answered with a nod and a smile. "Captain Langhorne was agreeable. Besides, this old bucket saved a lot of lives five years ago."

"Maurice was agreeable because the Army will pay him for use of his ship, and, trust me, I will see not a penny for my troubles. Where is the paymaster?"

"On the *Dixie*. A ruse, sir. We are taking all precautions."

"Very good. Is it here?"

"No, sir. I. . . ."

"I have schedules, Constantine," Kellogg fired back. "You know. . . ."

Ambroise made himself interrupt this family friend. "Yes, sir, I am aware of that, as is the Army, as is your boss." He had already found and withdrew another letter from his pocket, and passed it over to a frowning Homer Kellogg. "I apologize, Captain, but with the recent storms . . . well, you'll read it for yourself. We learned of the situation this morning, and I met with Captain Langhorne immediately. As you can see from his letter, he is agreeable to this request as well. I hope it will not inconvenience you, or your passengers and crew."

Chapter Seven

A wrought-iron fence, laced with Cupid's bow and arrow, and dying lawn surrounded the three-story Greek Revival home of Dr. Charles LeBreton. Sight of the marble columns and whitewashed stone made Laura Kelley remember Green Haven in all its glory, and her heart sank as a vision of orange flames and churning black smoke replaced it. Despite needing a new coat of paint and a good groundskeeper, LeBreton's home stood out among the mansions along tree-lined Esplanade Avenue, although all were small compared to the Parker family plantation near Alexandria. *At least,* Laura thought, *until recently.*

The filigreed gate squeaked as she pushed it, sending a chill racing up her spine. Laura steeled herself and, with Valdez and Randow following, walked up the stone-lined path to the front door, rang the bell, and heard the faint sound of the chimes from inside. Next, footsteps echoed, and the door opened to reveal not a servant, as Laura had expected, but Charles LeBreton himself.

His curly hair, once dark and long, had thinned and grayed, yet his mustache remained thick, brown, and waxed. He wore a sack coat, unbuttoned, and his black silk cravat had been loosened. Laura tried to remember the last time she had seen LeBreton. It seemed like only months ago, but that wasn't right. It had been at her wedding at Green Haven in 1861. They had simply corresponded since then. Seven and a half years ago, he had been as spry and dashing as Theodore Wilson Kelley, but now looked weary, run-down, yet his dark eyes sparkled when he recognized her, and he lifted her hand to his lips.

"Laura Parker Kelley, *chérie,* why you haven't aged a bit."

"Nor have . . ." — she started, but a roll of the doctor's eyes stopped her, and both grinned. He gazed past her, and she introduced Valdez and Randow, and the doctor invited all inside. A newspaper rested on a table beside an empty tumbler and bottle of brandy. Laura stared at *The Daily Picayune,* wondering if it contained news of her crime.

The clock down the hallway chimed twice.

"Do I know you?"

LeBreton stared at Randow, and Laura explained his situation — hers would have to wait — as quickly as possible. The doctor ran his long fingers through his hair, then tried to comb over the balding spot atop his shiny head.

"Laura," he finally said softly, "I haven't practiced medicine in three years."

"I know, Charles, but I thought. . . ." She really didn't know what she had been thinking.

"*Hélas,* I did take an oath." He took a deep breath and slowly exhaled. "I'll look at him. *Jeune homme,* if you would kindly come upstairs to my office." Randow offered a blank nod, and LeBreton told Laura: "It might help to have his friends with him. You both may join us."

Her heart sank, but Valdez surprised her. "No thanks, Doc. If you don't mind, I'll stay downstairs, maybe read the paper." He wasn't looking at the *Picayune,* though, but the brandy. "No offense, but I'm scared of doctors. You might find something wrong with me, even while you're looking at Captain Randow."

LeBreton chuckled. "*Naturellement, monsieur.* Help yourself to my *eau-de-vie.* You should find a clean glass in the bar."

Charles LeBreton's second-story office overlooked the banana trees in the back courtyard. Furniture was spartan, and Laura realized that, indeed, the entire house appeared practically bare, making their footsteps echo hollowly throughout the mansion. Even the bookshelves in his office sat vacant. It hadn't been like that in the late 1850s when she had first met the graduate of Cambridge and some French college whose name she had long since forgotten, but that had been before Ninette LeBreton, his radiant bride, had died of yellow fever while the doctor had been serving with the Confederate Army.

Laura declined LeBreton's offer of a rocking chair and watched as he helped Randow into the leather chair behind the doctor's desk. Gently he placed all of his fingers on the top of Randow's head and began feeling around the skull.

"Have either of you heard of *amnésie?*" LeBreton asked while continuing the head examination. "Amnesia is the English name. Memory loss."

"I think I've read about it," Laura answered; Randow didn't respond.

"No lumps." Shaking his head, LeBreton

moved around the chair, rested his back-side on the desktop, and lifted Randow's head into the light shining from a window without drapes. "A few scratches. Skinned knuckles. Bruising elsewhere, but his head looks fine. Usually *amnésie* occurs as a re-sult of head trauma, but I see no evidence of this." He wet his lips and scratched his chin. The doctor, Laura noticed, had not shaved today.

"What is your name?"

"Bobby Randow."

"And you served in which cavalry?"

"Ninth Texas. Under Colonel Sims."

"James Sims?"

"No, sir. William B. Sims."

"Your father? What of him? And the rest of your family?"

"Papa got killed at Shiloh. Brother Zack died in Vicksburg. Mama remarried, lives up in Shreveport."

"And what did you do last night, Cap-tain?"

"I. . . ." Randow swallowed and stifled an oath.

LeBreton reached into a desk drawer and pulled out a cigar, which he offered to his patient, who shook his head. The doctor stuck the cigar into his coat pocket.

"Have you ever experienced anything

like this before, *monsieur?*"

Randow smirked. "Would I remember it, Doc?" LeBreton laughed, and Laura smiled, but Randow quietly added: "I don't think so."

"Not even during the war?"

"No, sir. I've always had a rather good memory."

"Your mother? Your father or brother?"

His head shook again.

"*Juste ciel,* this is fascinating." LeBreton's eyes found Laura. "It is as you explained to me downstairs, my dear. I have not seen a case like this since Murfreesboro up in Tennessee." He turned back to Randow. "Did the Ninth fight there, Captain? I do not recall."

"Murfreesboro? No, sir, we were with Price's Corps then, had a scrap at Middleburg about that time, then got transferred to Van Dorn's cavalry corps in January of 'Sixty-Three."

LeBreton tilted his chin toward the door, and Laura moved to open it. "Captain, I'm going to say three words, then *Madame* Kelley and I shall step outside for a moment. When we return, I'll ask you to repeat these three words to us. Do you understand?"

"Sure. I'll try."

"Middleburg. Blue. And Laura. Those three words . . . Middleburg, blue, Laura."

"Middleburg, blue, Laura." Randow's head bobbed, and LeBreton followed Laura to the hallway outside, overlooking Hugh Valdez downstairs, sitting in a chair, reading the newspaper while sipping the doctor's brandy.

"You've seen something like this before, Charles?" Laura asked immediately. Her voice carried, and Valdez looked up but said nothing. A moment later, his head dropped back to the *Picayune*.

"Once, as I said, during the war. He was a strapping young Kentuckian, fit as a fiddle, one of Colonel Hunt's 'orphans', and, well, during the Yankee charge, this man had no choice but to plunge into Stones River or be slaughtered. I was with General Adams's First Brigade, and, after the carnage, this Kentuckian was being tormented by the Thirteenth Louisiana boys who had found him. They were calling him a coward, but God as my witness, Laura, those Kentuckians were anything but cowards. This was in late December, Laura. Stones River was freezing. Anyway, I intervened, brought the dazed, shivering soldier to a fire the surgeons had going near our hospital tent. This man knew his name, much like Captain Randow, knew everything about his past, but could not remember a stitch about the battle, couldn't even remember swimming the cold river. We learned that by guesswork later. Nor could he repeat my name until the following afternoon. The far past came easily to him, but more recent memories remained blurred, or black."

"What happened to him?"

"Most of his memory returned after a day or two, though he couldn't recall everything when I brought him back to Colonel Hunt's command, or what was left of it." LeBreton shrugged. "Whether he regained all of his memory, I do not know, for I never saw the poor fellow again."

"But this soldier's memory did return, so Bobby Randow's probably will? Is that what you're saying, Charles?"

Another shrug pierced Laura's heart. "I don't know. We doctors have learned so little about the mind. No one studies the human brain. I have read journals in which men receive blows on the head and forget everything about them, even their names, their families, but Captain Randow's case, as with the Kentuckian's, is so different. Is it hereditary? Perhaps. Brought on by distress, as in battle? It could be. I wish I had answers for you, and him." His hand gripped the knob, and he opened the door. Laura followed him inside.

"Captain Randow," LeBreton said, "I want you to repeat those three words now."

"Laura," Randow said quickly. She smiled.

"And?" LeBreton prodded.

His mouth opened, but he only sighed. "I . . . Laura."

"Oui."

"And, uhhh." Randow's shoulders sagged, and he let out a curse, and promptly apologized to Laura for his ungentlemanly language.

"That's fine, Captain," LeBreton said. "The Kentuckian could not remember a single word when I first examined him."

"Kentuckian?" Randow blinked repeatedly. "Do I know him?"

"No, *monsieur*. The Kentuckian is from my past, not yours. Blue and Middleburg were the other two words."

"So what do you think, Doc?" Randow asked hopefully.

"I wish I had an answer for you, Captain. What is the last thing you remember?"

"Playing cards at Number Eighteen Royal Street."

"Did you win?"

"Yeah. Had a good run for a while."

LeBreton let out a mirthless snort. "Fortune has not graced my company during recent visits to the Merchants' Exchange. What else, *jeune homme?*"

"Then I went to see. . . ." His mouth clenched, and the head shook angrily.

"Apolline Rainier," Laura answered. "She runs a. . . ."

"I am familiar with the reputation of *la mademoiselle,* and her occupation in the Swamp."

"He was staying at the Saint Louis Hotel," Laura added.

"If only I knew what had happened?" LeBreton tugged and twisted the ends of his mustache. "A fight," he suggested. "The Swamp is known for its brawls and murders. Why, this morning a man was found shot to death in one of our Cities of the Dead near that New Orleans blight. A notorious gambler whose name I do not recall." At the word gambler, his eyes focused on Randow.

Laura quickly opened her handbag and awkwardly withdrew a revolver. "This is Captain Randow's." She handed the .44 to LeBreton. "I. . . ." Well, her friend didn't need to know everything for the moment.

First, the doctor sniffed the barrel, then set the hammer at half cock and examined the cylinder. "All six chambers have been fired. *Juste ciel, monsieur,* you might well have been in a bit of a battle last night. Does that trigger any memories?"

Randow's eyes closed for a full minute, but he found no answer, no reason.

"The gambler's name, the one found killed," LeBreton continued, "it was Victor, Victorio, Vincent, De . . . De . . . De-something. Forgive me, I just heard of it at a. . . ." He stopped himself.

"I don't know, Doc. It's still all black."

LeBreton found the cigar Randow had rejected, bit off the end, and searched for a match. Finding none, he removed the long nine and sat on the desktop. "*Monsieur,* alas, there is little I can do for you. My recommendation would be that you retrace your path. Go see *Mademoiselle* Rainier, return to the Merchants' Exchange, the Saint Charles Hotel. If your memory does not return, I suggest you pay your mother a visit in Shreveport. You do not recall anything like this happening to your father or brother, but she might. Mothers do not forget." LeBreton groaned. "Forgive me, *monsieur.* My choice of words. . . ."

"It's all right, Doc. How much do I owe you?"

LeBreton's eyebrows arched. "Well, most

people would have forgotten to ask me that, Captain."

"You fought for the Cause, Doc. I can't forget that."

"Indeed."

"The South won, right?"

LeBreton's frown prompted Randow's soft chuckle, and the doctor bent over in laughter. "You have a grand wit, *monsieur*," LeBreton said when he regained control. "I dare say, if I were in your condition, I would not joke about it, but that is good, no, laughter?"

"How much?" Randow repeated.

"A dollar."

Laura watched with amazement as Randow reached inside his shell jacket and pulled out a wad of greenbacks. He handed LeBreton a five-dollar note.

"I . . . have no change."

"I didn't ask for any," Randow said. He turned toward Laura, waiting.

"If you don't mind . . . Bobby." She liked the sound of his name. "If you would join Hugh downstairs, I'd like a moment alone with Charles."

"Yes, ma'am," Randow said, and headed out the door.

LeBreton collapsed in the vacant chair

even before Laura finished her story. He sat there dumbly, paling, his fingers absently shredding the unlit cigar.

"I had nowhere else to turn, Charles. I. . . ." She found a handkerchief in her handbag, and wiped her eyes.

"*Chérie . . . chérie . . . chérie. . . .*"

"I don't know where. . . ."

Tears rolled down his cheeks when he looked up, crushing Laura's hopes. "Laura, I have no money, nothing to give you except Captain Randow's five-dollar note. I'm busted. What I don't owe to carpetbaggers, I owe to gamblers. Look at me, Laura. I am a drunk, a gambler, a dying old man. They'll soon throw me out of this house. I . . . miss . . . Ninette." He started sobbing, babbling in French, burying his head on the desk, and Laura left him there. She headed for the door, but stopped, and returned to the desk.

"Take care, Charles," she said softly in French. "I will be all right, and so will you, my darling." She doubted if he heard. Slowly she lifted Randow's Dance revolver and lowered it into her handbag.

Randow sat in the chair, poring over the *Picayune* as if searching for lost memories; Valdez, however, was gone.

"Have you seen Hugh?" Laura asked with an urgency that surprised her.

Randow looked up from the paper. "Do I know him?"

She bit her lip. She was getting sick of hearing that question. Laura looked around. The front door was open, and the clock chimed on the half hour. It was three-thirty. Valdez had been reading the paper and had left without an explanation. Or perhaps Valdez had told Randow, who had simply forgotten. Valdez might have read something in the *Picayune*, something about her crime, something about Randow, something that had sent him for the law. She'd never know, and couldn't take any chances. *Would it always be like this?* Laura wondered. *Worrying? Looking into the future? Playing detective? Running? Always running?*

"Let's go," she told Randow.

Chapter Eight

Inside John B. Schiller's Sazerac Coffee House, they sipped potent chicory after eating at some restaurant on Canal Street. Randow thought they were going to the Merchants' Exchange over on Royal Street, but Laura — her last name slipped his grasp — had grabbed his hand and led him into the quaint but crowded little building without a word. The last thing Randow remembered seeing before she almost jerked his arm from its socket was a New Orleans policeman walking up the *banquette* toward them. That, and the sky, which had turned almost pitch black toward the Levee. A storm must be blowing in, he had thought, until he detected the pungent odor of fat pine burning, and heard someone's remark about steamboats getting ready to shove off.

Food had done him good, for he couldn't remember the last time he had eaten. Nor could he recall ever tasting coffee like this, so strong it could likely float a spoon. Laura — *Kelley, that was it!* — apparently enjoyed hers, though. He made himself swallow more, set down his cup, and said: "Tell me about yourself."

She kept staring out the window, but turned suddenly, startled, and said: "I'm sorry. What did you say?"

Sounds like something I'd say, he thought.

Laura Kelley had pretty green eyes, although lined with red streaks from not enough sleep. She looked exhausted, but determination set her jaw. He couldn't guess how old she was, and wouldn't dare. His father had raised him better than to go around guessing a woman's age.

"You know everything about me." Randow grinned. "I don't know a lick about you. Don't worry. I probably won't remember what you tell me."

Her smile, soft but somewhat sad, managed to warm him, and she leaned back while the waiter refilled her mug. Randow put his hand over his cup when the young Creole started to pour more chicory in his. "My name is Laura Parker Kelley," she said after the waiter left. Her accent was Southern, not Cajun, a pleasant, gentle voice. "I'm a widow. My husband Theodore died during the siege of Vicksburg. I knew Apolline back home in Alexandria. We grew up together. I was coming to pay her a visit before . . . before leaving Louisiana."

"Where you going?"

"Texas, maybe. Then, oh, I don't know, California. The territories. I haven't given it much thought."

"Why? Why leave your home?"

Her eyes hardened. "There's nothing for me here, not any more, not since the war, really."

"So, I met you the other night?"

"At Apolline's." Her head bobbed.

"Why? Why help me?"

Laura's eyes relaxed, and she took another sip of coffee. "Charles, Doctor LeBreton that is, used to call me his little nurse. I was always helping, or wanting to help people, or animals. I thought I'd become a midwife, maybe even a doctor, but. . . ." She shook her head. "Well, ladies do not become doctors, Captain Randow, and daughters of wealthy cotton planters do not become midwives. So I was basically a . . . well, I helped Mother around the house, sneaked off when I could and looked after our horses, dogs, and, when I came down to New Orleans and lost my chaperone, I would assist Doctor LeBreton with his patients.

"Then I got married. I was old . . . twenty-six . . . and my parents thought I was bound to be a spinster. Surprised Apolline, everyone. You . . . you remind me of him. . . ."

"Of whom?" He silently cursed himself, his memory, for the pain he caused her.

"My late husband," she answered flatly.

"I'm flattered." *That's what I should have said to begin with!*

Her lips turned upward once more, but the smile had lost its warmth. "A horrible time to get married," she continued, "what with Louisiana at war. I hardly even saw Theodore after our wedding." She blinked often and took another sip to regain composure. "After Theodore died, I shut out everything but my parents, moved back home, took care of them. Father was an invalid after Brice's Cross Roads, lost his le . . . his limbs, and it was all Mother and I could do to take care of him after he came home. Then Mother died of pneumonia, and it was just me and Father. He took sick with a fever and passed away last summer, and the place proved too much for me. So . . . I left. Now, you're from Texas, is it everything I've heard?"

She wanted to change the subject, put the focus on him, and Randow almost let her. "You never been?"

Pain from her bad memories receded, her eyes danced with her laughter. "Captain Randow, I've never been east of Pontchartrain, north of Natchitoches, south of New Orleans, or west of, let's see . . . Huddleston. I've never left Louisiana, never seen anything but cotton, hurricanes, alligators, and swamps. I want to hear all about Texas."

"Well, firstly, let's forget that 'captain'. I never cared much for being called that during the war. The name's Bobby, if that's not being forward, ma'am."

"And it's Laura," she said, "please. 'Ma'am' makes me feel old."

"Yes'm, I mean, Laura. Texas, it's big. Haven't seen but a parcel of it myself."

"Full of wild Indians."

"None that I ever saw, but, yeah, they've had some Indian troubles. We lived on a farm outside of Sherman. That's in north Texas, Grayson County. Gently rolling, tall grass, not like New Orleans. No swamps, I mean, not much water."

"What's your farm like?"

Laughing, he shook his head. "There's no farm, ma . . . Laura. Tornado turned our cabin into kindling. That's why Mama sold the place, remarried, and moved to Shreveport. I haven't been back that way in years, since right after the surrender. Been to Waco, San Antonio . . . that's as far south as I've made it, probably as far west, too. Anyhow, for the past year or so I've gambled mostly in Arkansas and along the rivers, Fort Smith, Washington, Helena, Natchez, Memphis, Saint Louis."

"What about Jefferson?" she asked. "Jefferson, Texas? I thought I might settle there."

"Jefferson. Yeah, I've. . . ." Randow lifted his head slightly. *Jefferson. What was it about Jefferson?* He had gambled there, knew the city on Caddo Lake, could picture its red brick buildings and steamboats, pearl hunters, trappers, soldiers, children fishing in pirogues, the cypress trees, lily pads, Spanish moss, and that eerie black water. Yet something troubled him. He reached absently, feeling around his neck. *A cross,* he thought. *A pewter cross. I traded it for a cup of soup. But that's not it, either. It's something else.*

"Bobby?"

Whatever it was, he couldn't find it. He faced Laura again, and shook his head. "Sorry, what was I saying?"

"It doesn't matter," she said. "You want

to go to the Merchants' Exchange, or the hotel?"

He answered with a shrug, paid the tab, and followed her onto the busy street. The sky looked pitch black, and he smelled something burning. "Criminy," he said, pointing at the billowing clouds of smoke. "Must be a bad fire over that way."

Laura looked sad as she took him by his hand. "That's the Levee," she said. "Steamboats are preparing to leave. A man told you. . . . It doesn't matter. Let's walk over to Royal Street."

The Merchants' Exchange, better known by its address, Number 18 Royal Street, was a marble-faced, two-story building across from The Gem, another gambling hall. Laura considered waiting outside while Randow went in. After all, Number 18 Royal Street was no place for a lady, probably did not even allow women inside, but, if she stayed on the streets, she might be mistaken for one of Apolline's girls. So she let Randow take her by the arm and escort her into the smoke-filled gambling hall.

If anyone recognized Randow, or even noticed her, they paid scant attention. They wandered across the bottom floor, around tables already crowded, then walked upstairs, back down, and outside, crossed the street, and tried The Gem. Randow looked lost inside these places, though, and for once he didn't ask questions when he should have. Ten minutes later they were outside again, filling their lungs with clean air, instead of cigar smoke.

"Well," Laura said, "I guess it's the Saint Louis. Are you all right?"

"I . . . gambled here, right?"

"That's what you told us. Remember?"

Eventually he nodded. "It's six o'clock," he said. "I think I was playing poker there" — he pointed at the Merchants' Exchange — "late at night. Maybe I should come back later."

"Perhaps." She didn't want him coming alone, though. "Do you want to find a hack or walk to the Saint Louis?"

"Je vous demande pardon, monsieur, mademoiselle. . . ." The indignant *maitre d'hôtel* straightened, eyes widening in shocked recognition, and took two steps back when Bobby Randow turned. *"Pardonnez-moi, Monsieur* Randow, I did not recognize you nor. . . ." The distaste he couldn't hide on his face told Laura

that the mustached imp thought Laura was nothing more than a jill-flirt. "We worried about *monsieur* when he did not return last night, but now. . . ." He shot a lecherous glance at Laura and nodded slightly. As her blood pulsated and face blushed, she thought about ripping out his throat. "Would *monsieur* care for his key?"

Randow stood there dumbly, so Laura, having calmed herself down, answered for him: *"Oui."*

"Bien," said the Frenchman, leading Laura and Randow to the desk.

The new St. Louis Hotel — the original had burned in 1838 and been rebuilt three years later — stood on the corner of Royal and St. Louis Streets, perhaps the grandest hotel in any Mississippi River town, let alone New Orleans. It had a copper-plated dome, marble rotunda of various colors, and a staff that went to great lengths to keep rabble from bothering the paying customers. She couldn't really blame the *maitre d'hôtel* for thinking Laura and Randow were a couple of skipjacks. Both needed a bath and some clean clothes. At the desk, the Frenchman handed Randow a brass key, which he turned in his fingers.

"Does *Monsieur* Randow have any messages?" Laura asked, and took the key. Room 418.

"No, *mademoiselle*," he answered, after checking the row of boxes behind him.

"Let's go, Bobby," she said, and headed to the staircase.

The spacious room looked as Dr. Charles LeBreton's house once had: curtain-top desk with leather chair at a window overlooking St. Charles Street, maple chiffonier and matching bureau and hand-carved armoire, Turkish couch, overstuffed rocker, Chippendale mirror, and four-poster canopy bed. Randow, however, saw something else that interested him.

"Is this mine?" He picked up a grip, which he tossed on the Turkish couch, dropped to his knees, and opened without waiting for Laura's reply.

"I would assume so," she said, and opened the armoire. It was empty, except for a folded newspaper on the bottom. When she turned back to Randow, he was rifling through the luggage, tossing shirts, a badly folded frock coat, trousers, vest, unmentionables, socks, shaving kit, decks of cards, and other items onto the floor. The empty armoire and packed grip told Laura that Randow had planned on checking out of the hotel. He picked up a boiled shirt, sat on the couch facing Laura, and held it against his chest.

"It's your size," she said.

He turned up his nose. "Reckon I could use it now," he said. "I'm mighty ripe."

"We could both use. . . ." She stopped herself before she suggested the bath. That wouldn't be lady-like. Then, again, what would the prudes back in Alexandria say about a widow entering a bachelor's hotel room without a chaperone? She looked back at the armoire, picked up the newspaper, and walked across the plush carpet. She was heading for the overstuffed rocker, but, when she opened *The Daily Picayune*, she stopped, and sat on the edge of the bed.

"Bobby," she said, and motioned him over.

Inside the crumpled February 2nd edition on a page full of advertisements announcing the steamboat schedules, one item had been circled in ink.

**Leaves on THURSDAY, Feb. 4th, at 5 p.m.
FOR JEFFERSON, SHREVEPORT,
Grand Bayou, Grand Ecore, St Maurice,
Cotile, Alexandria, Norman's, Barbin's,
and all the way landings —
The light draft passenger packet**

MITTIE STEPHENS,
H. Kellogg, master, C. F. Hayes, clerk,
will leave as above. For freight or passage, apply on board, or to
W. M. SURLS, 2 Tchoupitoulas Street,
H. R. EPPLER, 4 Tchoupitoulas Street.

"What day is it?" Randow asked.

"February Fourth. I'm afraid the *Mittie Stephens* has steamed off for Jefferson by now," Laura said. "With Apolline and. . . ."

"Was I supposed to be on it?"

She sighed. He didn't understand, his mind still murky. Randow had moments where she thought he might remember everything, but then a fog would envelope him. Maybe it didn't matter. Earlier that morning, Hugh Valdez had told her it was perhaps better if Randow never remembered everything. So what if he couldn't recall what happened the previous night? He had known drunks who had suffered something similar but went on with their lives. Randow, however, was obsessed with what had happened to him.

He was back at the Turkish couch, pulling out a copper powder flask and tin of percussion caps. "No revolver," he said, and tossed the empty grip on the floor.

"It's in my handbag," Laura reminded him. "When I ran back inside Apolline's. . . ." She shook her head, tired of explaining everything to him over and over again. She had set the bag beside the wash basin on the bureau, and started to get it for him, but suddenly couldn't get her legs to work. She fell back into the bed, sinking into the plush comforter and downy mattress, and closed her eyes.

Chapter Nine

She rose stiffly, trying to gather her bearings, awakened by a light tapping on the door. Sunlight crept through the window's draperies. Morning. She had spent all night, hadn't even rolled over, asleep on Randow's hotel-room bed, only he was gone.

"Mademoiselle?" came a muffled voice.

Laura slid onto the floor, rubbed sleep from her eyes, crossed the room, and opened the door, surprised to see a rotund man smiling at her. "Is *mademoiselle* ready to have her bath drawn?"

"I'm sorry?" she began, bewildered.

"Monsieur Randow said you would like a bath. Is it too early? We can return. . . ."

"No, no." She shook her head, noticing the helpers behind him, the bathtub and buckets of water they had lugged up four flights of stairs. "Come in." She stepped away from the door. "Where is *Monsieur* Randow?"

"In the lobby downstairs, *mademoiselle*. He spent all night downstairs."

Laura smiled. Randow had not forgotten that he was a gentleman.

She almost didn't recognize him, sitting in an over-size couch in the lobby, newspaper in his lap, nodding politely at a gray-bearded gentleman in silk top hat and morning coat who sat across from Randow, engaging him in conversation about his shipping business on Conti Street. The merchant did all of the talking; Randow just sat there, head bobbing occasionally.

Gone were Randow's beard stubble and Confederate shell jacket. The boots were the same, although tan trousers were pulled over the tops. A brown frock coat, wrinkled and frayed, covered the red-and-white striped boiled shirt he had held up to his chest last night. No vest, no tie, and still no hat, but his hair had been trimmed and combed.

Laura waited for a pause in the merchant's monologue before introducing herself and greeting Randow with a — *"Bon jour."* — and a smile. She still wore the same dress she had on since Sunday, but the bath had refreshed her. The merchant crushed out a cigar she hadn't noticed, kissed her hand, and excused himself, saying how much he enjoyed "conversing with this charming young man. *Adieu*." When he had gone, Laura sat down.

"What were you talking about?"

"I don't know."

"Thanks for the bath, Bobby. That was very thoughtful."

"Ma'am?"

She shook her head. "Nothing. Did you get any sleep?"

"I guess so. I feel fine."

"You got your hair cut," she said. "And put on some other clothes." He smelled clean, too, but she didn't mention this. "Where did you go?"

He gave her an uncomfortable shrug. "I don't know. Some place on Royal Street. Like I told you, I was getting a mite ripe."

He hadn't forgotten that much. In fact, Laura thought, his memory kept improving.

"You could have come back upstairs, Bobby. I didn't mean to. . . ." A radiant couple in vivid clothes walked past them, stopping Laura from finishing her sentence. When they had passed, she started to ask another question, but Randow shot out an admission.

"Couldn't remember the room number.

Left the key upstairs." He sounded disgusted with himself. "Didn't want to ask."

"It's all right. What happened to your jacket, your other pair of trousers?"

"Left them somewhere, I think at the bathhouse. By the way, I checked out of the hotel. You wouldn't believe what they charge! Told the gent as soon as you came down, we'd take our leave. Hope that suits you."

Laura told him that was fine, although she would have loved to have spent a few more nights at the St. Louis, hiding from the law. She looked at the newspaper in his lap, then remembered. "Your grip. It's upstairs."

"My grip." Randow chuckled. "Oh, yeah. That's funny. I had packed it Wednesday night, thought about checking out then, but decided that, what for, if I got killed, they could. . . ." His mouth hung open as his eyes focused on that faraway place again, looking straight at Laura but not seeing a thing. *If I got killed . . . ,* he whispered. His face locked, and Laura didn't move, careful not to say a word, not to break his concentration.

A minute later, he let out another long sigh, and rose. "You hungry?" he asked.

After retrieving Randow's grip, they ate

121

omelets, fresh fruit, and toast, and drank chicory coffee in the hotel dining room before wandering back to Number 18 Royal Street for another fruitless journey through the gambling hall, then walking aimlessly along the French Quarter, finally stepping inside a mercantile where Randow bought a brown hat, and Laura purchased a green and white checked dress that she wore out of the shop and onto Canal Street.

By mid-afternoon, they had wound back at the Sazerac Coffee House.

"Hugh Valdez," Laura said, "suggested you forget. . . ."

"Who?"

"Hugh Valdez. You met him the other night at Apolline's."

"I see."

"Anyway, he suggested you forget what happened, what caused your memory loss, move on. You've lost a few hours. I don't think it's important that you know what happened. Probably nothing happened." That wasn't likely, though, considering Randow's empty revolver. "Let it go, Bobby." Especially, she thought, if Randow had killed that gambler Charles LeBreton had mentioned.

"That's not my nature," he said. "I know

that much about myself."

"Why?"

"What caused it? I don't want it to happen to me again. Why did it happen? And what is it that I can't remember? Is it something I can avoid, 'cause, trust me, ma'am, it's something I'd like to take a detour around the next time."

"I guess I understand, Bobby. Only, you're not supposed to call me 'ma'am'. Remember?" She cringed at her poor choice of words, but Randow didn't notice.

"What was it that doctor said?"

"Charles? About what?"

"Asking my mother. Maybe I should go to Shreveport. What was that steamboat's name?"

"The *Mittie Stephens*. It sailed yesterday, Bobby, remem. . . . But, yes, I think that's an excellent idea. You should visit your mother. Maybe Charles was right. Maybe something like this happened to your father or brother, or even your mother, but you never knew about it. Maybe she can help. Mothers always can."

"Here." He passed her the newspaper he had carried from the hotel lobby. She knew what he meant, and turned to the pages advertising the steamboat schedules.

"There are several leaving Saturday,

that's tomorrow, the *Selma*, the *Lulu D.* Or you could take one today for Red River, and connect with another packet for Shreveport. Or. . . ." A headline in the lower news column on the opposite page stopped her.

DELAYED

Departure of the passenger packet *Mittie Stephens*, scheduled to steam Thursday for Jefferson, Shreveport, &c was delayed. No reason was given. C. F. Hayes, first clerk, said the ship will leave Friday, Feb. 5th, at 5 p.m.

"I think," she said, "we should go to Tchoupitoulas Street and buy a ticket for you. I think. . . ."

She thought of herself this time, and quickly turned to the front page of *The Daily Picayune*, scanned the headlines, then looked inside at page two. Nothing, and her anxiety lessened, but when she found an article farther back in the paper, not about her, it caused her to tremble. "Does the name Victor Desiderio mean anything to you, Bobby?" She looked at him with trepidation.

"Victor Desiderio." He tested the name. "Do I know him?"

Laura exhaled in relief. The newspaper said Desiderio had been found shot to death in a cemetery Thursday morning. Apparently the man was a known gambler and blackguard whose presence along Gallatin Street would not be missed. City police had no clues. This was the man Charles LeBreton had mentioned.

"Do I know him?" Randow repeated.

"No, Bobby," she said, and continued her search of headlines. She closed her eyes tightly when she found it listed under the heading: **STATE NEWS**.

From Alexandria, we learn of the burning Sunday evening of Green Haven, a plantation overlooking the Red River once owned by Col. Hosiah J. Parker. "Everything was burned to the ground," it is reported. The home apparently was abandoned, and the Rapides Parish sheriff seeks an interview with Laura Kelley, daughter of the deceased Col. & Mrs. H. J. Parker, who has not been seen since the conflagration.

The wave of people practically pushed Randow and Laura along the Levee, past a mustached man standing on the back of a brightly painted ambulance, hawking something he called "Doctor Hennesy's Patented Miracle Elixir, Remedy for Gout, Headaches, Blurred Vision, and Other Ailments," through villages of carts, cotton bales, fruit peddlers, hogsheads of sugar, and myriad barrels labeled flour, pork, pickles, crackers, salt. . . .

They broke free of the mob and moved down the row of ships, Laura desperately trying to remember the directions H. R. Eppler had given them at his office on Tchoupitoulas Street. She read the names of the steamboats painted in big, black block letters on the wheelhouses: *Annie Wagley, New Era, Era No. 10, Gov. Allen, Bonnie of Riveroaks, Grey Eagle, General Quitman, Mollie Able,* and finally she saw it, a side-wheel packet, its main deck covered by hay bales, and from the back of the steamboat came the circus-like sounds of someone practicing on a calliope.

It was almost four o'clock, and the ship's stacks churned out thick plumes of wretched smoke. Steam hissed from the boiler deck, and the hull creaked.

She stopped at the plank leading from the Levee to the main deck, where a Union soldier stood talking to Julius Siegel. The major didn't notice Laura or Randow. She scanned the cabin and hurricane decks for Apolline, but saw mostly the *Mittie Stephens* crew and a few men smoking cigars.

"Well," Laura said, "this is where I leave you."

"You're not coming?" Randow asked.

She shook her head. "Apolline can take care of you from here to Shreveport."

"Apolline." Randow nodded. "Yeah, I remember."

"Are you sure?"

"Yeah. Redhead. Green eyes. I used to be her beau."

"That's excellent, Bobby." Discreetly she pointed at Major Siegel. "Do you remember him?"

Randow turned slightly. "The Yankee officer?"

"The man beside him."

He shook his head, and looked at Laura. "Do I know him?"

"No," she said. "You have your ticket?"

"Steerage passage. To Shreveport. I wish you were coming along, ma'am, I mean, Laura."

I wish so, too, she thought. He offered his hand, and she took it. He was improving. Last night, he would have asked her if she were going to Shreveport seven or eight times, and the night she met him, those questions would have doubled that. When they had purchased Randow's ticket at the office, she had considered buying cabin passage for herself, but deemed it too risky. The *Mittie Stephens* would stop in Alexandria, where someone might recognize her. If she wanted to leave New Orleans, and she would have to soon, her best bet would be to take a steamboat on the Mississippi, maybe get off in Memphis, or go as far as St. Louis, or as far as her money could take her at two cents a mile, cabin passage. Or she would sail into the Gulf of Mexico and head for Galveston or Indianola, disappear in Texas. Or try the railroads or a stagecoach and go east. *Or even turn myself in.*

"I'll miss you, Laura."

"God be with you." She dropped his hand, pivoted, and hurried into the crowd.

She stopped at a fort made of potato sacks to compose herself, wiped her eyes, and dropped the handkerchief into her handbag on top of the Derringer. When she looked up, panic seized her. Several rods in front of her walked Dr. Charles LeBreton, newspaper in hand — she couldn't tell the date, but something told her it was today's *The Daily Picayune* —

and animatedly talking to two men in sack suits and porkpie hats.

"Judas," she hissed, lowering her head and returning to the row of steamboats. Her old friend had turned her in, showed the item on the burning of Green Haven to a pair of detectives. Or maybe her suspicions of Hugh Valdez had been well founded. Maybe Valdez had returned to LeBreton's home with the authorities, looking to arrest Laura for arson. Valdez and LeBreton could be working together. Laura quickly scanned the Levee, but didn't see Valdez. That didn't mean anything. Valdez could be anywhere, or nowhere, could have nothing to do with LeBreton's sudden appearance. She cursed her distrustfulness, her unlady-like, animal instinct for survival.

The good doctor remained her first concern. LeBreton had mentioned his gambling debts, and maybe figured any reward the Yankee-run government was bound to post would surely keep him in his mansion on Esplanade Avenue a little while longer.

Of course, she had no proof, just a strong feeling in her stomach. LeBreton could have been, and probably was, simply looking for a game of chance, or had decided to flee New Orleans and his creditors. He also could have been looking for Laura, not to send her to jail, but to help her, yet she couldn't take that chance. Thoughts of turning herself in had been temporary. That would be like letting the carpetbaggers win.

She kept her head down, focused on her feet, walked rapidly, lifting her eyes to read the names of the ships she passed. *The Bonnie of Riveroaks, Gov. Allen, Era No. 10.* She paused, chanced a glance behind her, and couldn't see LeBreton, but, when she dared to lift her head and look down the Levee, the sight of three uniformed policemen walking in her direction frightened her. One held a placard, fueling her imagination again. *A description of Laura Parker Kelley wanted by the Rapides Parish sheriff.* She whirled on her heels, and almost ran.

Past the *Era No. 10* . . . *Gov. Allen* . . . *Bonnie of Riveroaks* . . . *Grey Eagle* . . . *General Quitman* . . . *Mollie Able.* . . . She heard the strains of the calliope, lifted the hems of her dress, and raced up the plank onto the *Mittie Stephens'* deck. Bobby Randow had vanished, likely hunting for a place on the main deck to call his home for the next week or so. Julius Siegel had also retired to his cabin or the ship's saloon. Apolline was still nowhere to be seen, so she asked a crew man checking the knots of ropes securing hay bales: "Excuse me, but who do I see about acquiring cabin passage to Jefferson?"

The man answered without looking up. "Cal Hayes, first clerk. He's in the galley, upstairs, ma'am, in the port wheelhouse."

Chapter Ten

Lieutenant Constantine Ambroise enjoyed his leisurely stroll around the *Mittie Stephens*. For the time being, he felt relaxed. The Army payroll — $100,000 in gold coin — had been loaded, secretly, the previous night and locked in the ship's safe. The 5,000 coins packed in leather sacks had almost filled the entire vault, which was huge. Only Captain Kellogg and the ship's clerks knew the combination, and Kellogg said he trusted his clerks, which was good enough for Ambroise.

Although a few passengers had cursed bitterly while hurriedly transferring their luggage and themselves onto Captain Langhorne's *Bonnie of Riveroaks*, most had accepted the delay without complaint — or had been bribed into shrugs and acceptance by Kellogg's offer of free supper in the dining room and, for the men, one free round in the saloon.

Even before Ambroise rounded the stern on the cabin deck, sweet sounds of a harmonica reached him despite the cacophony of voices, whistles, and barking dogs from along the Levee. He tried to place the tune while walking toward it. "All Quiet Along the Potomac". Yes, that was it. Why, he had not heard that song since the war.

The music stopped, followed by a friendly voice: "Now, you try it, son."

Ambroise found a skinny Negro sitting beside the ship's calliope, passing the harmonica to a young black boy. The man wore old blue trousers and even older boots, military issue but in poor condition; the boy was dressed in calico shirt, duck pants, and sandals. Between the man and the boy, who Ambroise guessed was the harmonica player's son, rested a trumpet, a book of music titled "The *Mittie Stephens* March", and a ball-peen hammer.

The boy brought the harmonica to his lips, but the noise that came out did not sound musical. After a few tweets and toots, he lowered the small instrument, revealing a wide grin, matched by his father's.

"That didn't sound like that song, did it?"

"You needs practice is all, Matthew." He

took the harmonica and dropped it in a shirt pocket. "Jus' like I needs to practice on this steam pianer." Scratching his chin, he leaned forward over the calliope.

Ambroise cleared his throat, startling the two musicians.

"Keep your seats, gentlemen," Ambroise said. "I only wanted to compliment you on your music. It's been a few years since I heard 'All Quiet Along the Potomac'. Where did you learn it?"

The man answered with a nervous shrug.

"In the war?" Ambroise asked. "Were you a colored volunteer?"

"No, sir." Still no eye contact, except from the wide-eyed boy who kept glancing back from his father to Ambroise and back to his father. "Didn't fight in the war."

"He fought Injuns," the boy shot out excitedly. "He was a hero in Texas."

Now the musician met Ambroise's stare. "Boy's exaggeratin', Lieutenant."

"No, I ain't, Daddy." The boy excitedly informed Ambroise: "He got hisself a medal. He must 'a' kilt a hunnert savages hisself, savin' ever'one on the Santa Saba, or somethin' like that." He looked back at his father. "Ain't that right, Daddy? You told me an' Emanuel that yourself, showed us your medal even. You's a hero. They should 'a' made you a colonel."

The musician's head dropped.

"Tenth Cavalry?" a smiling Ambroise asked.

"No, sir," came the barely audible reply. "Ninth." He stared at the calliope's keys. "Got an honorable discharge in November, and come home to get my family." He looked up quickly, and started firing out words almost as fast. "I lost that there discharge paper, Lieutenant. Lost it on a flatboat we taken comin' down from Convent after we paid Grandpa George a visit, so I ain't got me no papers, sir."

"It's all right, Mister . . . ?"

"Denton," the boy answered. "My daddy's name is Obadiah Denton. I'm Matthew."

"Hello, Matthew."

"I got a brother, too. His name is Emanuel. He's older than me. I'm seven. We got a mama, too. Her name's Zoë. How old are you, mister?"

"I'm eight."

Matthew Denton matched Ambroise's smile. "No, you ain't. You must be practically as old as my daddy."

"Practically," Ambroise said, and introduced himself before admitting to Mat-

135

thew Denton his real age — twenty-eight — and returning to his original question.

"Oh, I reckon some officers was partial to that song, sir," Obadiah Denton said. "They asked me to play it for them oftentimes, back in Texas."

"My mother gave piano lessons in Indiana, Mister Denton," Ambroise said, "but I never had the knack for anything musical. So you play the calliope?"

Denton blinked, studied the steam pipe organ briefly, and nodded. "Tryin' to, sir." He pointed to the hammer on the deck at his feet. "And I'm the ship's carpenter, Lieutenant." He looked at Ambroise briefly before dropping his gaze once more, this time focusing on the calliope. "Reckon I ought to practice on it a mite, sir."

"Certainly," Ambroise said. "Carry on."

Ambroise rounded the stern, starboard side, walked down the first flight of stairs he came to, and promptly discovered Nicholas Sloan leaning against the wheelhouse for support, head bent down.

"Surely, Sergeant," Ambroise said, "you are not sick. We haven't even shoved off."

Sloan straightened and turned, rubbing his right eye furiously. "No, sir, got a cinder in my eye is all, Lieutenant. All that pitch pine they're burning, sir. It's blacker than the ace of spades, and hotter than Hades."

When he lowered his hand, Ambroise found both eyes bloodshot.

"Did you get any sleep last night, Sergeant?"

"No, sir, but I feel fine. I spent the night at the safe, Lieutenant. Didn't want to take any chances."

Ambroise frowned. "Did Emmerich or Silvia relieve you?"

"No, sir. I ordered them to get some shut-eye on deck."

"Which is where you should have been, Sergeant Sloan." He never enjoyed rebuking anyone, especially a man like Nicholas Sloan, but, if something happened to the Jefferson payroll, General Napoleon Alexander Bishop would have Ambroise facing a board of inquiry or general court-martial. "The idea of having a small detail to guard" — he looked over his shoulders, lowering his voice to a whisper — "that much gold, Sergeant, and transferring the payroll onto a civilian ship in the middle of the night is secrecy." He no longer felt relaxed, no longer was enjoying his walk around the *Mittie Stephens*, and had forgotten all about "All Quiet Along the Potomac", Obadiah Denton, and the black musician's son.

"I don't want you anywhere near the ship's safe, Sergeant, nor do I want Emmerich or Silvia there. We watch it from a distance until we reach Texas." He painted on a smile. "We have a peaceful excursion for the next week, Sergeant. You should enjoy yourself. Play some cards, have a few drinks in the saloon. Mingle with the passengers and crew . . . act like there's nothing that concerns you on this steamboat and especially in the ship's safe. Keep your mouth closed, and make sure Emmerich and Silvia do the same." The latter was probably a pointless order considering the thickness of the German and Italian accents. "Understood?"

"Yes, sir, Lieutenant."

"Now get some sleep, Sloan." He shook his head and headed toward the bow.

"Lieutenant?"

Ambroise stopped, sighed, and pivoted.

"There's this gentleman asked to speak with you, Lieutenant. A provost marshal named Siegel."

Ambroise's eyes narrowed. "Did he say what he wanted to talk to me about, Sergeant?"

"No, sir." The sergeant's chin jutted toward the Levee. "But that's him over yonder by the hay bales. Bearded gent, holding the fancy cane."

Provost Marshal Siegel did not appear to be in good humor by the time Ambroise reached the ship's bow. He and a tall, well-dressed man exchanged harsh whispers, and Siegel clenched the cane so tightly his knuckles whitened. Ambroise considered turning around — he didn't feel like talking to a provost marshal anyway, and wanted to pay Homer Kellogg a visit in the pilot house — but the tall man spotted him, straightened, and told Siegel they had company. The marshal was grinning beneath his graying red beard when he turned.

"Lieutenant." Siegel held out his hand, introducing himself and his associate, Hugh Valdez.

"I was told you desired an interview with me, Major," Ambroise said stiffly after the handshakes. Julius Siegel. The name ran through his head. *Julius Siegel . . . Julius Cæsar. With a name like that, the major must have been tormented as a boy.* Ambroise would log that entry in his diary this evening.

"Certainly, sir. If you'll excuse me, Valdez."

The tall man nodded. "Sure, Major. I'll be in the saloon. Lieutenant Ambroise, a pleasure meeting you, sir."

Ambroise didn't reply, and, as Valdez headed toward the main staircase, Siegel sat on a hay bale and massaged his left knee. "Excuse me, Lieutenant. This blasted thing troubles me from time to time. Took a Rebel ball at Gettysburg." He looked up. "Were you there, Mister Ambroise?"

"No, sir. I served out West, here in Louisiana mostly, and Mississippi."

"Are you from here?"

"No, sir. I grew up in Madison, Indiana."

"I see. Well, be glad you missed the ruction in Pennsylvania, but we sure showed those Secesh who was their better, though they were game."

Ambroise was in no mood to relive the late war. "How may I help you, Major?"

"I thought I might offer you my services, Lieutenant."

The hair raised on the back on Ambroise's neck, and the coffee in his stomach soured. He hoped his face remained unreadable, but wasn't sure when

140

Siegel smiled. *Does he know about the gold?*

"Major, I have no deserters from my command that you can track down and return for court-martial. No one else accused of any crime, no pillagers, no weights and measures in need of regulating. My men and I are on our way to Jefferson." He had never been good at lying, and kept making this up as he went along, hoping Major Siegel would accept it. "Those are our only orders. Once we reach the barracks and I receive my orders from the commanding officer, perhaps I shall need your services, but until. . . ."

Siegel held up his hand. "I'm offering my assistance as one federal officer, Lieutenant, to another. Some people say the war is over, has been over almost four years, but I think it's not. Louisiana and Texas are chock-full of unreconstructed Rebels, brigands, and black-hearts, especially in East Texas where we're going. You have a sergeant and two soldiers with you. I have my deputy, Mister Valdez, my clerk, Sidney Paige, and my executioner, Jules Honoré. Eight is stronger than four, Lieutenant, if you run into any trouble. That's all I'm saying. No need to take offense, sir. I know provosts leave some soldiers with a strong distaste, but I'm here to help."

Ambroise felt the need to retreat and regroup. "My apologies, Major," he said. "I have the utmost respect for provost marshals and their ugly tasks, and did not mean to insinuate anything." That was another lie; most provost marshals and associates were only slighter more agreeable than the civilians who tracked down wanted men for bounties. "I appreciate your offer of assistance, sir, and, rest assured, that if I run into any trouble, I will come to you and your men quickly." He smiled. "But I don't think we'll have any trouble, sir. We're just taking a pleasant journey up The Big Drink, Red River, and Caddo Lake."

Siegel withdrew two cigars, handing one to Ambroise. "I pray you're right, Mister Ambroise." He used his cane to help stand. "Deputy Valdez and I share a cabin, Number Sixteen, on the larboard side. Misters Honoré and Paige are taking steerage passage."

"I'm in Cabin Twenty-One. Sergeant Sloan and my other two men are also on deck."

"That's the federal government for you, Lieutenant." Siegel fired up his cigar. "No need in spending money on cabin passage for everyone. Save some money. I'll take my leave, sir, and retire to the saloon."

Lost in thought, Ambroise barely heard Siegel and didn't notice the major had gone until moments later. He rolled the cigar in his fingers, thought about lighting it until he looked at the dry bales of hay, so he walked to the port side of the *Mittie Stephens*, sighed, and climbed the stairs to the cabin deck, leaned on the railing, and looked below. On the Levee, a blonde woman stood talking to a dark-haired man in a brown hat. *Probably her husband, and she's seeing him off.* Five men walked past them, up the plank and onto the main deck, and Ambroise's stomach started twisting into knots.

Julius Siegel might be right. In this part of the South, the war was far from over. Outlaws like Cullen Baker, Black Chivington, and Jeff Slade tormented the Army, Freedmen's Bureau, and civilians, and Ambroise cared not a whit for the looks of the five men who had just boarded the *Mittie Stephens*. Their faces needed a razor, and all but one wore gray woolen trousers with blue infantry trim. The one in dark denim cursed a black deck hand for getting in his way, and the others laughed before finding a spot to camp on deck. Former Confederates — or maybe, like Siegel had said, unreconstructed Rebels.

Ambroise spit a mouthful of bile over the side, and went to find Sergeant Sloan. Those five men, he decided, would bear watching.

Chapter Eleven

Slowly the *Mittie Stephens* backed away from the Levee, turning slightly, then stopped amid a string of clanging bells and hissing valves. Obadiah Denton leaned against the port-side derrick and held his breath as the steamboat began moving forward, hugging the Levee so close he could have leaped off the main deck and onto a docked ship. He had half a mind to do just that, simply abandon the *Mittie Stephens*, his dreams, even his family, and get off this thing before it rammed one of those docked boats, causing the boilers to explode, killing Denton and his family, and reducing the New Orleans Levee to ash and charred timbers.

A deck hand cackled when Denton shut his eyes and wrapped his bony arms around the tall derrick. "No need to fret. We're in safe water, and Mister Swain is one fine pilot."

Denton found a huge man of color grinning at him, more mulatto than the deep black of Denton's own skin, with a shaven head, arms thicker than Denton's thighs, a glint in his eyes, no right earlobe, and a gold ring piercing the left one. He wore green trousers, rubber boots, and homespun shirt with a yellow bandanna tied around his bald head.

"You'll be Obadiah Denton," the man said. "I'm Robert Erskine Thomas, but my friends call me Erskine. Mister Hayes said to find them boys of yours you bragged about. They supposed be my help in the hold."

Denton forced himself to release the white pole and accept the proffered hand, which resembled something more animal than human. He grimaced when they shook, for Robert Erskine Thomas's grip could crush alabaster. "What are your boys' names?" the crew man asked.

"Emanuel." He stared at his released hand, wondering if the blood would circulate again. "He's the oldest, ten. Matthew's seven. They with their mama."

"Well, I won't work them too hard, but they'll earn their keep. Mister Hayes, he's a stickler for that, him being first clerk and all. Biggest miser you ever laid your poor eyes on."

The pain in his hand had lessened, and he looked up curiously. *"Miser?"* he asked.

"Skinflint. Mister Hayes'd squeeze the coronet off an old half eagle. Come on, I want to meet them boys of yours, and your wife. Hear she cooks mighty fine."

"Zoë's a good cook," Denton agreed.

"Well, I'll reserve judgment for the time being because it's hard to make the scraps we gets fed edible. Now the passengers, they eat high on the hog, but the crew don't. Still, it's a good job."

They were walking now, although Denton wished they had gone to the other side of the boat. Those docked ships still looked too close. He kept his eyes on Robert Erskine Thomas's back, trying not to look at the Levee.

"You been on this ship long, Mister Thomas?"

"It's Erskine. And I'll call you Obadiah. Ain't no 'mister' on this boat, friend, unless you're addressing an officer or some other white man, but, yeah, I been on the *Mittie Stephens* since Capt'n Langhorne bought her. Worked for Capt'n Langhorne for nigh on ten years now. He owns this ship. 'Course, Capt'n Kellogg, he's more than a fair hand himself, and I've seen a slew of pilots, mates, capt'ns, and masters.

147

Been working decks on The Big Drink, Arkansas, Black, Ouachita, and Red since 'Forty-Two, and my pappie, he steamed the rivers East and West before that, till he was called to glory when we lost the *Pennsylvania*. Never was a slave, no, sir, and he wasn't either. We were freedmen. Come here, I want to show you something before we get your boys."

He hurried up the stairs. Denton wasn't sure he wanted to follow, at least, not until the steamboat cleared the Levee, but Thomas hollered to hurry up, so he tentatively climbed his way onto the cabin deck, and then up to the hurricane deck, where he found Thomas leaning on the railing, grinning, gesturing for Denton to look below.

Passengers crowded the decks, waving and being waved at by passengers and crew men on the docked ships. Denton couldn't understand any of the words, or what made Robert Erskine Thomas smile so. Finally Denton asked — "How many folks you figger on our boat?" — just to hear himself talk.

"Hundred, maybe more, with the crew and all. Look at them, Obadiah. What do you think?"

After another glance, he shrugged.

"Everyone is traveling," Thomas said reflectively. "Where are they going? Why? What do they do? You ever wonder about that?"

Denton shook his head.

"Every one has got some secret." Thomas turned to Denton. "Everybody's got secrets. I got mine. You got yours." He jutted his thumb at the decks. "They got theirs. Ain't that true?"

He didn't answer, and Thomas went back to looking below. "I like to stand up here when we're shoving off, look at them folks below, make up stories about them. About their secrets, their names, what they're doing and why. You ought to try it, Obadiah."

Denton's lips trembled when he spoke.

"What's that, Obadiah? Speak up, friend."

"Said I don't care much for secrets, is all. I mind my own affairs."

Thomas was facing Denton again. "You got no imagination, Obadiah Denton," said Thomas, shaking his head but still smiling. "Well, we best get down below before Mister Swain or Mister Hayes accuses us of lollygagging."

Matthew took to Robert Erskine

149

Thomas immediately, but that was just like the boy, unless his big brother seemed frightened — like when they met the cripple on the Levee the day before — and Emanuel wasn't intimidated by the hulky form of the deck hand, although he didn't say much.

"I'm gonna show the boys around today, Mizzus Zoë," Thomas said with a grin. He had to shout to be heard above the groaning of the pitman, a long pine timber reinforced with iron that, as best as Denton could tell, made the paddle wheels turn. "Ain't gonna work them none tonight, but they'll get plenty of chores come tomorrow. I'll have them back to you for supper. Your man says you cook mighty fine."

Zoë cast Denton one of those looks he had never learned how to read. "You make sure my boys don't drown, Mister Thomas."

"Won't be anywhere near the sides," he reassured her, then put a ham-sized hand on both boys' shoulders. "You boys don't smoke none, do you? Pipe, cigars, or cigarettes?"

"They's too young for that, Mister Thomas," Zoë fired back, and Denton could read that face. "If you plan on messin' with my sons' morals, we'll put ourselves offen this here ship right now and walk to this Jefferson, Texas and the territories."

Thomas never lost his grin. "Don't you go to fretting, Mizzus Zoë. I ain't got the habit myself. It's just that we're carrying some cargo where it pays mind not to go around striking lucifers. Come on, boys, let me show you around the *Mittie Stephens*."

With a shrug from Zoë, Thomas led the boys closer to the hard-stroking pitman, keeping his hands on their shoulders. "Since y'all are sleeping here, your first as-signment . . ." — he looked from side to side at the boys — "Emanuel, this will be your chore. You keep an eye out on this arm, the pitman it's called. Every morn you wake up, and every evening before you go to bed, you study this, make sure it ain't shrinking none, make sure the wood ain't rotting. If the pitman bursts or shrinks up on us, we'll be stuck like a fat heifer in a mud bog."

Emanuel stood a little taller with his first assignment. "Yes, sir," he said.

"Now let's get away from all this noise, boys, and I'll show you the hold."

Denton called for his sons, and knelt on the floor when they came. Robert Erskine

151

Thomas stayed put.

"Emanuel, Matthew," Denton said, "I don't have to tell you boys to mind Mister Thomas, now, do I?"

Both boys answered as he knew they would.

"All right, you be careful, and pay attention to what he tells you. And boys . . . let's not be talkin' none about your daddy's affairs in Texas."

"But . . . ," Matthew began.

"But nothin'. There's a lot of strangers on this here boat, and lots of 'em likely don't hold no truck with colored soldiers, or us bein' freedmen. Emanuel, you know this better than Matthew. He's still young, so you make sure he don't go to braggin' none. And, Matthew, you mind your big brother."

Matthew mumbled a — "Yes, sir." — which he followed with — "But you was a hero." — that Denton barely heard above the noise of the pitman, churning faster now as the ship picked up speed.

"Well, white folks, and some our color, might think us braggin', and you know your mama don't like braggin'," Denton said.

"That colonel didn't mind none," Matthew argued.

Denton felt blood rushing, but he managed to hold his temper, forced a smile, and tugged the boy's earlobe. "That was a lieutenant, Matthew," Denton said, "but not everyone'll be like him. You jus' do what Mister Thomas tells you, and don't go to talkin' about me bein' a soldier and all. Once we get settled in the territories, after you makes friends, you can brag all you want. All right?"

"Yes, sir," both boys said, and Matthew looked up hesitantly. "But will you let us see your medal tonight when we gets back?"

"Sure, Matthew, if you do like you're told. Now, run along, and be careful."

She felt imprisoned in her cabin.

It was pleasant enough, but small, with barely enough room for a built-in bunk, bureau, wash basin, and chamber pot. The owner of the *Mittie Stephens* had decorated its white walls with three hooks for hanging clothes, an oil painting of New Orleans by an artist she had never heard of — with good reason, considering the poor quality — and a small mirror with a tiny crack in the bottom left corner.

For the first time in months, Laura Kelley cried.

She was a fugitive from justice, a widow with one dress — which she was wearing while laying on the brick-hard mattress — a little bit of money, a handbag, dirty handkerchief, broach, tintype of her parents, and a .41-caliber pocket pistol made by Henry Deringer, Jr., which she didn't know would fire. She had no plans, no future, and a past she needed to forget.

Wallowing in self-pity sickened her, so she sat up in the bed, pulled the soiled handkerchief from the handbag, and dabbed her eyes. Tempting as it might be, she couldn't spend the entire voyage in her cabin, but she should stay out of sight whenever the *Mittie Stephens* put to shore. At some point, she would seek out Bobby Randow, if he still remembered her, and Apolline Rainier.

She was growing accustomed to the noise of the steamboat, and stood, sighing, then looked in the mirror. Laura reached into the handbag, but laughed. No brush. After another sigh, she combed her hair with her fingers, wet her lips, and headed toward the door.

A man's voice startled her, but not as much as the woman's. *Apolline!* Talking to one of Major Siegel's men, Paige. Yes, Paige, that was the name. Their voices and footfalls passed her cabin, and she carefully cracked open the door and looked down the ship.

Apolline nodded at Sidney Paige and his escort before disappearing inside her cabin. Laura made a mental note of its location and quickly shut the door before Paige and the crew man turned around. She heard their footsteps pass her cabin, and then nothing but the creaking of the ship, paddles striking water, and other mechanical noises. She opened the door again, saw no one on the deck, and hurried to Apolline's berth, knocking on the door in a panic.

Her friend's reaction mirrored the expression she had back in her New Orleans bordello. So did her words: "Laura, what on earth are you doing here?"

"Can I come inside, Apolline?" she asked breathlessly, and pushed her way past before her friend had answered.

Apolline closed and latched the door. "Where's Bobby?" she asked.

"He's on board. Deck passage. I haven't seen him since. . . ." She collapsed on the bed. "It's a long story."

A bottle of brandy and shot glass appeared in Apolline's hands as if by magic. She filled the glass, pressed it into Laura's trembling hand, and leaned against the bureau, taking an unlady-like pull from the bottle. Laura killed the shot, feeling the alcohol warm her body as it rolled down her throat. She set the glass on the floor, and stared at Apolline warmly.

She didn't expect Apolline to come to her, to wrap her arms around her, and squeeze her tightly, but that's what happened. When Apolline pulled away, tears welled in her eyes. "I'm glad . . . in a way . . . you're here. When Hugh. . . ." She shook her head and held up the brandy. "Another shot?"

"No, thank you." Laura pursed her lips as Apolline's words maneuvered through the brandy. *In a way?* Apolline had also mentioned Hugh Valdez's name, which made Laura's fists clench. Valdez must be on the ship. Maybe Laura had been wrong about him. Perhaps Valdez hadn't fetched the law, hadn't joined Charles LeBreton on the Levee to capture her, but Valdez had abandoned her and Randow. Why?

"Where are you staying?" Apolline asked.

Laura held up her key. "Six doors down," she answered.

"Have you seen . . ." — Apolline took another pull, a longer one — "Julius?"

156

"Before I got on. That's when I knew you were on the *Mittie Stephens*. When I read in the paper that the departure had been delayed, I thought you might have gone on another ship."

"We were in no hurry." Apolline shoved the cork into the bottle, which she placed on the bureau.

"He, Major Siegel, that is, didn't see me . . . or Bobby." Laura didn't know why she said that, or why she secretly questioned Apolline's statement about being in no hurry. Hugh Valdez certainly had been.

"He'll find you both," Apolline said. "This is the *Mittie Stephens*, not the *Richmond*. Why don't you tell me what happened."

Music sounded down the stern as soon as Laura had finished talking, a rollicking little tune played on the pipe organs that had become so popular on steamboats since the war.

" 'The *Mittie Stephens* March'," Apolline announced. "You'll hear it once a day till we reach Jefferson. It means supper is served. Trust me, girl, you'll be sick of it before the week is out."

"You've traveled on this boat before?"

157

"Just once," Apolline said, and braced herself with another swallow of brandy. "Went up to Jefferson and back a couple of weeks ago. Took the *Mittie Stephens* there and the *Dixie* back." She hurriedly added: "I was looking for a place in Jefferson."

Apolline changed the subject by offering to loan Laura two dresses for the voyage. Laura started to decline, but Apolline made a strong argument: "You're a lady traveling cabin passage, not steerage. If you show up at dinner in the same dress . . . *that dress!* . . . passengers and crew will become suspicious." Apolline checked a watch. "In fact, we should get ready now, for supper."

"I don't know about supper. . . ."

A knock stopped her, but Apolline seemed unconcerned as she tugged on the lock of her luggage. "Will you get that, Laura? It's only Julius, coming to escort me to supper."

I'd rather it be Sheriff Risseau from Rapides Parish, she thought, *than Major Julius Siegel.* She stepped back once she opened the door. So did the man who had knocked, almost upending the crew man who had escorted him to the ladies' cabins. They looked at each other in surprise, mouths hanging open, until Hugh Valdez swept the black hat off his head and bowed.

"I owe you an apology," he said, "and an explanation."

Chapter Twelve

Laura's nausea and fear receded slowly as Hugh Valdez made his excuses, told his side of the story, why he had left LeBreton's office without explanation. His brother had suffered some mortal injury at a sawmill near Port Caddo, Texas, and Valdez wanted to see him before he died. To make amends. To say good bye. It was a good story, Laura thought, although one her father would have called, if he didn't know Laura was eavesdropping, "cock-and-bull and a poor one at that."

Yet she found herself wanting to believe Valdez. All the running, all of her fears, the overwhelming exhaustion of the past few days had turned Laura's nerves raw. She felt a wreck, about to collapse, and she found a gentleness in Hugh Valdez. She just didn't believe him, not totally. He was lying to her, but hadn't she lied to him? At the least, neither had been completely honest with one another.

What she kept coming back to was the simple fact that Valdez had not turned her in. She had been wrong about that. Valdez hadn't joined LeBreton, hadn't contacted the New Orleans police. If Valdez had wanted Laura or Randow in jail, he would have betrayed them by now. He was hiding something, though. But what?

After supper, they stood outside, enjoying, or pretending to enjoy, the music, the rhythm of the paddle wheels, and she stared at him, listening to him tell another story about his past. When he finished, Laura smiled, although she had only half listened. The fear began roiling inside her, however, when he moved closer.

"I know I have done nothing to earn your trust, Laura," he spoke. "I was a coward at the doctor's office. I do trust you, my dear. I hope someday you shall trust me." He leaned forward and kissed her. To her surprise, she kissed him back, just briefly, before pulling away, expecting to see him wielding manacles he was about to slap on her wrists. He only gave her a warm smile. His hands were empty. She felt foolish, and again silently cursed her . . . what was the word she had read in one of the medical journals? . . . yes, paranoia.

"Everybody needs to trust somebody," Valdez said.

"I. . . ." Laura stopped. *I want to trust you. I need to trust somebody or I'll explode like a boiler.* She wanted to say these words, but she also wanted to run. Her fear, her distrustfulness had suddenly been replaced by confusion. She wanted to lock herself in her room, only she couldn't move, and she let Hugh Valdez kiss her again.

After the hay bales had been covered with heavy tarpaulins and supper had been served, activity on the deck died down, but all during the night crew men constantly came for the firewood stacked underneath and beside the bow staircase. So Bobby Randow had moved his bedding — which consisted of his grip and hat — behind the port wheelhouse where the rhythmic splashing of the wheels lulled him to sleep.

He woke up at sunrise, tossed his coat aside, and stretched before standing, but a pinching pain in his right calf sent him to the deck with a grimace. He cursed softly, noticing the bulge, while remembering he had shoved the .44 revolver inside his boot top. A voice rolled through his memories: *That's an old Dance you had, Bobby. Texas-made during the war, more likely to blow off your hand than kill a rat. Leave it.* He couldn't remember who had said it, or why. Or why he still had the weapon, concealed. He pulled up his trousers leg, withdrew the revolver, and checked the copper percussion caps, placed on all six nipples.

"It's a wonder I haven't blowed off my foot," he said softly, and started to remove one of the caps, but stopped, leaving the gun fully loaded. He didn't return it to his boot though, reasoning that walking with a two-and-a-half-pound chunk of case-hardened iron, brass, and walnut jammed against his ankle and calf would leave him crippled. Instead, he opened his luggage, but decided against that as well. Finally Randow shoved the Dance in his back waistband and pulled on the frock coat he had removed during the night to use as a blanket. He brushed off his crumpled new hat, popped out the crown, and pulled it down low on his head.

The stiff wind whipping off the dark river was cold this morning, carrying the aroma of coffee boiling from the ship's galley. Yet he didn't feel hungry or thirsty, despite having skipped supper last night. He picked up his grip and walked to the bow, careful not to wake the sleeping passengers, and sat on the covered hay bales to watch the sun rise. A strange-looking steamboat churned its way toward the — *What was the name of this boat?* Mittie Stephens? *Yes, that's it!* — and Randow stared at it. One of those double-hulled snagboats, he determined, that the late Captain Henry Miller Shreve had designed to help clear the Great Raft on the Red River. What it was doing on the Mississippi, steaming south toward New Orleans, Randow couldn't figure out.

At least he knew it was a snagboat, even knew its inventor, and the name Shreve reminded Randow of his destination: Shreveport, to see his mother, to see if she knew anything that could help him understand his memory loss. He slid off the canvas-covered bale and onto the deck, resting his back against the hay, and fishing inside his grip for . . . anything.

He pulled out a new deck of Lawrence and Cohen cards, a pair of one-cent proprietary tax stamps still on the unbroken cover, with a cancellation date of January 12, 1869. The date meant nothing to him, but the cards reminded him of how he relaxed. If this condition was brought on by distress, as he seemed to recall someone had told him, maybe if he relaxed it would go away, and he'd remember everything clearly. He opened the deck and began shuffling the stiff cards. Randow had never learned how to play solitaire — that had given the card-playing boys of the 9th Texas plenty of chances to abuse him during the war — so he dealt five-card stud to two imaginary players and himself.

King of diamonds up for the first player, six of diamonds for the second, and eight of spades for *Monsieur* Randow. He checked his hole card — ace of clubs — and dealt again. Seven of hearts, ten of spades and, for himself, ace of spades.

My luck's still good.

Eight of clubs, five of diamonds, two of diamonds.

No help for anyone. Good chance I'll win this hand.

Ace of hearts, queen of hearts, three of spades. Ace-king would bet. Queen high would probably fold, and Randow, feeling confident the ace-king would not have that fourth ace, would raise. Ace-king would call or fold.

Randow turned over the cards. Three of clubs for the ace-king, while the queen-high held the fourth ace. Randow gathered up the cards and reshuffled. He could pass time like this, merely play poker by himself on the deck until the *Mittie Stephens* reached Shreveport. The snagboat passed, tooting its whistle, which the *Mittie Stephens* pilot returned in a friendly greeting. Well, not so friendly, for the noise awakened some steerage passengers.

Randow pursed his lips and pushed back his hat. Why play poker with himself? Why not see if this steamboat had a place for gambling? He'd never know if he could play cards for a living with his faulty memory unless he tried. Randow pulled out the roll of greenbacks from his coat pocket and counted his money. He had more than three hundred dollars — and that was after paying the whopping bill at the hotel — *Hotel? What hotel?* — and buying passage to Shreveport.

"The Saint Louis," he said aloud, remembering the hotel's name. Another image flashed through his mind, and he whispered the name: "Laura Kelley."

He dealt the cards again.

Five of spades, nine of diamonds, six of spades. Randow checked his hole card — two of clubs — and continued to deal. Two of spades, four of spades, four of clubs. Again: queen of spades, three of hearts, nine of spades.

"This stinks," he said, and dealt the final round. King of clubs, five of hearts, two of diamonds. A pair of deuces. He looked at the other hands: King-high's hole card was the four of hearts, while nine-high held the seven of spades. Randow had won again — with a lousy small pair. He chuckled to himself, then felt the men staring at him.

Gathering the cards, Randow looked up at five corncob-rough men. Four wore Confederate infantry trousers, and the fifth man, sporting a bushy black beard and cleaning his fingernails with a giant Arkansas toothpick, grunted something unintelligible.

"Do I know you?" Randow asked. He ground his teeth, hating the sound of that question again, despising the feeling of ignorance it brought on.

"Do you know me?" The man with the big knife laughed. The four others joined in.

"I'm Bobby Randow," he said, and wished he hadn't. He cursed his memory again.

"Uhn-huh," one of the old Rebs said. None of them gave a name, and Randow didn't ask. You never asked a man his name. If he wanted to give you one, he would.

"This bucket's got a saloon," Arkansas Toothpick said. "Capt'n even allows a few honest games of chance, Bobby Randow. You believe in games of chance, don't ya?"

With a shrug, Randow opened his grip, gathered his cards, and shoved them inside the wrapper. These men weren't interested in cards or gambling. They wanted to kill him, take his money. He'd put the cards in the grip and pull out the Dance.

"I'd be happy to accommodate you," Randow said as his hand disappeared in his luggage. He felt around. His mouth turned dry. *Where did I put that revolver?*

He felt the gun pressing against the small of his back, and remembered, knowing it was too late.

Simultaneously the five men stepped toward him. The big one lowered the knife with a black-toothed grin. Suddenly all of them stopped and looked behind Randow.

"You boys head back to your sty and find a bottle of oh-be-joyful. And be joyful."

Cautiously Randow chanced a glance behind him.

A tall man, pale eyes and black hair, pulled back the gray coat that matched his trousers to reveal a star pinned on the lapel of his black striped vest.

"This your affair, Yank?" the smallest of the Rebels asked.

"Indeed. This is Captain Bobby

Randow, my friend. His memory is troubling him. Seems he can't recall what happened recently, and I've been asked to take care of him till he reaches Shreveport."

"His memory?" Arkansas Toothpick asked.

"Bobby," the man said, "I saw you playing poker from the cabin deck. What was your last hand?"

Randow focused on where he had dealt the cards. "I. . . ." He could answer anything. No one could have known what he had, especially someone looking down from the cabin deck, but he couldn't bluff them now, not after the long pause and dreadful look on his face.

"It's all right," the man said. "Now do you boys want to go along peaceable?"

"Five against one," the Reb with the waxed brown mustache said.

They weren't counting Randow. He moved his right hand behind his coat.

"Yeah," said another. "I ain't met no Yank I couldn't whup to the nethermost."

The man with the badge and silk hat laughed. "*Yank?* Boys, I hail from Thoroughfare Gap, Virginia. Rode with Mosby during the war."

"You wear a Yankee badge," Waxed Mustache said with a sneer.

"Yes, and I work for the Yanks. Isn't that right, Sergeant?"

"That's right," said a new voice, and Randow forgot about his Dance and looked to his left, finding a strapping, white-bearded soldier holding a stout piece of firewood in his massive right hand.

"You can start the ball," the Virginian said easily, "or crawl back into your hole."

Arkansas Toothpick pivoted with a snort, and the four others followed him.

"Thank you, Sergeant Sloan," the Virginian said, and held out his hand toward Randow.

Randow stared at it briefly, then understood, and let the man help him up. "You're . . . ?" Randow began.

"Hugh Valdez, Bobby. This is Sergeant Nicholas Sloan. We're your pals."

"I see." Bobby grabbed his grip and stepped around the hay bales.

"I thought you might enjoy some breakfast, Bobby, and I'm sure you won't mind the company of this lovely lass."

Valdez stepped aside and doffed his silk hat. Randow looked up the flight of stairs and quickly recalled his manners, removing the wide-brimmed hat he had bought the other day. The morning sun caught Laura Kelley's hair perfectly, and her face shone as she smiled.

"Miz Kelley," Randow said.

"It's Laura," came her reply.

"I remember," he said. He did, too. Not much else from the past few days could he recollect, but he knew her, and wasn't likely to forget her.

He had visited better dining halls on steamboats, and many more a lot worse. Thick red carpet showed its age and stains, the wallpaper had started to peel at the ceiling in a few places, and the brocades no longer looked lush. Randow had traveled on steamboats with ornate, carved columns, skylights, and crystal chandeliers.

Back when my luck was good, he thought.

He ordered coffee, ham, and biscuits; so did Hugh Valdez and Laura Kelley. After the waiter left with their orders, Randow stared out the window at the passing trees on the shoreline.

"I owe you an explanation and apology, too."

Randow turned at the sound of Valdez's voice.

"I explained all this to La . . . Miss Kelley . . . last night before supper," Valdez said. "It was cowardly how I left you at Doctor LeBreton's house . . . without a word, without even a note explaining my hasty departure."

Randow had no idea what he meant. He glanced at Laura Kelley, hoping she might fill him in, but she, too, was staring out the window at the Mississippi. No, Randow realized, she was looking at Valdez.

"I mentioned that I wanted to see my family. They live at Port Caddo. I haven't seen my brother since the war. He, too, rode with Mosby. Anyway, he has a wife and three young children . . . one, the only boy, is named after me. Well. . . ." He shook his head. "I received a letter from my sister last week that Henry, that's my brother, was gravely injured in an accident at the sawmill. It was providence that Major Siegel received orders to travel by the most convenient method of transit to Jefferson. I thought I might visit my brother, comfort him before he . . . passes on. It is that serious. But then Major Siegel asked me to stay with you, and I agreed, for the major knows not of my dear brother's plight. My brother's strong, Bobby, and I still expect him to pull through despite my sister-in-law's letter. At least, that's what I told myself . . . how I explained my delay to myself."

Valdez shook his head sadly. "Until I was

172

sitting downstairs at Doctor LeBreton's, sipping the gracious doctor's *eau-de-vie*. I realized then that I was nothing more than a craven coward . . . that I had chosen to stay behind because I feared seeing my brother on his deathbed. So I ran. Ran as fast as I could to get on board, only to learn that the ship's departure had been delayed. I did return to Doctor LeBreton's, but you were gone, and the doctor was not home. I couldn't find you, so I returned to the Levee."

He reached over to pat Laura's hand. "God has blessed me in one regard, though. Now I shall enjoy your company all the way to Shreveport, and even Jefferson with Miss Kelley." He smiled warmly at Laura.

The waiter arrived with coffee, leaving china cups and a fancy silver pot on the table top, and reported that breakfast would be served momentarily.

"I offer my handshake in apology, sir."

Randow took the hand and looked Valdez in the eye. Valdez offered a smile and a sigh of relief before thanking Randow for his understanding and forgiveness. Randow reached for his coffee cup.

"I pray that your brother's injuries are not as serious as you have been led to believe, Hugh," Laura said softly, and dropped two cubes of sugar in her coffee. "Don't you, Bobby?"

She looked up at him with those beautiful eyes, and Randow nodded. He couldn't forget the way Laura had cared for him. Criminy, if Valdez had cheated at cards and Laura had asked Randow to forgive him, Randow probably would have, just to make Laura happy.

"We have five more days together, Bobby," Valdez said. "Then, old chum, you leave us at Shreveport. I shall cherish our time together. You remind me of my brother."

"I pity your brother," Randow said.

Valdez laughed, and said: "And I love your wit. Perhaps we shall enjoy a friendly game of poker tonight after supper."

Breakfast arrived before Randow could answer, and he felt an overpowering hunger. The ham, maple-glazed and thick, was tender, the biscuits light and flaky, and he understood why the *Mittie Stephens'* owner had commissioned a march to announce supper every night. If supper tasted as good as this breakfast, he'd make sure he ate here. The ship might not be much, the dining hall's glory fading, but the food bested anything

Randow had tasted on a Mississippi riverboat.

"Poker, Bobby?" Valdez repeated. "Say eight-thirty?"

"I'd enjoy it," Randow replied. He would, too. He could read a man's face, and Hugh Valdez was one mighty poor liar. Oh, he might have Laura holding onto every word he said, but he couldn't bluff Randow.

The problem, Randow thought with regret, *is I probably won't remember any of this by the time I finish breakfast.*

Chapter Thirteen

The Soda Lake Saloon was long and narrow, its ceiling raised slightly above the hurricane deck, allowing long, side skylights made of orange glass to bathe the hall in warm light during the day. As dark as the sky was tonight, however, the lights did nothing more than poorly reflect the flickering glow from the wall lamps inside and torches outside. Speculators, merchants, and planters, ragged out in their finest duds, lined the long cherry-wood bar, their hats almost hidden by the smoke from their cigars and pipes, their right hands clutching glasses filled with gin slings and brandy smashes.

Randow wasn't interested in a drink, or a smoke, although he wouldn't turn down the offer of something to cut the phlegm. Instead, he made a beeline for the tables in the back of the barroom. A hand-painted sign had been placed prominently on the wallpaper above five felt-covered tables.

GAMBLE AT
YOUR OWN
RISK!

Once he spotted Valdez waving him over with his silk hat, Randow headed to the table, standing while Valdez introduced the others who remained seated: Major Julius Siegel, provost marshal; Sergeant Nicholas Sloan; Jules Honoré, Siegel's executioner; Gustavo Aquiles, a New Orleans merchant bound for Pineville on business; General Cyrus K. Granville, a Mexican and Civil War veteran from Ohio, now retired and living in Proctors on Lake Borgne, steaming to Shreveport to attend his niece's wedding; and Lieutenant Constantine Ambroise, Sergeant Sloan's commanding officer, ordered to Jefferson with his small command.

Siegel looked familiar to Randow, and it occurred to him that Valdez worked for the red-headed major. The sergeant, he recalled, had assisted him in the morning, although Randow couldn't describe any details. The others, he did not know. Or did he? If Honoré worked for Siegel, perhaps he had met him. That lean, ugly face seemed familiar.

"Let me apologize in advance if I forget

your names," Randow said after the round of handshakes, dropping his grip behind the vacant chair and sitting down. He had nowhere to store his luggage on board, so kept lugging it around like a simpleton, carrying it as if the old piece of leather and thread carried all of his memories.

"*Señor* Valdez has explained your condition to us, *Capitán*," the Spaniard said. "It is my sincerest wish that this infirmity does not incapacitate you for a long period of time."

"*Gracias.*" He clucked his tongue. *Well, now I know I know some Spanish,* he thought.

"I just sat down myself," the lieutenant said. "You are a captain, Mister Randow?"

"Was." Randow laid his money on the table to buy chips from the game's banker, General . . . ? He had already forgotten that name. "And I was on the opposite side, Lieutenant. Ninth Texas Cavalry."

"And what's this about your memory," the lieutenant continued, "if I'm not being forward, sir?"

Randow shrugged. "I'm having a little problem remembering stuff that happened not long ago. A whole night is black. . . ."

He couldn't even remember how long ago! "And most of what's gone on since then is blurred."

"Still no luck, eh, Captain?" Siegel said before firing up his cigar.

Randow didn't answer, and the general announced the rules as dealer's choice, no limit on betting or raises, table stakes. He began dealing cards face up. "First jack gets the opening deal," he said. "And lest any of you fear for Lieutenant Ambroise's career, that he will be reprimanded for fraternization with Sergeant Sloan, rest assured that, as a brigadier, I have breveted Sergeant Sloan to the rank of second lieutenant for the duration of our friendly game."

"I don't think we have to worry," Siegel said. "There are no other soldiers on board, except two immigrants under the lieutenant's command who can hardly speak a word of English."

"They're occupied anyway," Sloan said, "rolling dice on the boiler deck."

The general stopped dealing. "There's the jack. You have the deal, Captain Randow."

Randow looked down. Sure enough, the jack of clubs lay in front of him. He took the deck from the general and hoped he wouldn't make a fool of himself tonight.

"Grub pile!" Zoë shouted, and Obadiah Denton watched as the crew swarmed to fill whatever would pass as plates or bowls with boiled potatoes, and the remnants of the day's meats and custards the passengers hadn't eaten.

"You boys best eat," Denton told his sons, but Matthew and Emanuel remained at his side, although neither could barely stand.

"Ain't hungry," Emanuel said weakly, and Denton fought the urge to laugh.

"Reckon Mister Thomas worked you pretty hard today," he said pleasantly. "Well, you need to eat your mama's cookin' so you be strong enough to give him another day's work."

Emanuel groaned. "How long before we get to Texas?"

"Long time. Now go eat."

"I like workin' with Mister Thomas," Matthew said. "He sings and tells stories while we work, but he ain't never fought no Injuns."

Denton dropped to a knee quickly and firmly turned Matthew around to face him. "Now, Matthew," he said, "you haven't forgotten what I told you. . . ."

"I ain't told him nothin', Daddy, and you can ask Emanuel. I done like you tol' me to do. All I was sayin' is that I likes Mister Thomas. He got some mighty interestin' stories to tell."

"That's a good boy." He patted his son's shoulder. "Now both of you, get in line 'fore all that good food's gone to waste."

A swarthy white man snorted as he passed them, holding a bowl and steaming mug of coffee. "It's already gone to waste, laddies," he said, staring at his supper, "but it's somethin' in your gut, at least."

Denton made certain his sons fell into the rapidly moving line before he walked outside onto the main deck. He leaned back against the wheelhouse and stared ahead at the rippling brown water that reflected the outside torches and lights from the staterooms as the paddle wheels pushed the *Mittie Stephens* toward the bank. They were stopping again, pulling onto the shore to pick up firewood, and he'd have to help with the load. He should go back inside, take his place in line, and wolf down some of his wife's cooking — well, she had done the best she could with scraps and potatoes — but his bowels fermented and his hands turned clammy.

He'd likely feel sick until he was settled in Colorado.

"I don't know if luck smiled on you before, Captain Randow," General Granville said, "but your affliction certainly makes you one fine poker player." He tossed his cards onto the deadwood in disgust and reached for his tall tumbler of liquor.

Valdez clucked his tongue. "You can't tell if he's bluffing," he good-humoredly told the players, "because you're not even sure if he remembers what's his hole card. But I'll call you, Bobby, to keep you honest. It's what you see on the table. Jacks and eights." He flipped over the facedown card, a meaningless four of diamonds.

Randow showed his hole card. "Three sevens," he said, and raked the chips into his modest pile while staring at Valdez's losing hand.

Jacks and eights. He leaned back, remembering. He had jacks and eights at Number 18 Royal Street, had called an unemployed sailor, bluffing a full house, and cashed in his chips before returning to the hotel. Another phrase tore at him, clawing its way into his memories. *Keep you honest.* But what did it mean?

"Are you ill, *señor?*" the Spanish merchant asked.

Added Siegel: "Remembering anything?"

Randow didn't reply, kept thinking about that night in New Orleans. He had busted the monkey, so Randow had tossed him a dollar chip, cashed in, and returned to the St. Louis Hotel. Closing his eyes, he could see himself now, packing his belongings, cleaning and loading his revolver while staring at his winnings, wondering if he'd ever have the chance to spend all of that money. He had picked up the grip, planning on checking out, then laughed at himself, and tossed the luggage down, pulled on his old shell jacket, and left the room, dropping his key at the desk, heading into the chilly night. He saw himself walking — he could walk for miles, should have served in the infantry instead of the cavalry — down the slippery *banquettes* to the Swamp, to some house he couldn't picture clearly, recalling how he had pushed open the door with his left hand, keeping his right on the butt of his revolver — holstered, not concealed. Either no one had noticed, or they had not cared. He had stepped inside. . . .

"Apolline?" he heard himself calling . . .

and . . . nothing. The door to his memories slammed again.

"Captain Randow?"

Captain Randow. He was somewhere else now, chilled by the voice. A cemetery, at dark. *Why would anyone be in a cemetery at night?* "Captain Randow . . . ," the speaker had said, only that wasn't it. No, it had been: "*Preacher* Randow. . . ." But that was all he could revive.

"Captain Randow?" Siegel's voice returned him to the present, and he stared at the cards Valdez had handed him.

"It's your deal, Bobby," Valdez said.

"Sorry." Randow fumbled with the cards. "Thought I remembered something from that night, but it was nothing," he lied. He gave the men at the table a grin and shrug, noticing the empty chair, remembering that the sergeant had called it a night a few hands ago. He could recall that much. Maybe he was getting better.

Laura Kelley had borrowed Apolline's cloak to fight off the Mississippi River's winter chill as she ascended the stairs to the hurricane deck. Above her, on the texas deck, she heard the sounds of laughter and music from the black families traveling on deck. Most riverboats reserved part of the texas deck for Negro steerage passengers, calling it the "freedmen's bureau".

The singing took her back to Green Haven, listening to slaves in the cotton fields, or at their Sunday revivals in the ramshackle quarters her father had built for them. She had never enjoyed the knowledge that her family owned slaves, and, when her mother had assigned a timid girl barely in her teens to be Laura's servant, Laura had defied her parents for the first time. "I can dress myself and pour my own tea," she had told them. She had forgotten the rest of her words, but she would never forget the look of despair her mother and father gave her, and how it had made her relent. She had wanted to become some independent woman, a doctor, anything, but had been roped into the moralities of Rapides Parish. Oh, she had managed to escape every now and then, secretly assist Charles LeBreton when in New Orleans, help patch a few cuts on her horses, dogs and — sometimes — slaves, swearing them to secrecy.

Yet she was a belle, or had been, so prim and proper, respectable — before burning Green Haven.

"Well, well, well. . . ."

Laura whirled at the man's voice, backing away instantly, and the bearded face in front of her lost its smile and frowned, retreating a few paces as well.

"I . . . uh. . . ." Sergeant Nicholas Sloan reeked of whiskey and tobacco. The frown turned into that wicked grin again, and he stepped forward. "You look lovely, ma'am." His accent was Southern, slurred, and he pressed his hands on the wall, trapping her, leaning his stinking face closer.

She made herself talk, never taking her eyes off this Yankee. "I did not thank you for helping Bobby Randow this morning, Sergeant. I'm sure Captain Randow has, but I thank you, too."

"Well." Sloan chuckled. "Your capt'n thanked me by taking a month's wages from me tonight, ma'am. But I think you can thank me real proper. Yes'm."

She had heard about men like this, polite unless in their cups, then nothing more than savages. Sloan inched closer, and Laura pressed her back against the wall, wishing she had brought her handbag and the Derringer with her on this evening stroll. She could scream — the joyful singing upstairs wouldn't drown out her cry — but she didn't want to give this Yankee the pleasure. Yet if he moved closer, she would claw through his grizzled beard and lash his face.

Another voice — "What is going on there?" — gave her hope, and Sloan jerked his head toward the figure hurrying down the staircase.

"Nothin', Capt'n." Sloan backed away from Laura. "I thought this lass was somebody I knew."

The scent of pipe smoke and weathered face told Laura that her rescuer was the ship's captain. She was safe from the likes of Sloan.

"You're drunk. You stink of John Barleycorn. If I were you, I would retire to my bunk, Sergeant, unless you want to be put off at our next landing and face a court-martial in Texas."

Sloan tipped his kepi. "My apologies, ma'am. Didn't mean to frighten you none." He snorted and spit phlegm over the railing, then hurried down the stairs.

"I am Homer Kellogg," the captain said, doffing his cap. "If you desire, ma'am, I will throw Sergeant Sloan off the *Mittie Stephens*. I'll order Mister Swain to put us to shore immediately."

"It's all right, Captain," she said. "He did not hurt me, or frighten me . . . too much."

187

"As you wish, ma'am. We cater to gentlemen and ladies on the *Mittie Stephens*, and I regret this incident. If you would allow me, it would be my honor and duty to escort you to your stateroom, Miss . . . ?"

"Wilson," she lied, choosing her late husband's middle name for her alias. "I am Laura Wilson. It would be my pleasure, Captain." She slipped her hand inside Kellogg's elbow and let him lead her down the stairs, pretending to be that proper young belle one more time.

"A pleasant evening," Laura said as they walked down the cabin deck.

"Yes, though a tad on the cool side, but the weather should warm up quite nicely in the next day or so. Maybe the clouds will lift, too. It's so dreadfully dark on these rivers without the moon and stars. Are you traveling all the way to Jefferson, Miss Wilson?"

"Yes."

"Enjoying the passage?"

"Yes, supper has been divine."

They ran out of conversation and covered the last part of the journey in silence. She thanked Kellogg for his chivalry and opened the unlocked door to her berth.

"You should lock your door, ma'am," Kellogg warned her, "whenever you leave your room or whenever you are inside. As I said, the *Mittie Stephens* is a good packet, with good passengers, but we do pick up a few ruffians."

"As I learned tonight, Captain Kellogg. *Merci bien*. And good night."

Inside, she shut and latched the door, pulled off Apolline's cloak, and tossed it on the bed. She had just turned up the lantern on the bureau, when she saw his reflection in the tiny mirror. Laura whirled, feeling desperately for the door handle, and choked back a scream.

Chapter Fourteen

"It's me," Randow told her.

"Bobby!" Feeling her knees start to buckle, Laura dropped on the bunk. He stood in the corner, hat in one hand, grip in the other. "You took ten years off my life, sir, and . . ." — she lowered her voice; if a principled man like Homer Kellogg found Randow in her room, they'd both be put ashore — "what are you doing here?"

Randow let the luggage slide to the floor. "Six men were trying to kill me," he said. "In New Orleans . . . at. . . ."

She finished for him: "The cemetery, the one where the body was found. Victor. . . ." She had always suspected that, after the discovery of Randow's empty revolver, the story she had heard from LeBreton and read about in the newspaper.

He picked up immediately: "Desiderio. I

shot him. . . ." He quickly added, "In self-defense, Laura."

"I know," she said. At least, she thought she knew. How well did she really know Bobby Randow? How well could she know anyone who didn't even know himself? Her eyes brightened. "You remember . . . everything?"

She barely heard his sigh and curse. Randow stepped away from the wall and slapped his thigh with his hat. "No. That's the . . ." — he shuddered down another oath — "irksome thing. I only remember part of it, and small parts . . . the cemetery, shooting Desiderio . . . and most of it's smudged. Somebody called me 'reverend', and this was either before or after I shot the guy. It was after I went to see Apolline, though. She wasn't there."

Just as Apolline had admitted that night in her bordello. "That's wonderful, Bobby. I mean you're starting to remember."

"Yeah . . . I even remembered your room number, came straight here after playing poker."

"Why did you come here?" The man who had remembered he was a gentleman and stayed up all night in the St. Louis Hotel lobby while she slept in his room had no such reservations tonight.

191

"Because there were six men, Laura, and I killed one. Five of them are going to be trying to kill me, to finish the job. And I don't know why, and I still don't know who."

Her heart quickened. "Five men." She pictured the rowdies on the main deck this morning, the man wielding the big knife. "I think we should tell Hugh."

Words fail to describe the scope of the Mississippi River here, for it spreads more than a mile, and, as I am told by Mr. Lodwick, the capable steersman of the *Mittie Stephens*, it sinks more than 200 feet in places. The banks on either side reach maybe fifteen feet, not enough, Mr. Lodwick says, to hold "The Big Drink" during floodwaters, with no trees to speak of, mostly plantations of sugar, but with little activity these days, four years after the suppression of the rebellion. Today we reach Baton Rouge, and by nightfall, Coupee. Sometime tomorrow night, we bid the Mississippi fare-the-well and continue our course up the Red River.

From his perch on the hurricane deck, Lieutenant Constantine Ambroise set aside his pen and reread the passage. Mostly, however, he kept his eyes on the five unreconstructed Rebs passing a brown clay jug among themselves, laughing and belching while they stretched out on the main deck. He blew on the ink before closing the journal and caught the scent of pipe tobacco, which caused him to smile.

"Good morning, Captain," he said before craning his neck to find Homer Kellogg standing a few paces away.

"Constantine," Kellogg said. "I did not wish to intrude."

"You are not intruding, sir." He hooked his thumb at the deck below. "I'm keeping a watch on those no-accounts."

Kellogg removed the pipe from the crease in his lip and walked closer, studying the group with reserved curiosity.

"They are not worth a row of pins," Ambroise added.

"It doesn't make them picaroons," Kellogg said. "Rebels, certainly. Rowdies, I suspect. But I doubt they are a threat to your cargo." He returned the pipe, chewing nervously on the stem.

Ambroise grunted as he climbed to his feet. "Sergeant Sloan thinks otherwise, sir."

"Sloan." Kellogg said the name as if it

were a curse, followed that with a sigh, and began hesitantly: "I would desire a few words with you about your sergeant. . . ."

It was Ambroise's turn to groan. He had been troubled all night by Sloan, or rather his own actions. He liked Nicholas Sloan, perhaps trusted him too much, and had shown poor judgment. "A mistake on my part, Captain," Ambroise began. Kellogg removed the pipe and arched his eyebrows. "Seating myself at a card table with the sergeant was a breach of military etiquette, an error I shall not make again, sir. It's fraternization. It won't happen again."

The captain blinked. "You played . . . cards . . . with Sloan?"

"Yes, sir. I thought. . . ." He took a deep breath and slowly exhaled. "In the Soda Lake Saloon." He paused, trying to collect his thoughts. Soda Lake Saloon? Well, where else would he have played poker? It was the only gambling parlor on the *Mittie Stephens*. "Major Siegel and a few of his men, a former Rebel suffering memory lapse, General Granville, who I believe you know . . . you. . . ." Kellogg hadn't heard about the poker game. Something else troubled him. "What . . . what is it about Sergeant Sloan, Captain?"

"It's nothing, Constantine. Forget I troubled you."

She played the game again, asking Randow to try to remember three words. Laura Kelley, however, didn't know if she would recall her selection herself. The *Mittie Stephens* would arrive at Baton Rouge later that morning for a three-hour layover, and Laura knew she needed to lock herself in her cabin. Valdez had complicated matters by suggesting they dine together that evening and perhaps enjoy a dance or two. The thought of waltzing with Valdez thrilled her; the thought of being led down the gangplank in manacles terrified her.

They sat at a table overlooking the east bank of the Mississippi, waiting for breakfast — Laura, Randow, Apolline, Major Siegel, and Valdez, who had arrived in time to order coffee before the waiter left.

"An enjoyable game last evening." Wearing a wide grin, Valdez patted Randow's shoulder before taking his seat. "Well, perhaps more enjoyable for you, old chum, than the rest of us. How much did he skin you for, Major?"

"Forty-eight," Siegel grunted.

"I think I lost three dollars, maybe four,"

Valdez said, "but Aquiles, he must have lost a hundred or more. Sloan went bust early, and the lieutenant said he dropped ten dollars. I know Jules didn't quit the game ahead . . . he plays poker worse than my Great Aunt Sallie. I think you were the only winner, Bobby."

"The general won his share of pots." Randow stared at the napkin in his lap. "All big ones, too."

"You remember that, eh?" Siegel asked dryly.

"Can't remember his name, though."

"Cyrus K. Granville," Siegel said bitterly. "A buckeye Yank."

Randow, head still bent, gave the major a quick glance — Laura barely detected it — before returning his focus on the napkin.

"How much did you win, old chum? You can answer. We're among friends."

Randow's sigh revealed annoyance. He looked up, mouth open as he formed his thoughts, but the waiter had returned with the coffee. "Not as much as the general," he replied, and Valdez laughed with appreciation. He was still sniggering when he picked up his cup, almost spilling coffee on the tablecloth.

"Do you remember the three words?" Apolline asked. "The three words Laura told you a few minutes ago."

He leaned back, wet his lips, breathing silently.

Laura clasped her hands under the table and watched with apprehension.

"Turkey . . . ," Randow began. He seemed to breathe easier when no one corrected him. "Alexandria . . . and. . . ."

He blinked, stared at Siegel, and finished: "Buckeye."

Laura groaned and closed her eyes briefly. "No, Bobby," she said. "It was button. Buckeye was something Major Siegel just said."

"Two out of three, though," Valdez added. "It's a good start. I'd say you are well on the road to recovery."

"Buckeye," Randow repeated. His eyes never left Siegel, who slowly lowered his coffee cup and lifted his cherry-wood cane.

"Julius called General Granville a buckeye," Apolline explained. "It means he is an Ohioan, *amant*. Does 'Ohio' mean anything to you? Or 'buckeye'?"

Neither, Laura thought. It wasn't what Major Julius had said; it was the way he had said it. The bitterness. *A buckeye Yank*. He had momentarily dropped the screeching Yankee whine and sounded almost Southern. Randow and Siegel stared across the table at each other, Randow's face blank, Siegel's malevolent. She feared the provost marshal would slam that long cane against Randow's skull.

The tension broke, however, when Valdez started laughing. This time he spilled coffee all over his fancy coat and the stained tablecloth. "You had best explain yourself, Major," Valdez said. "Your remark about General Granville being a buckeye Yank has aroused suspicion."

Siegel blinked rapidly and lowered the cane. "It was in the war." He shook his head. "Hugh and I always said Ohioans might as well have been fighting with the Secesh. They were the absolute worst in our regiment, so I called them buckeye Yanks. . . ."

"In his best Southern drawl," Valdez added, thickening his own. "No offense, Bobby, ladies."

"That's right, Hugh. I have little use for gentlemen from Ohio, especially generals who served alongside us. I've often wondered if it was not a Southern ball that felled me on the fields of Gettysburg, but one . . ." — with a wink, he returned to his Southern accent — "sent by a poor-aimin' buckeye."

"Buckeye. . . ." Randow stared at

Apolline, then at Laura. "Button."

"That's right, Bobby. It was *button,* not buckeye." She was looking not at Randow, though, but the smiling Hugh Valdez.

"What's the matter, Laura?" Valdez asked as he led her off the dance floor.

He was a splendid dancer, too, much better than Theodore Wilson Kelley had been. Laura had let Valdez persuade her to dine and dance with him that evening, after they had departed Baton Rouge, after Apolline had convinced her that the only people who boarded the *Mittie Stephens* at the state capital had been a family of four, traveling steerage passage to Norman's Landing.

"Anyone who knows you, dear," Apolline had said, "anyone from Alexandria or Pineville would travel in a stateroom, not on deck." She had been mocking Laura's wealth, her gentry heritage, but it had not been a sound argument. The men who worked the fields at Green Haven — after the emancipation — had not been wealthy, and they would know Laura Parker Kelley on sight. Yet Laura wanted to be with Valdez, wanted to ask him, make him explain away the doubts that had been roiling inside her since breakfast. She had only picked at her meal then, and hadn't eaten since.

"We should have no secrets," Valdez whispered as he helped her in her chair. He rounded the table, picked up a glass of champagne, and sat down across from her. Still smiling, he drained the flute. "I am wondering if this jealousy I have of Captain Randow is not misplaced."

The thought of Randow and her started her. She was his nurse. Nothing more. She couldn't have feelings for him. Randow had served as a captain in the Confederacy. He had had a brother who died of disease in Vicksburg. In some ways — but certainly not all — Bobby Randow resembled Theodore Wilson Kelley. There were too many similarities. She would not develop feelings for Randow. She hadn't wanted to find herself attracted to Hugh Valdez, but Valdez never reminded her of her late husband. He made her laugh, made her forget her troubles — usually, that is, but not tonight. Tonight Valdez troubled her, worried her.

"Forgive me, Laura." Valdez looked hurt. "I should not have suggested a thing. It is true, that I am . . . well, any man would be fond of you, yet we have known each other only a short while . . . and my brother weighs heavily on my mind. I. . . ."

She slammed her fist on the table, over-turning her flute. "Will you stop sounding like some half-dime novel!" she shouted, and felt her face flush. The room had turned silent. The band had stopped playing, and her voice had carried across the ballroom. She wanted to apologize, but screwed her eyes shut. She tried to control her heartbeat, her breathing. The next voice was not Valdez's, but she did recognize it.

"Is there a problem, Miss Wilson?"

Laura looked up, and gave Captain Homer Kellogg a quick smile. The master of the *Mittie Stephens* had come to her rescue again.

"No, Captain," she said. "A woman's temper . . . 'Hell has no fury . . .' "

Kellogg grinned and returned his pipe. "I see, ma'am. Enjoy your evening, Miss Wilson . . . *monsieur.* I will see that your flute is refilled with champagne. Excuse me."

She made herself look into Valdez's eyes.

They apologized at the same time, stopped, embarrassed, and Valdez began mumbling something about how he always acted like a schoolboy when around a woman he "adored" — he said *adored* —

how he could play poker, arrest deserters, face down ruffians, but when it came to women. . . .

"Hugh. . . ."

He stopped.

"This morning, at breakfast, Major Siegel said you and he used to joke about Ohioans during the war."

"That's right. I served under him."

"Yesterday, though, when you faced down those men on deck, when you helped Bobby Randow. . . ." She made herself say his full name. "When you helped him, you told those ne'er-do-wells that you came from Virginia . . . I can't recall the town . . . and that you rode with Moseby."

"Mosby," Valdez corrected. "And the place was Thoroughfare Gap, Virginia."

"You couldn't have. . . ."

Valdez chuckled and waited for the waiter to wipe up the spilled champagne with a rag and refill Laura's flute and leave before continuing. "I am a liar, Laura. I am a compulsive liar at times. I am from Virginia, though. In fact, I grew up near Thoroughfare Gap. It's in the Bull Run Mountains. The Manassas Gap Railroad runs through there, right on the county line of Price William and Fauquier. That's all true. I hope you don't believe I could

202

make all of that up. When we get to Alexandria, we can go ashore and see if we can find a map of Virginia. . . ."

"No!" she shot out, again louder than she meant, but the thought of Alexandria frightened her. This time, however, the music had started again, and few people heard her.

Valdez lost his smirk and lowered his voice. "I'm from Thoroughfare Gap, Virginia, but I never rode with John S. Mosby, though Major Siegel and I certainly chased him enough. A Virginia Yankee I am, and it did not make me the most popular person in the county . . . or with my family . . . another reason I so desire to see my dying brother. I was lying to those men, Laura. Sometimes, you lie to men to give yourself an advantage, to avoid a fight. I didn't want to fight those men, but I would have . . . for Bobby Randow, but mostly for you. And I can't help it if that sounds like I write romances for Beadle's."

She felt like an idiot. She reached over and patted his hand and didn't pull away when he held hers. He had soft hands, a gentle touch. Randow's hands and Homer Kellogg's were callused and rough.

"I'm sorry, Hugh."

He lifted her hand and kissed it, then released it, and picked up his flute, motioning her to do the same. They toasted, and drank.

"Well, now that I've earned your trust again, I wonder if I might ask you a question," Valdez said.

"Certainly."

Whispered Valdez: "Why did the captain call you Miss *Wilson?*"

Chapter Fifteen

Zoë Denton could not be bribed with compliments. Obadiah Denton knew that much about his wife, whose face remained granite despite the praise Robert Erskine Thomas heaped on Denton's wife's cooking. She probably didn't believe the crew man, and with good reason. Denton doubted if a cook had ever lived who could improve the taste of boiled potatoes and a hodge-podge of broken bits of meat, vegetables, and bread.

"It's just right, Mizzus Zoë," Thomas said. "The *Mittie Stephens*' crew ain't never dined this well in all my years serving Capt'n Langhorne."

She grunted something unintelligible, and Thomas leaned over, winking at Emanuel and Matthew. "You don't believe me, ma'am?"

Another grunt.

"Well, you don't hear no one complaining about this fine meal, now, do you?"

Denton hid his smirk by filling his mouth with a spoonful of heavily salted mush. Since that first night out, none of the crew had ever really complained, at least not so that Zoë Denton could hear. Oh, a few made comments on the first couple of nights, but those had been more in jest than anything. Most ate in silence — perhaps because they found the food better than expected, or maybe because a woman as big and solid as Zoë Denton could intimidate even the most quarrelsome riverboat man.

As soon as she yelled — "Grub pile!" — every evening, they formed a line to fill their bowls and plates with whatever she dished up. She was the last to fill her own bowl, as she had this evening before settling her ample frame on the deck between her sons and across from Denton and Thomas.

Denton washed down his supper with coffee, which was good. Strong, hot, and bitter. If the food didn't keep a man going, the coffee would, but that's the way he had liked it back in the Army.

"Ship's turnin'," Matthew said with his mouth full.

"How can you tell?" Denton asked, curious. Matthew was becoming quite the sailor.

His seven-year-old son hooked a thumb toward the paddle wheel. "Turnin' east. Tell by how the wheels is actin', how the ship feels. Mister Erskine says a side-wheeler's easier to turn than a stern-wheeler. Says the wheels can act inde . . . inde . . . independently. Ain't that right, Mister Erskine?"

"That's right, Matthew," Thomas said.

Matthew's mother countered: "Don't talk with your mouth full."

"Yes'm." He swallowed, wiped his lips with the back of his small hand, and continued: "Side-wheelers are the best on the river, ain't that right, Mister Erskine?"

"Mostly. In shallow water, a stern-wheeler works better. In fact, the shallows can be right dangersome for a side-wheeler, but I'm in agreement with Matthew. I'll take a side-wheeler like the *Mittie Stephens*. We're leaving the Mississippi now, I warrant. Tomorrow morn I'll be showing you boys the Red River, show you how to catch a mess of fish when we land to take on wood at first light."

Denton groaned. "More wood?" he asked. The thought sickened him.

"That's what keeps us going, Obadiah."

He looked at his fingers and the blood blisters that had formed helping the crew load firewood. If this kept up, he wouldn't be able to play that fancy organ to announce supper for the passengers, or even grip a hammer. Maybe Zoë would pop them and put a poultice on them later that night.

"While your daddy and the crew is loading firewood, I'll take you to the fishing hole," Thomas said. "Now we gotta hurry, but the captain, he likes it, allows me to haul up some big ol' cats, and I'll put in a word so he'll let you go along. Then they skin and fry those fish and serve them to the fancy passengers. But I get to keep one or two for us to eat. Bet your mama can fry up a catfish. Just us."

"Stew 'em," she said.

"How's that, Mizzus Zoë?"

"Said I'd stew 'em. Stew 'em so the whole crew can taste somethin' dif'rent. Ain't fair for you to hog them fish for yourself, or ourselves. We's a crew, ain't we?"

Thomas stared at his empty plate in silence, and Denton chuckled. He liked the way Matthew had taken to the crew man, how he was learning about the steamboats, and earning his keep, too. He had made Obadiah Denton proud. So had Emanuel. Both were hard-working boys, always had been. Robert Erskine Thomas bragged on the two every night he brought them in, bedraggled, dirty, and sweaty, their little hands filled with splinters. Never did either complain, though. *They're a hundred times better than their old man,* Denton thought.

"Maybe," Zoë began, sounding like a woman rather than a gruff crone for a change, "what with us changin' course, maybe we'll get from underneath them clouds. I almost forgotten what the sun looks like."

"It's dark for certain," Thomas said. "I figure some old lady has witched us, or the good Lord's frowning on somebody on this bucket."

"Hush your nonsense," Zoë snapped. "You'll fill my boys' heads with nonsense."

Denton's appetite soured. He wasn't so sure Thomas had been speaking nonsense. Oh, he didn't believe in voodoo, or witches, although he had grown up around many, many who did. Denton did believe in God, however, and He certainly had reason to frown upon Obadiah Denton.

"What were the three words Laura told you at the beginning of supper?"

Randow had grown weary of this game, but he set his wine glass down and smiled warmly at Apolline, who reached over and took his hand, patting it gently, returning a lovely smile. He couldn't really remember loving her, but it must have been easy, he thought, although she was brazen, looking at him that way, smiling at him that way, holding his hand that way — all the while Major Siegel sat across the table, clipping a cigar. Apolline was the major's girl now, or so he had learned. Laura must have told him. Randow couldn't recall.

But the game — the game kept ruining his mood. They should start charging admission. One shinplaster to see if Captain Randow can remember three simple words forty-five minutes, if that, after hearing them. Laura did it every time they saw each other — at breakfast that morning, while strolling around the deck that afternoon, and now at supper.

He could remember the events of this day, most of them clearly. He drank coffee for breakfast — alone, for he had risen early, although Laura and Apolline came in later and sat with him, eating their breakfast while he kept them company and tried to recollect Laura's three words of the day (he had gotten all three right, pleasing the ladies immensely). Later, he had found a quiet place on the stern and whiled away the hours staring at the river, helping the crew load firewood when the *Mittie Stephens* had stopped at Tunica, taking a bite of plug tobacco offered by the colored crew man who played the calliope and that wretched tune cranked out every evening before supper. That had caused several stares — a white man accepting chewing tobacco from a black man, not even cutting off the piece with a knife, but biting it.

"Nigger lips," a grizzled fellow in denim trousers had said stiffly. The phrase had been directed at Randow.

"Do I know you?" he had asked, and the man had laughed and gone about his work without another word.

Later in the afternoon, he had visited the Soda Lake Saloon to drink a whiskey with Valdez, then had strolled around the decks with Apolline and Laura. He had retired to his spot on the main deck, dealt solitaire poker to himself and three imaginary players, and watched some young children fish from the riverbank, their laughter carrying across the wide river. He had watched them until the steamboat rounded a bend and they had disappeared. Valdez had found him a few minutes later, suggesting they freshen up in his cabin before supper. He had accepted the man's generosity, changed his shirt, and shaved in the stateroom, nicking his chin when the organ began that obnoxious *"Mittie Stephens March"*.

He could remember all of that, so he certainly could recall the three words Laura told him before they were seated.

"Oyster," he said — and his mind went as muddy as the river.

"You can do it, *amant*," Apolline said.

But he couldn't. He could remember only one lousy word, and he wasn't even sure "oyster" had been right.

He announced his defeat with a sigh, and Laura told him the other two words had been "snagboat" and "river". How could he have forgotten those stupid words? Well, he had gotten one right. Yesterday, it had been two, and this morning, three. Was his condition worsening? Or did it have something to do with distress? The doctor in New Orleans — Charles LeBreton, he could picture the man clearly — had said there might be some relation to anxiety and his memory lapses, but he had not been in any fights today. There had been no confrontation with the deck passenger helping load the firewood, the burly man with the big knife, although now — hours later — Randow remembered this was the leader of the group of rowdies who had been coming at him when Valdez had stopped them, Valdez and the Army sergeant named. . . . He couldn't remember the name, hadn't seen the soldier in a spell.

"Valdez," Randow whispered the name.

"What's that, old chum?" Hugh Valdez shook out the match he had used to light a cigar.

Randow shook his head. "Nothing," he said.

"*Tsk, tsk.* I had hoped you were inviting me to play cards tonight, to be a gentleman and give me a chance to win some of my money back. Say, eight-thirty?"

"It would be a pleasure," Randow said. *If I can remember the time.*

"Good," Valdez said. "Eight-thirty. That will give me and Miss Wil . . . Laura. It will give Laura and myself a chance to walk around the deck, enjoy the evening cool, if it would suit you, Laura?"

"It suits me," she said. Both rose, and Laura slipped her arm inside the crook of Valdez's elbow before the gentleman from Virginia escorted the lady to the exit.

"They make a handsome couple," Apolline said.

Major Siegel shrugged. "If you'll excuse

me, I desire a few words with an acquaintance."

That left him alone with Apolline — and most men would dream of such a situation — but he kept staring at the door.

"What are you thinking about, Bobby?" Apolline asked. "Don't worry about tonight . . . the words. You're getting better, I know it. You got all three right this morning. Remember?"

Chinaberry, Texas, and Dixie. Yeah, he even knew those words.

"Maybe it was the wine," Apolline said. "Maybe alcohol affects your memory, *amant.*" She let out a short chuckle. "Lord knows it affects the minds of most men I've known."

He wasn't thinking about the words, though, or the wine. He was thinking about Valdez, about Laura, and wondering. . . .

Not distress. Not fights. Not tension. Could he blame his memory on jealousy?

He leaned against the jackstaff and stared into the darkness, wondering if the moon, now in the last quarter, would break through the clouds. Men upstairs in the Soda Lake Saloon would bet on that. They'd bet on anything, but Randow kept his wagers to cards and horses. He had won again this night, only ten or twelve dollars, but he had won. Gustavo Aquiles had been the big winner, or, at least, had been when Randow decided to call it a night. The merchant steaming to Pineville had lost heavily the first time they had played poker, but his luck had turned tonight. That's the way cards go. Julius Siegel couldn't buy a hand. He had lost with three kings, had even dropped a substantial pot when his nines over sevens lost to General Granville's larger full house. Randow had folded three twos on that one, when the betting went crazy, and had been glad he had when he saw Granville's and Siegel's hands. They were still playing poker, would probably be at it until dawn.

"How can I remember all of that?" he asked himself in a whisper. "And I don't know who's trying to kill me."

"Kill you?"

His heart skipped as he whirled, reaching behind his back for the Dance but stopping when he saw her, her beautiful face and auburn hair illuminated by torches and metal cages filled with glowing pine knots.

"Who's trying to kill you, *amant?*" Apolline Rainier stepped to him, her face reflecting concern.

He started to tell her, but couldn't. What could he say? Who would believe him? Well, Laura had believed him.

"It's a dream," he lied. "A dream that makes no sense. What time is it?"

"After two." She came closer.

"You should be in. . . . You should be asleep, Apolline."

"Can't sleep." Smiling, she stepped around him. "I grew up in Alexandria. We'll be there tomorrow, or, rather, today, I mean. February Ninth, my birthday. I bet you had forgot. . . ."

"Happy birthday," he said. Of course, he had forgotten.

Her quick turn surprised him, and, before he knew it, she had wrapped her arms around him and kissed him. Before he knew it, he was kissing her back, kissing her hard until he pulled away and swallowed down his embarrassment and urge to kiss her more.

"You're still good as gold," she said. "And I do miss you, *amant*. And you do miss me."

"Ma'am?"

She laughed. "You asked me if you missed me. Back in New Orleans, when you came barging into my place. You asked

216

me if you missed me, and Laura and I laughed." She rested her head against his chest, wrapped her arms tighter. "I wish. . . ."

A door opened somewhere on the cabin deck, and she pulled away. "I should go," she said. "You should turn in yourself, Bobby. Who's trying to kill you, *amant?*"

"It's like I said. . . ."

"You used to be a better liar." She said something in French, shrugged, and left. "Be careful, Bobby. We don't arrive in Shreveport until the Eleventh. That's a long time on a riverboat." She disappeared in the darkness.

He drew the Dance, rubbed his thumb against the hammer, and returned the pistol into his waistband, but this time on his left hip, butt forward, still hidden by his frock coat but easier to reach. Apolline's words ran through his mind, triggering another deep memory. *You used to be a better liar. . . .* Yet something else she had said kept ricocheting inside his skull, refusing to rest until it reached the recesses of his memories where it meant something. *Your kisses are still as good as gold . . . as good as gold . . . as good as gold . . . gold. . . . Gold!*

Chapter Sixteen

As he sat in the dining room toying with both his breakfast and a morning entry into his journal, Lieutenant Constantine Ambroise saw the form of Sergeant Nicholas Sloan immediately fill the doorway. Ambroise glanced around the hall, finding it practically empty. A red-headed woman in a green dress sat at the neighboring table, talking to the blonde woman Homer Kellogg had introduced the other night as Miss Laura Wilson, and Captain Randow, the Secessionist plagued by memory lapses. The provost marshal and his associates were nowhere to be found this morning, probably sleeping late after an all-night poker game already being talked about. A couple of merchants and one couple sat farther away, and a black galley hand headed for the door with a pot of coffee and plate of biscuits, likely bound for the pilot house.

He motioned Sloan over.

"Begging the lieutenant's pardon," Sloan said once he reached Ambroise's table.

"Go ahead, Sloan."

"Those vagabonds, the five Rebs . . . they all disembarked at Barbin's, sir, early this morning."

"Are you sure, Sloan?"

"Yes, sir. Mind you, I didn't see them get off, but that darky carpenter told me, said he saw them get off, and they didn't get back on. Me, Emmerich, and Silvia spent the past hour combing all the decks, and they aren't on board, sir."

The blonde had been eavesdropping. Now she excused herself, stood, and nervously approached Sloan and Ambroise.

"Excuse me, Lieutenant," she said in a soft Southern accent, "but I couldn't help but overhear. Oh, please, Lieutenant, do not stand."

Ambroise settled back in his chair. He remembered now that the five Rebs had accosted Captain Randow earlier in the voyage, and she obviously was a friend of the cavalryman as well as Major Siegel's top man, Hugh Valdez. He had seen them dancing quite often the past few nights.

"Sergeant Sloan, this is Miss Laura Wilson. . . ."

"We've met," the woman said, her eyes never glancing in Sloan's direction. The sergeant, likewise, remained facing Ambroise.

"That'll be all, Sergeant," Ambroise said. Sloan offered a salute and retreated from the dining hall, apparently glad to get away from Laura Wilson. Ambroise recalled Captain Kellogg's visit the other day, when he had said he wanted to speak about Sloan but had wound up not saying a thing. He wondered if Laura Wilson might have been the reason but decided it was none of his affair.

"Sergeant Sloan reported that those five men got off at Barbin's, ma'am," Ambroise said. "I would fathom a guess that Captain Randow, and you, will not be threatened by them any more."

"That is a relief, Lieutenant. Thank you."

He bowed slightly before she returned to her table to tell her friends the good news. She was right, Ambroise thought, as he lifted his cup of coffee and whispered to himself: *It* is *a relief.*

She waited the rest of the morning, and much of the afternoon, in her stateroom, her face damp with sweat, knuckles whitening every time someone walked past her door. The *Mittie Stephens* had docked in Alexandria, and she worried her luck had played out, that Sheriff Risseau would be stepping on board to arrest her, or at the very least that someone would recognize her and turn her in to Captain Kellogg.

The other night, Laura had told Hugh Valdez everything. After Captain Kellogg had called her Miss Wilson, she had felt she had no choice, and the confession had eased the tension, the burden, the anchor around her neck. She had prayed that Valdez's relationship with the provost marshal would not force him to arrest her, or rather had hoped that her relationship with Valdez would stop him from doing so. He had squeezed her hand and kissed it.

"My dear," he had said, "you should have told me this long ago. I'll protect you, Laura. No one shall arrest you for keeping your property out of the hands of those thieving carpetbaggers."

There would be more stops before the steamboat reached Texas — Cotile, St. Maurice, Grand Ecore, Natchitoches, and Shreveport, to name a few — but she believed, if she could just get past Alexandria, everything would work out.

Laura looked at her fingernails, and couldn't believe it. She had bitten them down almost to the quick.

Footsteps again, and she held her breath, feeling her stomach overturn when they stopped. A light tapping followed, and then a voice she did not recognize: "Miss Wilson?"

She opened her mouth but heard no words, realized she hadn't said anything. "Yes," she answered timidly. A wave of nausea left her dizzy, but it passed quickly.

"It's Joe Lodwick, Miss Wilson, ship's steersman. Mister Valdez asked me to see if you would join him on deck, the main deck. It's against ship rules for him to come up here to ask you himself."

Laura collapsed on the bunk and blinked away tears. "Yes," she said, her voice still trembling. "Yes, Mister Lodwick, I know. Thank you, sir. Thank you kindly." She fell back, her heart still racing.

"Miss Wilson?"

"Yes?" She closed her eyes.

"What should I tell Mister Valdez, ma'am?"

Laura giggled and sat up. "Tell him I will be happy to join him, sir." It was clear, or Valdez would not have asked her to leave the cabin. In three days or so, she would be in Texas. She'd be free.

"Of course, ma'am. Port side, Miss Wilson, behind the wheelhouse."

He started away, but Laura shouted at him to stop.

"Yes, Miss Wilson?" he said.

"How much longer before we leave Alexandria?"

"We're shoving off now, ma'am."

"Thank you, Mister Lodwick. Thank you very much for your trouble."

"It was no trouble, ma'am."

Randow spotted Laura as he dealt Valdez the nine of diamonds on top of the ten of clubs, then tossed himself a four of spades to go with his queen of clubs. Valdez's back was to her, and he leaned back, smiling that big Virginia smile, and pushed back his silk hat.

"It's your bet, Bobby."

Randow checked his hole card. "Check."

With a shrug, Valdez bet fifty cents and Randow called.

They were passing time, mostly, playing cards on deck while the *Mittie Stephens* put back into the river and began steaming up the Red. Randow waited for Laura to get closer before he continued his deal.

"No more word on your brother?" Randow asked.

"None," Valdez said. "It's still your bet."

If my brother were dying, I'd pick a faster steamboat to get home, one that didn't stop at every way landing along the Red River. I would have ridden a horse, or taken a stagecoach. I would. . . . Randow stopped. His brother had been dead almost six years. Sometimes he wished his mind would let him forget those things instead of the more recent memories.

"It's still your bet, Bobby," Valdez repeated, and Randow tossed in a fifty-cent piece. Valdez raised two bits.

"Swanson's Landing, right?" Randow called Valdez's bet.

"Port Caddo."

"Port Caddo. That's right." He dealt the final cards. "And his name is William?"

Valdez grinned. "It's your bet, Bobby. Pair of fours beats a pair of threes."

"Right." He checked, and Valdez bet two dollars — high stakes for what they had been betting the past hour, but it was two-hand poker — not much of a game.

Randow raised a dollar.

"Checking and raising." Valdez shook his head. "That's not friendly poker, old chum. But I raise you back a dollar."

Laura stood behind Valdez, waiting patiently, not wanting to interrupt the game. Randow tossed in two dollars. "We were talking about your brother William."

"It's Henry, old chum." He arched his eyebrows. "Are you trying to catch me in a lie, Bobby?" He withdrew a dollar coin from his change purse and tossed it onto the pile.

"I've already caught you in one, old chum," Randow said. Their eyes locked, and Valdez's pale eyes narrowed. There was something beyond that boyish humor, something brooding, perhaps even merciless. Randow kept his face a blank, long enough to make Valdez wonder. Laura had heard the conversation, but Randow couldn't read her face, if she questioned this federal officer, this gentlemanly rapscallion. He broke the trance and developing tension with a soft chuckle before adding: "I just can't remember what it was." He turned over his hole card, the four of diamonds.

With a sigh, Valdez collected his cards and tossed them away. "Can't beat that, Bobby. I wonder where . . . ?" As he turned, he saw Laura, and quickly stood, removing his hat and walking to her. Randow collected the cards, coins, and paper money, shoving them into his coat pocket, and pulled himself up.

"Laura." He removed his own hat.

"Bobby." She smiled at him, but slipped her hand through Valdez's arm. "It's a lovely afternoon, for once. No clouds. Warm."

"Yes'm," Randow pulled on his hat. "You two taking another stroll?"

"That's our plan, old chum," Valdez answered, his eyes jovial again. "Would you care to accompany us?"

He shook his head. "No. I'll stay down here, maybe see if I can't bribe someone upstairs in the galley to give me a cup of coffee."

"Well," Laura said happily, "we sha'n't be gone long, Bobby. Here. Try to remember these three words . . . home, future, and Caddo. I'll test you in a half hour."

"Home, future, Caddo," Randow said. "I think I can remember those, Laura."

"I think he can, too," Valdez said. "His memory is fast improving."

"It is," Randow said. There was an edge in his voice, but Laura, happy to be outside, happy to be with Valdez, happy at something, didn't notice.

"That's wonderful, Bobby," she said.

Her smile turned upside down, and she stepped closer to him. "Do you remember . . . ?"

He shook his head. "No. That night's still muddy, but things are clearing up. Home, future, Caddo." He smiled, first at Laura, next at Valdez.

"It'll come to you, Bobby," Laura said. "Don't rush things."

"Yes," Valdez said as he led Laura away. "Don't rush things, old chum."

Is he threatening me? Or am I just jealous? He had tried to catch Valdez lying in front of Laura, but Valdez had not stumbled. His dying brother was named Henry and lived in Port Caddo, not William in Swanson's Landing. Randow had remembered the name and place clearly, could remember almost everything now — everything except what had happened at the graveyard at midnight in New Orleans a few days ago. Maybe Valdez wasn't lying. Maybe Randow was jealous. What did he really know?

Well, he knew five men were trying to kill him. He knew that as certain as he knew his own name. Laura had suspected the rowdies, but they had gotten off the *Mittie Stephens* that morning, and no one had boarded the steamboat at Alexandria.

227

His journey would end in Shreveport in less than forty-eight hours. He'd see his mother, and be shut of Hugh Valdez, Julius Siegel, and the *Mittie Stephens*. He should relax, but he knew the men wanting him dead remained on this ship. Well, he felt it at least, but it was a strong feeling — like the feelings he had developed for Laura Kelley, only she would not reciprocate those. He hadn't asked her, hadn't even told her how he felt about her, and couldn't bring himself to, not now, not after seeing how she looked at Valdez.

He kept trying to tell himself that, honestly, he couldn't be in love with Laura Kelley. He barely knew her. She had simply cared for him, helped him when he was practically helpless. It was only natural to develop feelings for her. It was only natural that he was a little — well, more than a little — jealous of Valdez.

Valdez . . . Major Julius Siegel . . . the clerk whose name he couldn't remember . . . and Jules Honoré, a lousy card player but one hardcase. Four men, though, not five. Unless he had been mistaken about the number, unless he had killed another man beside Victor Desiderio that night in the City of the Dead. He cursed his memory, his uncertainty.

Unless the fifth man was not a man, but a woman. Apolline Rainier? Apolline was Siegel's girl, and before that had been Randow's. That was a strong connection, but he couldn't see Apolline trying to slice his throat, couldn't picture her murdering anybody, especially him, after they had kissed last night by the jack staff. Or Laura Kelley? What was she doing at Apolline's place that night? Why was she so concerned with his memory? Why was she seeing Valdez all the time?

"Well," he said to himself, and pinched the bridge of his nose. He felt a headache coming on. "That's obvious, *old chum*. She's in love with the shoat."

Chapter Seventeen

The poker game lacked the friendliness on the night of the 10th, even though most of the players were the same. Sergeant Sloan, of course, was not sitting in, and hadn't played with Lieutenant Constantine Ambroise since that first night. Gustavo Aquiles had departed the *Mittie Stephens* at Alexandria and taken a ferry across the river to Pineville. Sidney Paige, Major Siegel's clerk, and a cotton buyer named Frederick Ashland, bound for Jefferson, had replaced those two players, joining the regulars — Hugh Valdez, Julius Siegel, Jules Honoré, Bobby Randow, and General Cyrus K. Granville, along with Ambroise — for the nightly pastime after supper.

Yet only Granville and Ambroise appeared to be enjoying themselves — and they weren't even winning big. Granville hadn't won a hand in hours; Ambroise figured he was about even.

"The ship's master was bragging on you, Lieutenant, at our table during supper," the balding, rheumy-eyed Ashland said to make conversation as Honoré dealt five-card draw.

"Don't believe everything Captain Kellogg says," Ambroise said lightly, and looked at his cards: seven of spades, queen of spades, five of spades, six of hearts, queen of diamonds. For once, he had a solid pair worth betting.

"Balderdash. You were a hero, sir, saved the lives of many passengers when the *Princess*'s boiler blew on the Mississippi ten years ago. In fact, you saved Captain Kellogg's life."

Jules Honoré snorted. "Is that a fact? You mean we're playing poker with a by-gawd hero? Well, hero, it's your bet."

He bet five dollars, hoping to run most of the players out of the game. Valdez and Randow promptly folded, Siegel called, Paige folded, Granville called, Ashland folded, and Honoré raised five. After the remaining players called the raise, Ambroise drew three cards. He picked them up — eight of hearts, nine of spades, ten of spades — and placed them alongside the pair of queens. Everyone else also drew three cards.

"Your bet, *hero*," Honoré said.

"There's no need for cynicism, young man," Ashland said. "The lieutenant was a hero."

"I did what anyone would have under those circumstances," Ambroise said, without looking up. He wished Kellogg would quit bringing up that incident.

Honoré coughed slightly and reminded Ambroise he still had the bet. He tossed another five-spot into the pile. Siegel called, Granville folded, and Honoré raised ten. That chased Siegel out of the game, and Ambroise hesitated.

"Well, hero, do you think I'm bluffing? Call me, hero. See if my hand isn't as good as gold."

Ambroise looked at his cards again, and sighed. He wasn't much of a poker player, too big a skinflint, especially considering how little a second lieutenant made in this man's army. Besides, the game wasn't fun any more. He started to toss his cards onto the deadwood, but Captain Randow stopped him.

"He's bluffing," Randow said softly.

Honoré's eyes narrowed as he quickly faced Randow. "How'd you know? You likely can't even remember how many cards I took."

"You took three. Everyone took three."

"Yeah? You didn't. I chased your yeller hide out of the game."

"I had a lousy hand. I wouldn't have stayed in if you had bet a half bit."

Ambroise shifted his cards into his left hand and picked up ten dollars in chips and slid them toward the pot. "All I have is a pair of queens," he said, turning them over. "If you can beat that, sir, the pot belongs to you."

The dealer slammed his cards onto the table top and waved a bony finger in Randow's face. "It's your fault, preacher. I had him running scared till you opened your trap." Swearing savagely, he drank the shot of rye in front of him. "I should have killed you. . . ."

"Honoré," Siegel said sternly, "if you can't play cards like a gentleman, you should retire to the main deck."

When the swarthy man didn't budge, Valdez leaned across the table. "Good night, Jules," he said, and Honoré cashed in his chips, shoved his money into his deep pockets, and stormed out of the Soda Lake Saloon.

"My apologies, gentlemen," Siegel said. "Jules isn't much of a poker player."

"He isn't much of a gentleman either,

Major," Valdez added. Valdez's smile returned. "That little fracas has left me dry as a lime-burner's hat. Could I interest everyone in another round on me?"

Granville, Ashland, Siegel, and Paige readily accepted, but Ambroise shook his head. He had lost interest in playing poker tonight. "If you'll excuse me, gentlemen," he said, "it's late, and I think I shall turn in."

"Bobby?" Valdez asked.

The Rebel captain also declined the offer and called it a night. He had lost money tonight, not much, especially considering how much he had won recently, so Ambroise wasn't surprised when he quit the game, too.

"Sleep well," Siegel said as the two men left the saloon.

They parted company outside the Soda Lake, Ambroise climbing the stairs to visit the pilot house and Randow descending to the main deck. Ambroise talked to the ship's pilot, William Swain, briefly, then asked clerk Cal Hayes if he would mind escorting him to the ship's safe.

"Do you want to deposit anything, sir?" the clerk asked.

"No. Don't even want it opened." He shrugged and grinned. The poker game had unnerved him, and he wanted some reassurance that the Union payroll remained secure. It seemed a silly notion, but Ambroise couldn't shake the foreboding that had started at the poker game.

"Where you goin'?" his wife demanded.

Obadiah Denton shook his head. "Can't sleep. Thought I might wander up to the freedmen's bureau. That's the deck where they let the coloreds. . . ."

"I know what it is."

"Yes'm, well, I thought I might bring my harmonica or trumpet. . . ."

"You leave that tootin' horn in its sack, Obadiah Denton. Ain't no need in you wakin' up passengers with that thing at this time of night."

"Yes'm."

"And don't be gone too long."

He hesitated, though, and she rolled over. "Well, what's keepin' you? You want to go socialize, do it. Play your music. Maybe that'll help whatever's troublin' you so . . . since you can't talk to me 'bout it. Go on, now, before you wake up the boys."

"Yes'm."

He wished he could tell Zoë, but feared how she would react. It would be beyond disappointment, he figured. It wasn't like he had frequented the West Texas *jacales* populated with lewd women, or anything like that, but he surely had betrayed Zoë and his boys. He had betrayed a lot of people. He thought of the medal Matthew had stuck underneath his makeshift pillow tonight, as he had many nights. He wished he had never seen the piece of bronze and pretty ribbons.

Outside, away from the pitman arm and paddle wheels, he heard the music on the texas deck. The sky had cleared, and he gazed at the shrinking moon, the brilliant stars, the flickering torches. He started up the stairs, gripping the harmonica in a clammy hand, drawn by the music like a moth to a flame. The travelers on the texas deck sounded so joyous, laughing, clapping their hands, tapping their feet to the rhythm of someone's banjo and fiddle, drowning out the noise from the ship's saloon.

Maybe, Denton hoped, the music would help him forget, or provide an answer, a way to escape from the hole about to bury him.

He met Nicholas Sloan by the hay bales, smoking a cigarette while leaning against the staircase railing, surprised to find the sergeant up this late. Constantine Ambroise thanked Cal Hayes for his time, and watched the first clerk disappear up the staircase while he stayed behind to talk to Sloan.

"Where are Emmerich and Silvia?" Ambroise asked.

"Sleeping, I reckon, sir. Why?" He dropped the cigarette and crushed it out with his boot heel. "You expecting trouble, Lieutenant?"

"No . . .," Ambroise began. "It's a bad feeling, probably nerves."

They were past Natchitoches, past Grand Ecore, and would dock in Shreveport at midday. By the following afternoon, the *Mittie Stephens'* cargo would be safely in the hands of the paymaster at Jefferson.

"Let's go," Ambroise said, and headed up the stairs.

"Where we going, Lieutenant?"

"To the pilot house. I'll feel better there, for some reason."

Sloan laughed, and followed him up the steps. "Maybe you were born to be a riverboat pilot, after all, sir."

Ambroise moved past the cabin deck to the hurricane deck, heard the music down the texas deck, and then a figure appeared in the shadows. "Lieutenant!" the voice

237

called out, and a man stepped into the light. Ambroise unfastened the holster flap covering his Remington revolver. Behind him on the stairs, hidden in the dark, Sergeant Sloan held his breath.

"Captain," Ambroise greeted Bobby Randow. He turned his head and mouthed at Sloan to remain in the shadows and keep quiet.

"If I were you, Lieutenant," Randow began, and Ambroise gripped the revolver's walnut butt. "If I were you, I'd transfer that payroll to another ship at Shreveport."

Ambroise's throat turned dry, and his stomach see-sawed. He clutched the Remington tighter but did not draw the weapon. No words. He couldn't think of anything to say, and blinked rapidly, running his tongue over his cracked lips. Finally he said: "I don't know what you mean, Captain."

Randow's soft chuckle surprised him. "I don't know what I mean half the time, either, Lieutenant, but I've a strong hunch I'm right about this."

Ambroise turned to Sloan. "Find Emmerich and Silvia," he whispered urgently. "Don't leave the safe."

"Yes, sir," Sloan said, and his footsteps

echoed in the darkness as Ambroise faced Randow again.

How did this slipshod Secessionist know about the payroll? Ambroise wondered. *Who told him, a gambler who couldn't remember what he had for breakfast? Or was it just an act? Shreveport? Wasn't Randow leaving the steamboat at Shreveport? Is that why he wanted the gold transferred to another ship? Too many questions. No answers.*

"I know you don't believe me, Lieutenant," Randow said. "Can't say that I blame you. But five men are going to try to steal that gold from you between Shreveport and Jefferson."

"How?" Ambroise quickly laughed and added: "I'm not saying you're right, Captain, that there is any federal money on this ship, but you have aroused my curiosity." The laugh hadn't fooled Randow. Ambroise knew that. Randow was too good of a poker player, and Ambroise too poor of one.

"If I knew, I'd tell you, Lieutenant. When Siegel's man Honoré mentioned gold, it set something ringing in my head, and it came to me while I was wandering about the main deck, thinking. Gold. Someone else said something about gold a while back. It's. . . ." Randow shook his head.

Don't trust him, Ambroise thought. *He fought for the Confederacy. He's probably nothing more than a cold-blooded killer and thief.*

"I wouldn't be telling you this, Lieutenant, if I meant to rob you." When Ambroise didn't move, Randow sighed. "You still don't trust me," he said.

Ambroise shrugged. "For all I know, Captain, you are Cullen Baker or Black Chivington."

With a laugh, Randow pushed back his hat. "I'm not Baker, Lieutenant, and Black Chivington was killed by Jeff Slade in Benton, Texas three weeks ago. I. . . ." He stepped back, slamming into the railing as if he had been shot. "Jeff Slade," he whispered, spun around, and ran down the deck. Ambroise started to draw his revolver, to go after him, but, no, he thought, it could be a trap. He was torn, indecisive — upstairs to find Captain Kellogg, downstairs to guard the safe with his men, or chase Randow into the dark?

For the first time, Bobby Randow had danced with her. He had cut in on Hugh Valdez during a waltz after supper.

"Let's see if I can remember this," he had said with a smile.

He had remembered, too, had waltzed so well, and Laura had been amazed at how graceful he was, swinging her across the ballroom floor while other couples stopped to smile, bow, or applaud.

The song had ended all too soon, and Randow had escorted her back to the table, where Valdez sat waiting, sipping a brandy.

"A drink?" Valdez had suggested. "Before you retire for the evening till our card game?"

Laura understood the threat now, but hadn't then. Valdez was the jealous one, jealous of Randow.

"A pleasure," Randow had said, and Valdez nodded at a passing waiter.

"How did you learn to dance so well?" Laura had asked.

He had shrugged, and accepted the glass from the waiter, raising it in a toast to Valdez.

"To old friends," Randow had said.

They both downed their drinks, staring at one another, sizing each other up. Again, Laura had not noticed, or felt the tension, until now, hours later, as she lay on her bunk, playing the scene through her mind over and over. The music had started again, another waltz, and Valdez rose. "It's a shame, sir," he had said, "that you'll be leaving us so prematurely."

She had thought Valdez had meant that Randow would be departing tomorrow afternoon in Shreveport, but later decided that he had meant he had worn out his welcome dancing with Laura. Now she feared the deputy provost marshal had meant something entirely different.

"I'll enjoy our game tonight, though," Randow had told Valdez before tipping his hat, kissing Laura's hand, and heading for the door.

Valdez's words haunted her as she lay, still in her clothes, hands clasped, wondering, worrying. *"Perhaps it's time to raise the stakes, old chum."*

Randow couldn't be thinking Valdez was one of those men in the cemetery, one of those marauders who meant to kill him. She kept trying to tell herself that, convince herself that she was imagining things. Valdez and Randow were friends, although — maybe — they were jealous over her. *Her?* She had boarded the *Mittie Stephens* to escape the New Orleans constabulary, and now two men had fallen in love with her, and she had fallen in love with Hugh Valdez.

Or was she actually in love with Bobby Randow?

She sighed and rolled over, but it was too hot to sleep. The chill had made way for more typical Louisiana weather, even in February. *What am I to do?* Laura wondered as she closed her eyes.

The scream came next, and she bolted upright, breathing heavily, trying to tell herself it had been a dream, but the words that penetrated her cabin walls were no nightmare. Laura leaped out of bed, grabbed the cloak borrowed from Apolline, and opened the door as someone shouted again:

"Man overboard!"

Chapter Eighteen

Creeping clouds blanketed the bright moon like a shroud, covering the City of the Dead in darkness. The deep blackness reflected Bobby Randow's mood as he waited for his partners to arrive in the New Orleans cemetery. He nervously scratched the heel of his right hand against the holstered revolver's hammer. He should have brought another pistol, or, even better, one of those repeating Henry rifles Jeff Slade's men carried.

He should have done lots of things, he thought as the clouds parted and the brilliant moon again cast a haunting glow on the tombs and eerie mist. He could have gone straight to the New Orleans Police Department and revealed Slade's plot. He could have simply checked out of the St. Louis Hotel and headed to the Levee to board the first departing steamboat. He could have *rounded up any number of blackhearts from the Swamp and ambushed Slade and his men, then put in for part of the reward the United States attorney general had offered for the gunman's capture or death. Or he could have simply decided to go along with Jeff Slade. After all, $100,000 in Army gold held a strong temptation.*

Instead, he came here alone, with six shots in a Dance .44.

The iron gate squeaked, followed by soft footsteps on the stone path, and Randow knew it was too late to back out, too late to run. He pushed back his hat before hooking his thumbs in his gun belt, and hoped he could bluff his way past Slade, or change the killer's mind. He saw them now, walking through the thickening mist, led by Slade, who stopped a few yards from Randow.

"You're here early," Slade said.

Randow didn't respond. Instead, he looked past Slade and his men. Four men. There should be six.

"Where's Tennyson and . . . ?" He couldn't recall the man's name, the informant and turncoat. His memory had started troubling him earlier that night, first in the hotel and later at the poker

tables at Number 18 Royal Street, maybe from the tension that had been building inside him for weeks.

"At the gates," Slade answered. "Don't want nobody barging in on us, uninvited, you see."

"You look a mite pale," Victor Desiderio added.

Desiderio carried a Henry rifle, as did Sidney Paige and Jules Honoré. Slade had a Remington revolver shoved inside a yellow sash, and probably another gun, or more, hidden on his body. Paige was sweating, had been since he had arrived in New Orleans, and Randow doubted if the pasty little gent even knew how to work the lever. Desiderio, Honoré, and Slade, however, were murderers, and quite comfortable using firearms, even in a metropolis like New Orleans, even in a creepy cemetery after midnight.

Asked Slade: "Something on your mind, Randow?"

"You backing out, Preacher Randow?" With a dry chuckle, Honoré thumbed back the Henry's hammer but kept the rifle cradled in his arms. "I had you pegged as a gutless coward."

Randow checked his rage, knowing

246

Honoré wanted him dead, anyone dead, for no other reason than to increase his share from the robbery. He wet his lips while forming a sentence. His usually strong pokerface had betrayed him, he realized while clearing his throat and looking straight at Slade, but making sure the other men remained in his peripheral vision.

"I don't care much for your plan," he said, and waited for Slade to make his play.

Instead, Slade laughed. "It's not my plan, Randow. It was Black Chivington's, and me and the boys think it's a mighty good plan. So did you, back in Texas. Remember?"

He did remember.

Bobby Randow had been on the longest losing streak of his life, a run that had busted him and forced him to sell a pewter cross that had once belonged to his father for a cup of soup. That had been his only meal in days, and, thirty-six hours later, his shrinking stomach and aching head had steered him to the banks of Caddo Lake. He had stared at the rows of steamboats, thinking about trying to stow away on one and jump off at Shreveport. He'd go crawling back to his mother. Only he couldn't bring himself to do that — Texas pride, he had figured — so he had visited a Jefferson saloon and tried to sell his revolver. Maybe he'd have enough money for a small meal and deck passage — if he agreed to work on board — to Louisiana.

That's when he had met Roy Tennyson, and his luck had turned. At the time, Randow had thought it had changed for the better. Tennyson was an affable Virginian who had ridden with John Mosby's raiders during the late war. Randow's Confederate shell jacket had drawn Tennyson into conversation.

"A man who sells his six-shooter is a man who's not thinking straight," Tennyson had said, "especially a former Johnny Reb horse soldier. Fought for the Cause myself, with John Mosby. Let me stand you to a whiskey, old chum."

Randow had bristled. "I'm not selling it for a drink, mister. I'm not some walking whiskey vat."

"It's not what I was implying, sir, but the offer still stands." He had held out his hand. "I'm Roy Tennyson of Virginia."

Randow had accepted his hand, and

the whiskey. From the cut of Tennyson's clothes, the Virginian could afford to buy a stranger a drink.

"You looking for a job?" Tennyson had asked after downing the forty-rod that would blister a drunkard's tongue.

Randow had answered with a laugh. He hadn't done much manual labor since the war, had done little but bet on the turn of a card or the look of a horse. He had gotten his fill of hard work back in Grayson County, Texas as a boy. All of that he had revealed to Tennyson, who had a similar story to tell. They had ordered another drink — Randow promising to return the favor at some point — and talked about their families, the war, the sorry state of this thing the Yankee government called "Reconstruction".

Only after the third round did Tennyson bring up the job again.

"What I'm hiring for isn't much work at all, Bobby," Tennyson had said. "And it pays better than any poker game or Thoroughbred. If you're game, old chum, meet me at the first cabin on this side of Benton, the one with the cypress stump charred by lightning, on the Jefferson pike, at ten tomorrow night. Any questions?"

The whiskey had made Randow light-headed on his empty stomach. "The first thing I always ask about is the money," Randow had said.

"Your share would be ten thousand dollars," Tennyson had whispered. "Maybe more. And, no, old chum, we won't be robbing any citizens. At least, not citizens of the South."

So Randow had walked down the woods road toward the Caddo Lake town of Benton, had found the old cabin, and had met Jeff Slade, Victor Desiderio, and Jules Honoré.

The plan to rob the federal payroll had not originated with Jeff Slade, Randow had learned that night, but another un-reconstructed Rebel, perhaps one with a reputation even worse than Slade's.

Honoré had ridden with Black Chivington, who had learned of the gold shipment from an informant. Chivington, however, was going to pay his men only $5,000, so Honoré had mentioned the fortune to Jeff Slade after meeting Slade by chance in a card game at Swanson's Landing. Liking the idea, Slade had ridden to Benton and chopped Chivington, well in his cups, to pieces with a hatchet.

"A hundred thousand dollars is what the steamboat will be carrying," Slade had told Randow and the others. "You'll get ten thousand each. I get more for expenses and the likes. Tennyson gets a little more because he's my segundo. Honoré gets an extra thousand because we wouldn't be here if not for him. Agreed?"

Ten thousand dollars. *Randow had nodded. It all had felt like a dream.*

"And if anybody has the unfortunate luck to get killed, there will be more money for the survivors," Tennyson had added with a wink.

No one had left — Slade would have killed anyone who wanted out, Randow had understood — so the cutthroat outlined his plan. "Chivington and his informant caught up with the provost marshal outside Helena, Arkansas on their way to New Orleans, and murdered him and his associates. Right, Jules?"

"Aye, and their bodies won't be found, except by the blue cats feeding at the bottom of the Mississippi."

Slade had begun to fill a shot glass with whiskey and continued: "The plan was that ol' Black and his men would play the part of those lawdogs, board the steamboat, get cozy with the payroll guards." Slade had paused to kill his whiskey. "We'll keep that plan. What's more, once we've got the money, we'll drop a few rumors, let the Yankees and law think Black Chivington did the dirty deed. They'll be chasing a dead man . . . instead of us.

"When we force the steamboat to land, we break out the Henry rifles that I'll have stored in a berth. We'll have the guards, crew, and passengers outgunned for certain. You see, the Yankee plan, according to Chivington's informant, is that the guard detail for all that gold will only be four or five men. What we still need is somebody to play the part of the provost marshal's clerk. I got Apolline looking for a gent to fill that bill."

"Apolline?" Randow had asked dully.

"Yeah. You know her?"

Victor Desiderio had chuckled. "Who don't?" he had said, and everyone else had broken out laughing, except for Bobby Randow, who had frowned. His stomach had started dancing, but he couldn't shake the thought of $10,000. All that money. Yankee money. Requital for his father and baby brother.

"It seems to me," Randow recalled saying, "that the key to this is Black Chivington's man, and, since you killed Chivington, how do you get to the informant?"

"I've already done it, through Monsieur Honoré. Chivington was only offering him five thousand, too. I ain't greedy, boys. We'll meet up with him in New Orleans."

"Who plays the provost marshal?" Honoré had asked.

"I do," Slade had replied. "I have a pretty good Yankee accent. Used it oftentimes when I was spying for John Hunt Morgan. Tennyson is the deputy, Honoré you play the executioner. . . ."

"I like that," Honoré had said with a snigger.

"Apolline finds us a clerk. Desiderio, you and Captain Randow will travel as gamblers. That way we can talk about changes in the plan over a poker table without arousing the blue bellies' suspicion. It also will help if we get caught and arrested on the boat, in case someone on board happens to know this Major Julius Siegel. Any more questions?"

Randow had one. How could they get

away with that much gold?

"We bury the gold, except for enough to carry as spending money, then return in three months for the split. This is where you boys have to trust me. I know these woods. I know Caddo Lake. We meet back here in May. Agreed?"

Everyone had silently accepted. "We'll have horses waiting for us near Swanson's Landing," Slade had said, "not far from where the steamboat'll have to land. We split up, disappear for a spell, then come back and leave rich men."

That had led to Randow's final question. "How are you going to make that boat land?"

"That's easy," Slade had answered with a laugh.

Randow could remember that laugh now as he stood facing those killers in the cemetery.

"It's a good plan," Slade said. "It would have worked for Chivington, and it will work for me. Unless you got some conscience to keep you honest."

"By jingo, the preacher does want to back out," Honoré said.

Sidney Paige cleared his throat and

tried to play the peacekeeper. "Randow, you've told us how the Yankees killed your brother and father. Surely your share of that plunder will help ease your pain. Surely you don't have reservations stealing from the Yankee government."

It struck Randow as ironic. Sidney Paige was a Yankee himself, an embezzler and fraud, and here he was pleading to Randow's anti-Union sentiments. Also, Paige would be the first man Slade killed once they made it off the Mittie Stephens *and got away with the payroll. Slade had said he wasn't greedy, but Randow didn't believe him — not now. He probably had never really trusted him.*

"It's not robbing the Yanks that troubles me," Randow said. "But you're risking a lot of lives."

"One hundred thousand in gold doesn't come easy, Randow," Slade said. "We have to figure on some risks for ourselves."

"I'm not talking about us, Slade. I'm talking about the passengers and crew on that boat. That steamboat's not a Union transport. . . ."

"It used to be," Honoré said.

"But not now!" Randow snapped. He

stopped. *Argument seemed pointless. Slade wouldn't change his plan, or his mind. He also wouldn't let Randow leave the cemetery alive. Of course, Randow believed Slade intended to murder them all at some point, after they had gotten away with the gold. He had known that for days. His heart began racing.*

He had also known that it would come to this, come to his gun. He had realized that they would try to kill him, but he had come to the cemetery anyway, and come alone. It wasn't the police department's problem; it was Randow's. There was that Randow pride again. He had gotten into this himself, so he would get out of it himself — one way or the other.

Randow kept thinking about his father, dead all these years now, a quiet man, a good Episcopal, felled by a Yankee ball at Shiloh Meeting House while trying to comfort the dead and dying, Federal and Confederate. His father had always preached the value of honesty, the love of God, the love for neighbor whether red or white, or blue or gray. Bobby Randow hadn't done much in the way of honoring his father's memory lately. Maybe that's why he came to the cemetery, instead of running.

"I can't let you maybe kill a hundred innocent men, women, and children, Slade." Slowly he unhooked his thumbs and lowered his arms at his side.

Slade laughed. "Randow, we really don't need two gamblers for this plan to work. One will suffice. Ain't that right, Victor?"

He didn't wait, didn't have to, knew Slade was telling Desiderio to kill him. Randow swept the Dance into his hand, ducking and pirouetting while thumbing back the hammer. Desiderio was turning, jacking a round into the Henry, when the .44 kicked in Randow's hand. Randow moved to his side, began backing away from Slade and his men. He pulled the trigger again, and Desiderio buckled and collapsed, his rifle clanging against a marble tomb.

Above the reports of his pistol, he heard Sidney Paige's scream. A rifle boomed, and Slade cursed, but the clouds covered the moon again, turning the cemetery into a dark void. Slade and his men fired blindly, and Randow, surprised to be still alive, fired again and ran deeper into the bowels of the City of the Dead.

Chapter Nineteen

Randow recalled everything clearly as he ran along the hurricane deck, placing names with faces: Major Julius Siegel was really murderer Jeff Slade; Hugh Valdez was affable Roy Tennyson, who had dyed his graying hair with bootblack more from vanity than disguise; Jules Honoré was, as far as Randow knew, the killer's real name, a merciless butcher who had sold out his former boss, Black Chivington; Sidney Paige was a timid clerk who had absconded in Minnesota with funds from a tiny bank, and made the mistake of stopping at a New Orleans bordello. There, the charming Apolline Rainier had lured him into the federal payroll proposition because Slade needed someone to play the rôle of the provost marshal's clerk, and Paige — or whatever his real name was — had been too scared to tell the killer no, or too infatuated with Apolline.

Randow knew them all, remembered the fifth man, too.

What he didn't know was why he was running. Where was he going? He had no plan. What was he going to do? Find Honoré and Paige on the main deck and kill them, then go after the others? Bust into the saloon or cabin and capture or kill Tennyson and Slade? Randow's mind hadn't cleared from the fog; his judgment remained faulty. What about Apolline Rainier? She was in this deadly scheme. Was Laura Kelley a conspirator as well? And why had Randow run from the federal lieutenant in charge of the payroll? Why hadn't he barged into the pilot house and informed the *Mittie Stephens*' captain of the plot? Would they believe him?

Randow didn't stop, though. He was afraid of stopping.

Taking three steps at a time, he bounded down the stairs, didn't even pause on the cabin deck, leaped the final yard, and landed on the main deck, turned a corner and. . . .

A sudden blow to his head sent him crashing to the floor.

"You dull-brained Texican," a raspy voice sounded. "I would have made you rich."

Randow's head throbbed as he rolled over, and, through blurred vision, he made out a figure silhouetted by the torch on the wall. Randow never saw the boot, though, that caught him just below the sternum and knocked him against the railing on the ship's edge. He gasped for breath, thought he might die there from the kick to his chest.

Jeff Slade, alias Major Julius Siegel, stepped into the light, gripping the gold-handled cane tightly in both hands. "I should have killed you at Apolline's myself, never should have trusted Tennyson to do the job."

"Why . . . didn't . . . you?" Randow gasped, stalling for time, waiting for the pain to subside, praying for help. Maybe that Yankee lieutenant had followed him.

Slade didn't answer. He didn't have to, really, for Randow had already guessed everything. Randow owed Apolline Rainier his life. After Randow had fled to Apolline's bordello and Slade had caught up with him, Apolline must have convinced Slade that Randow wasn't faking his memory loss, probably pleaded that killing Randow would be too risky, that, if the police found his body in Apolline's place, their plan would be in jeopardy, and, if they tried to move the body, someone might see them and alert the law. Perhaps Apolline hadn't said any of this to save Randow's life, but if Slade had killed Randow, he would also have had to murder Laura Kelley. Apolline had her faults, but she wouldn't watch her best friend be killed in cold blood.

Apolline, however, had not been around when Slade had asked Roy Tennyson, alias Hugh Valdez, to stay behind in New Orleans with Laura and Randow. Tennyson was supposed to have killed the two when he had a chance, but hadn't gone through with the murder, maybe because he truly did love Laura Kelley, maybe because he enjoyed a friendship with Randow, maybe because he wasn't a heartless killer, or maybe because he simply didn't trust Slade and wanted to be on this steamboat, close to the $100,000.

Once Laura and Randow had boarded the *Mittie Stephens*, Slade must have understood the risks of killing them. If two passengers wound up dead or missing, the captain would have put to shore. There would have been an investigation, and the payroll would likely have eluded Slade's grasp.

Things had changed now, though, that

Randow had remembered everything. Slade had no choice. Bobby Randow had to die. Slade wouldn't delay another moment.

The killer twisted and pulled on the cane, and Randow glimpsed firelight reflecting off something long and metal — not the gold handle. As Slade lunged, Randow reached for the .44 on his hip. Randow gripped the butt, started to tug, but a sharp pain sliced through his left shoulder. Hot. Blood. A scream of anguish Randow recognized as his own. Tears welled in his eyes, and the air exploded from his lungs. He couldn't move, dully realized Slade had straddled him, pinned his arms, one on the deck, the other across his abdomen. Randow arched his back, tried to buck the gunman off, but lacked the strength, and then felt the tearing, agonizing torture as Slade jerked the cane-dirk from his shoulder.

Cursing, Slade pulled the weapon over his head. Desperately Randow tried to draw the Dance, but Slade was too powerful, had almost broken Randow's right arm with his crushing weight. The Dance's hammer bit into Randow's thumb; the barrel dug into his side. Useless.

The hidden dirk started its descent —

and Randow felt a sudden, surprising sense of relief, of freedom. Slade had been hurled off Randow and onto the deck, rolling over, cursing louder. Randow glanced up, saw a figure on the hurricane deck staring down at the fighters. *How could a man way up there have stopped Slade?* flashed through Randow's mind before someone moved to his left. It wasn't the man upstairs who had saved Randow's life, but someone down here. Lieutenant Ambroise? Maybe another steerage passenger awakened by the fight, although most folks would have minded their own business. Such was the law on the lower deck.

Randow couldn't see clearly through tears and agony. He plugged his left hand against his shoulder to stanch the pouring blood. His shirt front was already soaked. On his knees now, he tried to draw the Dance with his right hand, to help his rescuer, whoever he was.

The cane-dirk rolled toward the stairs. Slade, also, had climbed to his knees, and reached for the boot pistol, but went down again, kicked senselessly by Randow's savior. Randow started to stand, mumbled something — he had no idea if what he said was understandable — and the figure standing over Slade spun quickly, ignoring Slade, and charged Randow, stepped into the light, gripped Randow's right hand like a vise, twisting it savagely.

The Dance splashed overboard. Randow felt himself being spun around, and he tried to stomp the attacker's feet with his boot heels, but the man's fingers dug into the dirk wound, and Randow shrieked in blinding pain. A moment later, he felt himself shoved into the openness, nothing under his feet, the cold wind biting his face. Then freezing water stunned him. Momentarily Randow blacked out, felt as if he were on fire, knew he was drowning. He was underneath the Red, swallowing muddy water, remembering at last how to swim. He kicked up, broke the surface, filled his lungs with precious air, and tried to shout out for help.

"Man overboard!"

Only Randow hadn't said anything, had done nothing except gag and vomit. The water seared his shoulder wound. His face and hands turned numb. The day may have been warm, but the water here, especially at night, was beyond chilly. He wondered if the cry had been produced by his imagination.

"Man overboard!" came the shout again,

and lights began appearing all over the *Mittie Stephens*. The gentle rhythm of the paddle wheels stopped. Steam hissed. More lights.

Randow realized he was treading water. He kicked forward, pushing himself toward the boat, calling out in a hoarse voice: "Over here! I'm over here!"

Another splash, and a moment later, a strong arm wrapped around his chest.

"I got you, mister," a stranger said. Randow didn't know what was more comforting, the smooth voice or the arm tight underneath his armpits. His shoulder didn't hurt so much now.

"I can swim," Randow said. He didn't know why he said it, although he had always been a great swimmer.

"That's fine, mister." His rescuer spit out a mouthful of water. At first, Randow thought it was the ship's carpenter and calliope player, but, no, as they neared the *Mittie Stephens*, Randow saw this was another man of color. "But I gonna help you back to the ship anyhow," the Negro said.

Laura Kelley fought her way down the staircase and through the assembly, breaking free just as three crew men pulled two men from the river. She didn't recognize the black man pulled from the river, but, when they laid Bobby Randow on the deck, a fear chilled her, and she stopped, wondering if Randow were alive. Randow spit out more water, coughed, and she closed her eyes in a quick prayer of thanks.

"What happened here, Mister Thomas?" Laura recognized Captain Homer Kellogg's voice. More torches were brought, illuminating the *Mittie Stephens'* stern, and Kellogg leaned closer to the shivering crew man. "Get some blankets!" Kellogg shouted, then repeated the question to the crew man.

"I heard someone cry out 'man overboard', Capt'n," the black man answered. "Heard some sort of fisticuffs before that, then a splash. After that second 'man overboard' holler, I stripped off my shirt and shoes, and jumped in. This fellow here was in the water. I'm mighty cold, Capt'n."

Kellogg whirled. "Where are those blankets?" he demanded sharply. A second later, a big black woman Laura had seen near the galley charged into the light, followed by two young boys, all of them loaded with blankets.

"You didn't shout that warning?" the ship's clerk asked as the black woman draped a dark woolen blanket over the crew man's shoulders.

"No, sir, Mister Hayes. I just heard it. Heard it twice. From up yonder."

Laura couldn't tell which deck he meant.

"Who shouted the warning?" Kellogg yelled.

No answer.

Brow knotted, eyes blazing, Kellogg repeated the question. When no one came forward, he sucked in air, exhaled like an angry whale, and started to say something else, but stopped when one of the boys pointed at Randow, and said: "Mama, this man's bleedin'."

The boy's mother knelt beside Randow, pulled back his torn shirt, and grimaced before finding Kellogg in the masses. "He's been stabbed, Capt'n."

Laura started forward, tried to hurry, but a crew man stopped her. "Let me go," she demanded, and another man pushed past them despite the mate's protest. A second later, Laura's stomach turned queasy when she heard the smooth Virginia accent of Hugh Valdez: "What happened, old chum? Who stabbed you, Bobby?"

If Randow answered, Laura didn't hear him. All she heard was the terrifying wail behind her. The crowd turned as if on cue.

A woman had fainted, and the people parted as Kellogg and two crew men charged forward.

"What is it now?" Kellogg growled.

Laura stood on her tiptoes to see. Two women were fanning the fainted lady's face, while a slack-jawed drummer in a sack suit pointed a chubby finger toward the stairs. The clerk crept closer, and, when he held up a torch, a cacophony of voices, gasps, and sobs rang out all around Laura. One of the gasps had been her own.

Leaning against the corner wall, sitting in a pool of blood, sat Major Julius Siegel. He was clutching some sort of black stick protruding from his chest, mouth open, blood staining his beard, vacant eyes focused on his boots.

"If you killed Major Siegel in self-defense, lad, now is the time to come forward." Captain Homer Kellogg spoke in a soothing tone. "He was stabbed with his own cane, Mister Randow . . . the same weapon that apparently wounded you . . . and witnesses say he lost a good bit of money to you during our voyage."

Lieutenant Constantine Ambroise waited for Randow to reply, but the Texican's eyes darted, and Ambroise cursed his judgment. He should have followed Randow, instead of heading to the pilot house to ask Kellogg and his crew for help.

"Come on, old chum," the deputy marshal named Valdez pleaded.

They sat in the Soda Lake Saloon, gathered around the stove, staring at the blanket-covered Randow, his shoulder bandaged, his eyes dancing with confusion.

Laura Kelley knelt beside Randow, holding his hand, while Sergeant Nicholas Sloan stood at attention on Ambroise's right and breathed heavily, bitterly, hardly controlling his anger. Behind Randow and Kellogg stood Hugh Valdez. Across the room, by another stove, sat crew man Robert Erskine Thomas, who had pulled Randow from the Red, First Clerk Cal Hayes, and the big galley cook. The rest of the passengers and crew had been ordered back to their berths, bunks, or posts, and the *Mittie Stephens* had resumed its course to Shreveport.

"Bobby," Laura Kelley whispered again.

Valdez gave Randow a shot of brandy. Dazed, Randow stared at the liquor briefly, finally downed it, and dropped the empty glass on the floor. Randow hadn't muttered an intelligible sound since being pulled out of the river.

"Son, I need to know if it was self-defense," Kellogg repeated.

This time, Sloan's rage boiled over: "Self-defense? Captain, this man murdered Major Siegel, a provost marshal for the United States Army. I don't know why we're standing around here like it's a prayer meeting. We ought to be hanging this Reb from the jack staff!"

"That'll be enough, Sergeant," Ambroise said softly.

"But. . . ."

"But nothing, Sloan," Ambroise raised his voice. "Get below, Sergeant. Get down there with Emmerich and Silvia. Don't leave your post until I relieve you."

"Yes, sir," Sloan muttered underneath his breath, and stormed out of the saloon.

Ambroise looked back at the shivering, frightened Randow.

"Bobby?" Valdez pleaded, and this time Randow spoke.

"What's happening to me?" he cried out. "Why can't I remember anything? Who are you? What's going on?"

Laura Kelley's head dropped, and she began to sob.

Laura explained Randow's condition to

the kindly Captain Kellogg in the pilot house, where she sat with the ship's clerk, pilot, and steersman, along with Valdez, Lieutenant Ambroise, and Apolline Rainier. For the most part, Laura told the truth, although she omitted her own crime at Green Haven, the killing of Victor Desiderio, and her growing suspicion of Valdez and the minor discrepancies in his stories.

"His memory was improving," Laura said sadly, staring at the coffee cup held in her lap, its contents now cold. "But I think when he went into the river, the shock, it. . . ." She shook her head, remembering Charles LeBreton's story of the amnesiac Kentuckian who had been forced into the frigid waters of Stones River during the war. Cold water, coupled with the apprehension of battle, might have been a factor in the soldier's memory loss, LeBreton had said.

"And what can you tell me of Major Siegel?" Kellogg asked. "He was not a temperate man . . . forgive me for being so blunt, Miss Rainier . . . and had lost heavily at cards."

Apolline laughed. "Siegel could be a louse, Captain. Bobby wouldn't have murdered him."

Captain Kellogg sighed. "If only there was a witness."

"There was," Laura said suddenly. "Somebody shouted the warning when Bobby went overboard. He must have seen what happened."

No one spoke for a while. Kellogg lit his pipe, let out a sigh, and spoke to Valdez. "What is the Army's desire in this matter, sir?"

Valdez shrugged. "Captain Randow was bound for Shreveport. What time will we arrive?"

The pilot answered: "Eleven in the mornin'."

Added Kellogg: "We have a five-hour layover."

"Well," Valdez continued, "we should turn Randow over to the local authorities. You shouldn't transport him out of state, out of Louisiana's jurisdiction."

"I had no intention of doing that, sir," said Kellogg, bristling.

"We'll let the sheriff sort out this mystery," Valdez said, "and I'll wire General Butler in New Orleans, tell him of Major Siegel's death." Valdez patted Randow's back. "Looks like this is the end of the line for us, old chum, but I'm sure everything will work out fine."

"Does that satisfy you, Constantine?" Kellogg asked.

Ambroise nodded dully.

"All right," Kellogg said, "when we reach Shreveport, Mister Lodwick and Mister Hayes will escort Captain Randow to the sheriff, who also serves as a deputy United States marshal. Mister Valdez, will you accompany us?"

"I . . . ," Valdez stammered before his head bobbed slightly. "Naturally, Captain."

Laura squeezed Randow's hand and said, more to him than Kellogg or Valdez: "I will come along, too."

Chapter Twenty

The very thought of entering the Caddo Parish sheriff's office frightened Laura, but she had promised Bobby Randow — and wouldn't break her word. Besides, what was the maximum punishment for arson, for a grieving widow, nonetheless? Over the years, Laura had befriended lawyers in New Orleans, Pineville, and Alexandria who would defend her in a trial, if it came to that. This close to the Texas border, however, she had no plans of turning herself in. On the other hand, if found guilty of murdering Julius Siegel, Bobby Randow would hang. Of that, she had no doubt.

Most of Randow's memory had improved by daybreak. He knew his name, remembered he was bound for Shreveport to visit his mother, even knew Laura, Apolline, and Valdez. The last thing Randow recalled was talking to Lieutenant Ambroise on the hurricane deck earlier that night. After that, everything turned dark — why Randow had fought with Siegel, if indeed he had, and who had thrown him over the railing and into the Red River. Ambroise had admitted to talking to Randow, but said they had chatted about the weather and cards. Something in Ambroise's face left Laura questioning the officer's truthfulness, but she couldn't picture him stabbing Randow and killing Siegel; he wasn't big and strong enough to accomplish that.

Did Randow remember killing Victor Desiderio in the New Orleans cemetery? Did he recall everything that had happened on that night? Laura didn't know. She hadn't had a chance to speak to Randow alone, and likely wouldn't now that the *Mittie Stephens* had arrived in Shreveport.

As soon as the steamboat had docked on the levee near an old sawmill, Laura had made her way to the texas deck, where Randow was being detained in the pilot house. Fifteen minutes later, Joe Lodwick and Cal Hayes led Randow down the steps. Randow gave her a kind smile and made the motion of tipping his hat, although the hat he had purchased in New Orleans was lost, either during the scuffle or when he had been thrown into the river.

If he was thrown into the river, she suddenly thought. *He might have jumped overboard to escape. He might have really murdered Siegel.*

She dismissed those foolish ideas, and followed the escort downstairs, where Valdez, smoking a cigar, met them near the covered hay bales. They were the first to descend the plank onto the Commerce Street levee; other passengers had stayed back, wanting a glimpse of the suspected killer of a provost marshal. As they started up Cotton Street, Laura realized the original reason Randow had bought passage on the *Mittie Stephens.*

"Where does your mother live, Bobby?"

He answered easily. "Common Street. Yellow house on the east side between Fannin and Caddo."

She didn't know Shreveport, however, and chewed on her bottom lip. A street number would have helped, or directions, but she feared asking Randow again, afraid he might not know, or perhaps what really scared her was the sight of two federal soldiers walking down the street toward them. Whatever the reason, the clerk came to her rescue, pointing a long finger southwest.

"Common Street's about six, seven, no

more than eight blocks straight ahead, ma'am. Fannin's five or so blocks that away."

"Thank you." Quickly she turned from the approaching soldiers.

"You want me to call you a hack, ma'am?" the clerk asked.

"No. I'll walk, thank you."

Laura didn't walk, though. She ran.

They had allowed him privacy in the jail cell to visit with his mother, but Randow had asked Laura Kelley to stay as well. Laura had introduced herself to the sheriff as Laura Wilson, and that plagued Randow's mind for he felt quite certain her last name was Kelley. Randow said nothing, though, not now. He might speak of it later — if he remembered.

Valdez, the *Mittie Stephens* officers, and Sheriff Joss Geringer left the jail for the connecting office, and Randow, separated from his visitors by the iron bars, smiled at his mother.

Leigh Powell looked as Randow remembered. At least his mind hadn't botched that up. She was a big woman, gray hair kept in a tight bun, wearing a red calico dress, and toting a big handbag. Her eyes were blue, her face sunburned, hands

277

scarred and callused from a hard life in Grayson County, Texas, and an even harder one living with that plug-ugly Jim Powell.

"You're no man-killer, Son," his mother said in that throaty voice that never hit a musical note during camp meetings in Sherman or Shreveport. "How's your shoulder?"

"Little stiff," Randow said. "Little sore." Actually it hurt worse than that.

"You don't remember who done it?"

He shook his head. "Don't remember a thing, much."

"It's the same. . . ." Sighing, Laura Kelley shook her head before telling his mother what had happened in New Orleans, how they had met. When she whispered the name Victor Desiderio, recognition struck Randow like a pole-axe, and he saw himself surrounded by tombs, drawing his weapon, firing at the gambler, at others. His memory began clearing.

"You recollect somethin', Son?" his mother asked.

Randow shook his head, not enjoying lying to her, but he certainly didn't want to tell her he had indeed killed at least one man before Major Siegel, even if it had been in self-defense.

With a sad groan, Leigh Powell directed a mouthful of snuff into the spittoon in the cell next to Randow's. "Jus' like your pa, Bobby. Jus' like your pa."

"How's that?" Randow and Laura asked simultaneously.

"Zachary was a good man. Didn't imbibe in intoxicatin' liquors, didn't gamble." Randow's mother glanced at Laura. "Zachary was Bobby's pa, got kilt by the Yankees. My youngest boy was named after him, an' the Yanks got him, too." She spit again, and softly cursed.

"What about him, Mama?" Randow said.

"Well, he got caught in a blizzard oncet, when we was livin' near Sherman. Gosh, Son, you must 'a' been no more'n four or five years old then. I thought he was dead for certain, but Willis Holiman . . . this was our neighbor, Miz Wilson . . . he found Zachary by the creekbed, half out of his mind. Didn't recall nothin' for a spell . . . how he got there, what he was doin', even my name or Bobby's . . . little Zack, he hadn't been born yet. I thought I'd have to bury him, or be saddled with a brain invalid the rest of my days, but he got better."

"How soon?" Randow asked.

"He recollected my name, us bein' married an' all, after I got some broth into him, remembered you, too, an' even Mister Holiman, though he kept askin' Willis what he was a-doin' there. Oncet the norther blowed through an' the snow stopped an' the sun come out, he started recallin' more. Day and a half later he was good as he ever was. That was the first time that plague struck him."

Randow blinked several times. "The first time?" He felt suddenly weary. "It happened more than once?"

His mother spit before answering. "Yeah. Seven or eight years later, he woke up in the middle of the night, screamin', moanin' somethin' fierce."

"I don't remember that, Mama."

"You had gone off on a huntin' trip with Lucas Bledsoe. Woke up little Zack, but I tol' him his pa was just havin' a bad dream." She wiped her lips with the back of her hand after another spit. "That one lasted till morn. But he recovered, Bobby, same as you will."

"Any more times?" Randow asked.

His mother shrugged. "Not that I know of. Could 'a' when he went off fightin' Abe Lincoln's tyrants, but I never heard tell of it, if it did happen. My man got kilt at

Shiloh, Miz Wilson. Baby Zack died, too. Bobby's the only family I got left, lessen you count that addle-brain' fool I married after my Zachary was called to the streets of paradise."

"I know," Laura said softly. "Bobby told me. Did you ever take your husband to a doctor?"

She snorted. "An' let ever'one in Grayson County be talkin' 'bout Zachary an' me behind our backs? No, ma'am, we wouldn't tolerate none of that. Wasn't 'bout to have ever'one think my man was some simpleton, 'cause he wasn't. He was a right smart fellow, college educated, should 'a' gone into one of those seminary schools an' spread the Word. A temporary brain affliction is all it was. That's what my Zachary called it. Happened twice in his fifty-six years."

"A doctor we saw in New Orleans suggested the condition could be brought on by anxiety," Laura said, "the cold, trauma."

"Well, I don't know 'bout that, but we had some anxious, cold, an' traumatic times in North Texas. Gettin' caught in a blizzard, that's cause for distress. An' that time he woke up screamin', well, we was all mighty worried. After we up an' let Bobby go out a-huntin' quail with Lucas Bledsoe

281

on the prairie for two nights, we learnt that the Kioways an' Comanch' was actin' up. Zachary could hardly sleep that night he was a-frettin' so. I tol' him not to worry, but he didn't pay me no mind. Paced the cabin half the night before he went to bed, then woke up in a fright."

"I don't remember any Indians, Mama."

" 'Course you don't. We never saw any, not where we lived. But they raided over a few counties west of us."

Randow swallowed a curse. He had gone through a brutal war and never been afflicted. *Why now?*

His mother answered as if she read his mind. "Jus' the good Lord's doin'. He don't give us no guarantees. But you'll be all right, Bobby." She started to open her handbag.

The sheriff tapped lightly on the door, which creaked open, and the lawman whispered: "Mizzus Powell, I need. . . ."

"Give me two more minutes, Joss. Private-like."

The door closed, and his mother spit. She shot a glance at Laura, faced Randow again, and hooked her thumb in Laura's direction. "You trust this gal, Bobby?"

"Yeah," he said without looking at her, or hesitating.

With a grunt, Leigh Powell reached into the handbag and pulled out a brass-framed, four-barrel .22 Sharps, which she slid between the iron bars. Randow took the small pistol quickly, and slid the hide-away gun into his trouser pocket. His mother's eyes locked on Randow's, but she spoke to Laura: "Like I said, Miz Wilson, he's all I got left, an' I ain't a-gonna let them Yankees hang him for somethin' I know he ain't done."

"I know he wouldn't kill anyone," Laura said, "not without justification."

"You get away, Bobby." Tears welled in his mother's eyes. Randow wanted to take her hands, but she stepped out of his reach, found a handkerchief in her handbag, and blew her nose. "An' don't come back here no more. You go with this gal, give me some grand young 'uns, find a peaceful life . . . somewhere you ain't likely to get that brain affliction, an' that ain't to be found in them grog shops and gamblin' dens."

Still stepping on my toes with her sermons. "Yes, ma'am." Randow grinned. He wanted to see Laura's reaction, but embarrassment, or perhaps fear, stopped him. His mother was trying to marry them off, and Laura likely entertained no such notions of settling down with an itinerate gambler with "temporary brain affliction".

The door creaked open again, and Sheriff Geringer stepped inside, followed by Hugh Valdez. "I'm sorry, ma'am," Geringer said, "but I'll have to ask you to leave now."

Leigh Powell nodded. "I best run hire my boy a lawyer," she said.

"That's a good idea, Mizzus Powell," Geringer said.

"What time do that steamboat leave?" she asked Laura.

"Captain Kellogg said four o'clock."

Telling me when I need to be on board, Randow thought, *when I need to plan my escape.* His mind was working fine — for now.

"Well, you best get on board, too, Miz Wilson. Thanks for befriendin' my Bobby."

"I'll escort you back to the levee," Valdez said, and Laura nodded slightly.

Valdez's accent made Randow shiver, and another name popped in his mind: *Roy Tennyson. His name's not Valdez. He's Roy Tennyson!* "Come on, Miss Wilson."

Laura gave Randow a hopeful look as she passed his cell, whispering: "Three Twelve. Be careful."

Her room number on the *Mittie Stephens.*

Randow remembered that, too, and he would be careful.

"What time is it?" Randow asked the sheriff after the visitors left.

"Little after one. Reckon I'll go round you up some grub."

By his best guess, it was three o'clock, so Randow picked up the empty tin cup, and started to rake it furiously against the bars, yet he stopped after one swipe. Joss Geringer, Caddo Parish sheriff and deputy United States marshal, was no fool, wouldn't come into the jail with his keys, especially with a noisy prisoner pricking his nerves with a tin cup. Well, Geringer obviously hadn't searched Randow's mother's handbag, but that had been out of respect, decency, and friendship. Geringer had trusted Leigh Powell, but he wouldn't trust a suspected killer.

Randow glanced at the empty plate on the floor, remembering. When Geringer brought him his dinner, he had told Randow to step back, then opened the door quickly, set the food and coffee on the dirt floor, and left. When would the sheriff come take away the dirty dishes? Or would he even bother?

Randow briefly fingered the .22 in his

pocket. Maybe he shouldn't have waited this long. The cup dropped to the floor, and Randow rubbed his temples. Bring Geringer in anyway? Draw the Sharps, back the sheriff into a corner, shoot the lock, and pray for the best? No. *Think straight!* What about asking for bail? That wouldn't work, either. He wouldn't be arraigned until after a coroner's inquest, tomorrow at the earliest. Find a lawyer with a writ of *habeas corpus?* This was Shreveport, ruled by carpetbaggers and Reconstruction Yankees, and the victim was a provost marshal.

Only he wasn't a provost marshal. Randow pinched the bridge of his nose. "Jeff Slade," he whispered, and a flood of memories sent him reeling to the bunk.

He opened his eyes at the sound of the thick door opening, and heard Geringer's voice moments later. "Now stay where you are, sonny." Randow looked up as the sheriff slid the key into the lock, turned it, and pulled the iron-barred door open. As Geringer reached down to pick up the cup and plate, Randow withdrew the Sharps, pressing his finger against the sheath trigger, his thumb on the hammer.

At the *click*, Geringer froze in a crouch. Slowly the sheriff lifted his gaze. "Where'd you get that, Randow?" he asked dryly.

Randow grinned. "I can't remember."

"Don't be a fool," Geringer said, still not moving. "You'll make matters worse, have them federals scouring the country for you. They'll be more likely to shoot you than bring you in alive. You stand a chance with me, sonny. I know your mama, and she's a fine lady."

Randow's finger tightened on the trigger, and Geringer stopped talking. *Tell him the truth,* Randow thought. *About the plot. About Roy Tennyson, Jeff Slade, the others. They can stop it all before the* Mittie Stephens *leaves.*

"Julius Siegel is dead," Randow began.

"Yeah, everyone knows that. That's why you're here."

Randow shook his head savagely, and muttered an oath. "No, no, no! Siegel was murdered by Black Chivington in Arkansas. Then Chivington was killed in Texas by Jeff Slade. That wasn't Siegel, Sheriff, on the steamboat. It was Jeff Slade. Shave off that beard, wash the dye out of his hair, and you'll see it's Slade. They. . . ." He saw the hopelessness of it all. "You don't believe me."

Geringer wet his lips. "I don't know what to say to that story, Randow. Now, I ain't about to take a corpse to Luke Nolan's tonsorial parlor for a shave and hair wash, but we can talk to some folks, get you a lawyer. . . ."

Randow couldn't blame the lawman for stalling, for not believing a story he scarcely believed himself. "What time is it?" he suddenly asked.

"Clock said three-twenty when I came in here. It usually runs five minutes slow."

No time. By the time Randow convinced Geringer, or anyone, of the truth, the *Mittie Stephens* would be a wreck, and those killers would be rich. *And Laura?* Randow leaped to his feet. To Randow's surprise, Geringer also stood, blocking the open doorway.

"You won't kill me, Randow. Not in cold blood. I do believe that about you, sonny. Now hand me that little pistol."

Randow drew a bead on the center of Geringer's chest. "What's to stop me from killing you, Sheriff? I probably won't remember doing it anyhow."

Chapter Twenty-One

"You ain't said much," Obadiah Denton's wife muttered as he fumbled inside the ship's toolbox for a screwdriver. "Ain't hardly spoke three words to me or our boys since last night."

"Uhn-huh." Denton found the flat-head, and briefly caught Zoë's burning gaze as he straightened his aching back. "Been busy."

She mimicked her husband. "Uhn-huh. One man dead, 'nother stabbed and bleedin' like a stuck pig, and Matthew and Emanuel sees it, sees the dead body and that poor fellow. It ain't good for boys that age to be exposed to such sights, Obadiah. Ain't good at all. And all you can say is 'uhn-huh'."

Looking for help, Denton found himself alone. The boys would be with Robert Erskine Thomas, firing the boilers with pitch pine. The rest of the crew men were also busy preparing the *Mittie Stephens* for departure. Denton fumbled with the screw-driver as his wife's tirade continued.

"You knowed that fellow that got stabbed. Told me how he borrowed some Navy plug offen you when you was loadin' firewood."

"Don't make him no friend of mine!" Denton had found his voice. "White man like he was . . . is, I mean. Yeah, I'm sorry he got hurt, sorry for that major, too, but I ain't seen a thing."

Zoë's eyes narrowed, and Denton realized his error. "I didn't ask you if you saw anything, Obadiah," Zoë said, her voice softer. "What ain't you been tellin' me?"

He kept talking, jamming the screw-driver handle against his thigh, hoping she would forget, but knowing she wouldn't. "I got work to do, woman. We'll be in Texas by tomorrow," Denton said, without looking at Zoë again. "Meet up with that feller gettin' settlers for that freedman's town in Colorado Territory, be stakin' our own claim pretty soon. Everything'll be all right then." Denton headed toward the starboard side, running from his wife, from the truth, the way he always ran.

"*Uhn-huh!*" Zoë shouted to his back.

After leaving Geringer locked in the windowless cell, Randow stole the sheriff's porkpie hat and corduroy jacket from a deer antler rack hanging on the wall, then cautiously stepped outside. Despite the warm afternoon sun, he pulled on the jacket as well as the hat, but found the latter about two sizes too small. The disguise would have to work, though. The keys to the jail cells he dropped in the nearest trash bin, and he walked quickly past an elderly woman cooing over a young redhead's *carte-de-visite* of her beau. Neither gave him a second glance, and Randow decided his odds had slightly improved.

Shreveport was noisy this time of day, and Randow was glad of that. With luck, he might have an hour or more before someone heard and investigated the muffled shouts from the sheriff's office. Randow felt the small Sharps in his trouser pocket as he hurried east toward the levee. The sky in that direction had turned black from the steamboats preparing to shove off.

Randow picked up his pace. When he reached the bustling Commerce Street levee, he tried hard to recall where the *Mittie Stephens* had docked. *Sawmill*. He remembered the old sawmill, and hurried north, passed two snagboats and a smaller packet before he spotted the bold, black letters on the wheelhouse: *Mittie Stephens*. Thick smoke billowed from her twin smokestacks, and Randow leaned against a pork barrel, wondering how to get aboard. A crew man stood beside the plank near the jack staff, collecting money from a passenger. The clerk would likely stop Randow, demand to see his ticket or greenbacks. Randow had found his wallet in the top drawer of Sheriff Geringer's desk, but he didn't want to be stopped, to have someone recognize him. Although Randow didn't know the clerk — this wasn't the same fellow who had led Randow to the sheriff's office — others on board were sure to remember him.

The clerk and passenger stepped aside, allowing a brawny black man to bring aboard a sack of grain. Others followed, backs bent underneath the weight of the sacks, and Randow found the source: an ox-drawn cart just a few rods from the steamboat. Pulling the ill-fitting hat down lower, Randow wandered through the people, wagons, barrels, bales, hogsheads, and "monkeys" to the wagon, fell in line with the workers, and grunted and cursed as he hefted a 250-pound bag over his shoulder.

He weaved a path, staggered by the weight, earning newfound respect for the men who did this daily, and almost fell off the plank. A white-bearded man behind Randow laughed, but no one else paid him any attention, and, if the laborer wondered what a weakling stranger was doing bringing cargo on board, he kept silent.

Randow dropped the grain onto a stack near the boilers, staggered back against the wall, and massaged his left shoulder. The bandage underneath his shirt felt wet again. The strain of lifting the sack had opened up his wound, but the dark jacket would hide the bleeding, for a while. He needed to find shelter in a hurry.

"Three Twelve," Randow said to himself as a reminder, and wandered toward the stern, where fewer passengers waited. As he stepped around the wheelhouse, however, he collided with another man.

"*Achtung, dummkopf! Langsamer!*"

Randow looked into the face of a mad federal soldier, one of Lieutenant Ambroise's men. *Should I tell him about the plan?* Randow shook off the thought. He didn't know who he could trust now, except Laura Kelley. The Yankee said something again in German, and Randow muttered an apology, not knowing if the private understood much English. "Sorry, soldier. Stupid of me. I'll buy you a drink later in the Soda Lake Saloon." Randow kept shaking his head at his carelessness, smiling, trying to move past the guard, whose hard blue eyes never blinked.

Randow moved around him, and walked faster, feeling the soldier's eyes boring through his back, expecting the Yankee to shout a warning but hearing only another: *"Ach!"* Randow kept moving, head bowed again, heart pounding. *Maybe he doesn't recognize me.* Randow nodded at the thought. After all, Randow had only passed the payroll guards a time or two.

Randow gripped the balustrade tightly, feeling comforted by the railing, let a little girl bolt past him, and smiled warmly at the mother chasing her. A quick glance told him the stairs were empty, and he hurried up them, stopping quickly at the sight of a black man standing over the calliope. Randow knew this man from somewhere, but his memory plagued him again, and his shoulder ached. The Negro didn't look up, and Randow hurried out of his sight. By now, Randow was sweating profusely. He halted again, and peered around the corner. A porter helped a young woman and toddler boy into a berth. When they disappeared inside, Randow hurried down the path, glancing at the red numbers on the doors, but stopped when one swung open behind him. The noise hadn't stopped him; it was the knowledge that he remembered that musician's face.

The memory staggered Randow, and he spun around, ready to confront the musician. Instead, Randow ran into a couple, almost knocking the woman down. Randow fell against the wall, his shoulder throbbing, and tried to mumble some apology to the woman, but then he recognized her. Apolline Rainier's mouth hung open as she stared at him in bewildered recognition. Randow's eyes swept to the man on her right. *Hugh Valdez . . . no, his name's Roy Tennyson.* Softly Randow cursed his luck.

"Hello, old chum," Tennyson said with a smile. "Let's get back inside your room, Apolline. After you, Bobby."

"Let's see if you can recall these three words, Bobby," Tennyson said as soon as he had closed the door and slid the bolt. "Gold . . . Slade . . . Tennyson." Tennyson's right hand disappeared behind his frock coat. When it reappeared it held a New Orleans boot pistol. Randow recognized that, too. It had been Jeff Slade's. Slade had put the weapon down on a table beside Randow back at Apolline's place in New Orleans, practically daring Randow to grab it. That, Randow now understood, had been a test to see if Randow really had lost his memory. If Randow had reached for the weapon, Tennyson or someone would have charged in, and killed him.

"Yeah," Randow said dryly. "I can repeat those words: Murderer . . . Judas. . . ." His eyes fell on Apolline Rainier. "And. . . ."

"Don't say it, old chum." Tennyson chuckled. "She saved your life back in her house of many pleasures. Talked Slade out of nailing your hide to the barn. And you owe me your life, as well. Slade was on the irritable side when I told him I hadn't slit your throat. And Laura's throat, too. Sit down. You can thank me for your life later."

Randow obeyed. "Is that what you call saving my life, Roy? Killing Slade and throwing me into the river."

"If I hadn't killed Slade, Bobby, *you'd* be dead. And I threw you overboard knowing you could swim. You bragged about your swimming when we first met in Jefferson. Told me, after I bought you a few whiskies,

296

how you once swam the Tallapoosa for five Yankee dollars."

Randow's laugh held no humor. "Yeah, you were helping me out, me with a hole in my shoulder." Mention of the wound caused him to reach inside the jacket. Tennyson cocked the .50-caliber pistol, and Randow paused, slowed his motion, and brought out his hand, holding up his blood-stained fingers for inspection.

"You should take better care of yourself, Bobby," Tennyson said. "How did you get out of the jail?"

"I don't remember."

Tennyson laughed again. After lowering the hammer, Tennyson tossed the pistol to Apolline. "Watch him, dear. I'll be back later."

As soon as the door closed, Apolline latched it and leaned against the wall, keeping the big-barreled pistol pointed at Randow's chest.

"You with him now?" Randow asked bitterly.

"Be a gentleman, *amant*. Slade would have gotten us all killed . . . gotten a lot of innocent people killed. That's what turned you against this to begin with, remember? Roy's a lot of things, but he isn't a butcher."

"He killed Slade."

"You don't see me shedding tears over that, and I don't see you sobbing. Slade was about to kill you. Like Roy said, he could have let Slade put that knife in your heart first."

"Where are the rifles?" he asked. "In your berth or Roy's?"

"They're here. Slade figured they'd be safer in an unmarried woman's berth. Gentlemen don't search ladies' quarters. But don't get any capricious notions, Bobby. I'd hate to kill you, but there's a lot of money at stake."

"And Laura?"

Apolline sighed. "I wish to God you two hadn't gotten on board, Bobby. Believe me. I tried, tried to keep you both out of harm's way. I wish your memory hadn't returned, or were you play-acting all this time? No, you weren't acting. I know you well enough to know that, and I hope you know that I never wanted to see you and Laura hurt. You believe me, *amant?*"

When he didn't answer, Apolline let out a hoarse laugh. "You keep patting your leg, lover. You used to be a better poker player. What is that in your pocket, Bobby, a Derringer?"

"It's nothing," Randow said, but

Apolline cocked the pistol loudly, and he slid his hand inside the pocket, keeping his eyes on her, moving slowly as he told her the truth. "A Twenty-Two Sharps four-barrel. My mother gave it to me. That's how I got out of jail."

Apolline chuckled. "You best keep it, *amant*, but don't try to use it on me or Roy."

Randow stared at her blankly, unbelieving. Apolline eased the hammer down on the percussion cap, and waved the barrel at a chest of drawers nailed securely to the far wall. "There's a flask of brandy," she said, "top drawer." Randow felt the ship beginning to reverse, heard the paddle wheels slapping water, but couldn't look away from the prostitute.

Apolline shrugged. "Woman's prerogative," she said. "Maybe I still love you, *amant*. Now get that flask. We have a long wait."

Darkness fell like an anchor, but Laura lacked the strength to turn up the lantern in her berth. She closed her eyes, felt her lips trembling, an aching in her heart. She had no idea how long she laid on her bunk, listening for the hopeful sounds of someone knocking on her door, hearing

Randow's urgent whisper. They were moving now, heading for Texas, and Randow hadn't come. Maybe he had forgotten her room number. Maybe. . . . She tried to stop thinking.

The music began from the stern, as it had done every night around this time, and activity sounded in the cabins around her as the calliope player pounded out "The *Mittie Stephens* March" again. She waited for the song to end, the commotion to die down, then hated the quietness that came with it.

Laura cursed herself, her cowardice and stupidity, and made herself stand. She couldn't go on like this, couldn't leave Louisiana, not knowing if Randow were alive, in jail, dying, or dead. She resolved to find Captain Kellogg, tell him everything, something she should have done days ago. Let him know about her own crime. She'd do anything to learn of Randow's fate, to have the chance to help him again.

After turning up the lantern, she found the cloak she had borrowed from Apolline, tossed it over her shoulders, and heard the gentle rapping on the doorjamb.

"Bobby!" She rushed forward, opened the door, and stared up at Hugh Valdez.

"No, Miss Wilson," Valdez said smugly. "It's not Captain Randow, but I. Did you not hear that dreadful pipe organ? It's suppertime, my dear. I was hoping you would accompany me."

Valdez held out his arm, and Laura hesitated before accepting. He patted her hand gently, led her outside, and allowed her to close the door. *It would work out anyway,* she told herself. She would find Captain Kellogg in the dining hall, make her confession there. As they walked down the aisle, Valdez hummed that awful march.

"Hugh," she said, "the dining hall is the other way."

"I know, Laura. First I thought you'd like to see a dear friend."

Chapter Twenty-Two

Obadiah Denton had skipped supper — didn't have much of an appetite, anyway — and walked to the freedmen's bureau to listen to the singing, but found he wasn't in the mood for music, either. So he wandered the upper decks for hours before finding enough nerve to go downstairs and face his wife.

Zoë was there, darning one of the boys' socks, oblivious to the noisy pitman arm. Robert Erskine Thomas, smoking a pipe, stood beside her. Denton scratched the beard stubble on his chin. *What's he doing here? And where are my boys?*

Thomas saw Denton first, withdrew the pipe, and said something to Zoë, who set her sewing project at her feet, and stood. Denton couldn't read her face, and took his time heading over to Thomas and Zoë.

"Where's Matthew?" Denton asked. "Where's Emanuel?"

"Got them helping out in the boiler room," Thomas answered.

"So's we can have a word with you, Obadiah Denton," Zoë said sternly.

Denton ignored her, wouldn't even look her in the eye. Instead, he turned to Thomas. "You best get them boys of mine back up here, Erskine. We'll be taking our leave when we put into Mooringsport later this evening. I'm quittin'."

"You're runnin', fool," Zoë said. "From what?"

Angered at being humiliated in front of practically a stranger, Denton whirled toward his wife. "You hush up, woman."

Her backhand staggered him, and he would have fallen against the pitman arm if Thomas hadn't grabbed him by his collar and kept him on his feet. Denton gingerly touched his stinging cheek, stunned by a blow that would have staggered most men, especially a rawhide little cuss like Obadiah Denton.

"You saw what happened when that major got kilt," Zoë said calmly, but emphatically. "You know if that white feller murdered him, or if it was self-defense."

"I don't know what. . . ."

Thomas cut him off. "I recognized your voice, Obadiah. You were the one who yelled out 'man overboard'. I never told the capt'n because. . . ." Thomas shrugged. "Well, I guess because I'm fond of your boys. Figured you had your reasons and all. And I didn't want to hurt them none. That's why they ain't here."

Denton cringed when Zoë moved her arms again, but this time she rested her bruising hands on her hips. "But you're tellin' us . . . *me* . . . the truth, and right now, Obadiah. Else you can get off at Mooringsport or anywhere you want to, but Matthew, Emanuel and me won't be goin' with you. You understand that, mister?"

The only noise came from the rhythm of the hard-stroking pitman. Denton lowered his arms. His shoulders sagged.

"Was it murder, or did that gambler kill the major in self-defense like the capt'n believes?" Thomas asked at last.

Denton's eyes met briefly with Zoë's, and he knew how much he wanted to tell them everything. He needed to tell them. With a sigh, he sat down.

"Wasn't the gambler that done it," Denton said. "I was comin' down from the freedmen's bureau when I heard the noise. Looked over the railin', and saw the major 'bout to kill that Randow fellow. Then another man come, pulled the major off Mister Randow, started whuppin' the tarnation out of the major. Suddenly he up and throwed Mister Randow off the boat. That's when I hollered. Was scared speechless a-fore that. I ducked back into the shadows. Didn't hear nothin', but I hollered again, heard Erskine come runnin' below. Mind you, I didn't see nothin' after that, but I reckon it was the major's friend that stabbed him, drug his body into the corner."

"His friend?" Zoë asked.

"The other gambler," Denton said. "Tall fellow ragged out in them go-to-meetin's, that bunked with the major. Think they called him Valdez."

The pitman slowed, and Denton felt the ship begin to turn — his own son Matthew had taught him how to tell the movements. Likely the *Mittie Stephens* was preparing to dock at Mooringsport.

"You got to tell the capt'n," Zoë said. "That Randow fellow might hang if you don't."

Denton leaped to his feet, shaking his head, and closing his eyes. "And I might hang if I tell."

"What you talkin' 'bout, Obadiah?"

Tears streamed down Denton's bearded

cheek when he found the courage to look at his wife. "That dead man was a provost marshal, Zoë. You know what a provost marshal does?" She shook her head. "They'll think I killed him!"

"You ain't makin' a lick of sense."

Thomas tapped his pipe against a column, and said: "Your man's a deserter, Missus Zoë."

"Nonsense." Zoë's face softened, and tears welled in her own eyes. She reached for Denton gently, but he backed away.

"Erskine's right, Zoë!" Denton exploded. "I ain't no hero. I took that medal offen a dead man, a friend of mine. Wasn't no real medal, jus' something us A Troop boys give Sergeant Street. But he was dead, and I figured I would be, too, if I didn't foot it out of there. Been runnin' ever since!" Denton shook his head sadly, remembering, the image causing him to grimace, but he kept talking. "We was on patrol on the San Saba, Sergeant Street and a handful of us boys. Didn't even see no Injuns. They come out of nowhere, like they was the devil. Sergeant Street jumped off his hoss, tol' us to do the same, and we dived behind these stones from an old mission, those of us still alive. Then Sergeant Street's head exploded . . .

I was blinded by his brains, woman . . . and I took scared. I wiped my face, grabbed his blouse, screamed at him that he couldn't be dead. But he was, and I felt that medal in his pocket. All this time, them Comanch' was yippin' like mad dogs, arrows and lead rainin' down on us, the few boys left, shooting back. Smelled like hell's brimstone, and I lost my mind. Went crazy, I did. Grabbed Sergeant Street's medal . . . don't even know why I done that . . . and I run. I run, Zoë. Run like a swamp-runner."

A gentle lurch told Denton the ship had docked. "Come on, Zoë. Get the boys, and let's go." As Denton reached for Zoë, this time she backed away from him.

"No," Zoë said. "We ain't runnin' with you, Obadiah. And you ain't runnin' from us."

A crew man opened the metal cage in front of the pilot house and began filling it with burning pine knots that glowed red as the *Mittie Stephens* backed away from the Mooringsport landing. Lieutenant Constantine Ambroise nodded courteously at the crew man, then climbed the steps, knocked on the door, and opened it.

"Permission to come inside, Captain?"

"Of course, Constantine," Homer Kellogg said with a smile. "Can't sleep?"

"Not this close to Jefferson, sir." Ambroise shut the door behind him and accepted a cup of coffee from steersman Joe Lodwick. "Are we in Texas yet?"

"You sound like an eight-year-old, Constantine, on his first steamboat trip. In about an hour or so. We're still in Louisiana for the moment."

"What time is it?"

Pilot William Swain answered. "Half past eleven." Swain sipped his coffee, and shuddered as he gazed through the glass. "I'd sell me soul for some moonlight."

"You know the course, Mister Swain," Kellogg said softly. "Be on the look-out for the *Dixie*. Captain Jacobs will be tied up for the night near Jeter's Landing."

"Wish we'd tie up," Swain said, "wait for dawn."

Kellogg chuckled. "After a day's delay in New Orleans, I imagine the passengers are in a hurry to get to Jefferson, Mister Swain. Right, Lieutenant?"

Ambroise grinned. "Right, Captain." Traveling at night in Caddo Lake had been done many times before, and Ambroise had confidence in Kellogg and Swain.

308

"Has anyone seen Mister Remer?" Kellogg asked.

Lodwick and Swain shook their heads, and Ambroise shrugged absently. Ambroise didn't know anyone named Remer. "Cal Hayes took sick in Shreveport," Kellogg explained. "Had to bring George Remer on as his replacement. Don't worry, Constantine. I trust Mister Remer as much as I trust Mister Hayes." Kellogg slid the pipe into his pocket. "All right, gentlemen. We'll pass Jeter's Landing in a half hour, then stop at Swanson's Landing. The ship is yours, Mister Swain, while I catch a few hours' sleep. Keep her steady, son."

Laura hated Hugh Valdez, Roy Tennyson, or whatever his real name was.

She sat in a corner next to Randow, and had been sitting there for hours, waiting. Valdez, alias Tennyson, had pleaded with Laura after admitting the truth, saying she should join him and the others, arguing that she hated the Yankees as much as Jeff Slade had. Hadn't she burned down her family plantation to keep it out of the hands of carpetbaggers?

What Laura couldn't get out of her mind, hours later, was the look Randow had given her upon hearing that bit of news. She should have confessed her crime to Randow, not Hugh Valdez–Roy Tennyson. So she hated Tennyson for lying to her, and for betraying her confidence.

Gripping her handbag, Laura found the nerve to look at Randow. The waiting had done him some good, for his shoulder had stopped bleeding. "I should have told you," she whispered.

"I understand," Randow said. "Likely would have done the same thing myself."

Apolline Rainier cleared her throat. "Let's not talk, friends. Don't want some passing crew man to think I'm running a bordello in my unmarried ladies berth."

Laura hated Apolline, too.

"One man's dead already, Apolline," Laura said defiantly. "Isn't that enough? Can't you stop this before someone else gets hurt?"

"A hundred thousand dollars," Apolline said, "in Yankee gold. And more than one is dead. The real Major Siegel is dead, and his men, and so is Black Chivington."

Tennyson stood beside the door, chewing on an unlit cigar. Grinning, he added: "You also keep forgetting the gentleman Bobby shot down in the New Orleans cemetery."

Randow let out a hardened laugh. "Victor Desiderio was no gentleman, Roy."

Someone knocked at the door, and Tennyson thumbed back a Remington revolver's hammer, gesturing at Apolline, who asked softly: "Who's there?"

Laura couldn't hear the answer, but Apolline quickly slid the bolt, swung open the door, and Jules Honoré, holding a Bowie knife, and Sidney Paige shoved a pale, bald fellow with a swollen right eye and bleeding lip inside.

"Meet George Remer," Honoré said with a smile as he and Paige hurried into the crowded berth. "Our banker."

Apolline bolted the door, and Honoré pushed the clerk toward Laura and Randow.

The smile faded quickly, and Honoré pointed the knife at Randow. "What's he doing here?"

"He's minding his own business, Jules, which is what you'll do," Tennyson said. "I don't want him, or Laura, hurt. Understand?"

"But he killed Slade."

Tennyson laughed. "No, I did." When Honoré spun around, Tennyson brought the pistol barrel down hard on the killer's hand. Honoré yelped, and the knife fell to the floor. Before Honoré could react, Tennyson had shoved him into Sidney Paige.

"Slade would have gotten us all killed!" snapped Tennyson, covering them with the Remington. "Listen to me. We still get the gold, but we do it my way."

Honoré rubbed his wrist, and shook his head. "I liked Slade's plan."

Tennyson snorted. "Yeah, set an old steamboat loaded with hay and gunpowder on fire to force it to land. That's a fine plan."

"It'd get the ship to land," Honoré said. "And them Yankee guards would be in a fret to get that gold safe. They'd need help, and, thinking us to be provost marshals, they'd get us to help them. Then we kill 'em and take the gold."

Tennyson cursed softly. "I fully expect to see the fires of hell someday, but I don't want to be burned alive before I'm damned by Saint Peter."

"We'd die game," Honoré said. His voice and face displayed a challenge.

"You're as crazy as Slade."

"This was a Yankee boat. It transported Yanks up the river during the war. I haven't forgotten that. Neither had Chivington. Neither had Slade."

"Criminy, Jules, the war's been over four

years. It's time to get on with our lives, and a hundred thousand dollars should pay us back plus interest."

Get on with our lives. Those words cut Laura to the quick. She had been little better than this den of thieves, cursing federals and carpetbaggers alike, blaming them for her misfortune. It was time to move on, to let her parents, Green Haven, and Theodore Wilson Kelley rest in peace. *Live.* If she got a chance after tonight, she would go on. Her hand moved, and, without realizing it, she locked fingers with Randow.

"I want this boat burned!" said Honoré, still defiant.

"Once we get the gold, I'll give you a match," Tennyson shot back. "But first we have to get the money . . . and not be burned alive doing it."

Honoré started to say something, but Sidney Paige spoke first, softly. "What's your plan?"

"Thank you." Tennyson let out a heavy sigh, and lowered his revolver. "We break out the Henry rifles, take over the pilot house, force them to land. We use Mister . . . I'm sorry, what's your name?"

"Remer," came the clerk's frightened reply.

"A pleasure, Mister Remer. Remer opens the safe for us, and we make the crew unload the gold. A Henry rifle is a good persuader, gents. No one will give us trouble. And no passing ship will come investigating the smoke from a steamboat set ablaze by a bunch of stupid, unreconstructed Rebs." Tennyson paused to read their faces. "After the gold is loaded, you can torch this ship, Jules. Not only that, we won't bury the gold in the woods the way Slade wanted. We split it up as soon as we clear Caddo Lake, and bid each other *adieu*."

"I like that idea," Paige said.

Honoré frowned harder. "I like Slade's plan better. Yours is risky."

"Risky? Riskier than setting us on fire?"

"The confusion," Honoré said. "The confusion will help us get away."

"The confusion will turn us into ashes."

Tennyson's face reddened with anger and exasperation, and Laura thought he might kill Honoré then.

Randow squeezed her hand, leaned close, and whispered in her ear: "I have a pistol."

Laura stiffened, remembering, and stared at her handbag. She had a weapon, too.

Another knock sounded, and Tennyson stepped aside to allow Apolline to move to the door. After a few whispered exchanges, Apolline opened the door. Laura's throat turned dry as Sergeant Nicholas Sloan stepped into the light, holding the cherry-wood cane that had belonged to Julius Siegel — rather, Jeff Slade.

"He killed Slade!" shouted Honoré, pointing at Tennyson.

"Shut up," Sloan said. "I heard you. Heard all of you. If I was Kellogg or some ship's mate, we'd all be finished."

Tennyson stepped in front of Sergeant Sloan. "We're doing it my way."

"No," said Sloan, twisting one end of the cane. A quick flash of metal caused Laura to gasp. She knew what was about to happen before Tennyson understood he had underestimated his colleagues.

Sloan rammed the hidden dirk into Tennyson's stomach.

Chapter Twenty-Three

No one in the room spoke, and only Tennyson moved, pressing both hands against his stomach to stop the blood, backing away from Sloan, at last stopping at Randow's and Laura's feet.

After wiping the bloody blade on the bed's quilt, Sloan slid the top of the cane into place, tossed the weapon onto the floor, and casually picked up the revolver Tennyson had dropped. Sloan stared at Apolline, and asked: "You gonna use that boot pistol, ma'am?"

With a shrug, Apolline lowered the weapon.

"Break out those rifles, boys," Sloan ordered. "As soon as them boys in the pilot house see the smoke, they'll put for shore."

Honoré dropped to the floor, and pulled a long box from underneath the bunk. As he worked on the lid, Sloan motioned the clerk to come over.

"We'll be walking down to the safe,

Mister Remer," Sloan said. "If you say anything, I'll kill you. All you have to do is open the safe, and keep your mouth shut. We'll be taking the gold off the ship once we hit land. These" — Sloan grinned — "provost marshals will be helping my men and Lieutenant Ambroise. If you say anything to alert them, you're dead, and so are them soldier boys. Savvy?"

The clerk's trembling head bobbed.

"Good. I'll meet you downstairs, gents," Sloan told Paige and Honoré. "Remember . . . Paige, you make a beeline to the safe. Honoré, you find Ambroise, tell him that I'm unloading the gold and have asked you to help. With the fire and all, he won't have time to debate."

"You're all mad," said Tennyson, fighting back the pain, his legs kicking like an infant fighting sleep.

"Maybe," Sloan said. "But I'm in agreement with Jules. The Yanks need to pay, and so does this steamboat."

"You're a Yankee," Tennyson said through clenched teeth. "I thought you were in this only for the money."

"Money's a factor for certain, but, before I put on these blue clothes, I wore the gray," Sloan said. "Fought at Mansfield. Saw more'n a few pals die, thanks to the Yanks

317

this ship brought upriver." Honoré and Paige were loading the rifles. "I've started the ball," Sloan told them. "Stuck a cigarette in the bales, and added a little forty-rod whiskey, so when the hay finally catches, it'll be a sight." Sloan swept a glance at Laura, Randow, and Tennyson, and whispered in Honoré's ear: "When the ship lands, there'll be panic. Women'll be screaming, kids yelling. Lot of confusion." Sloan either didn't care if Randow heard, or didn't believe anyone could hear, but there was absolutely nothing wrong with Randow's ears, just his memory — and it was working fine, now. "When that time comes," Sloan said, "kill them all, and meet me at the safe."

Sloan pivoted, grabbed Remer's shirt, and lifted him off the floor. "One word, and I kill you." Before Sloan walked out the door, pulling the clerk behind him, he told his men: "Remember . . . you're Major Siegel's men, helping us bluecoats save the federal payroll."

They were gone, and Randow slid his hand into his trouser pocket. He didn't trust the four-barrel Sharps, didn't like his odds against two .44-caliber repeating rifles, but he'd have to make his play anyway — soon.

Unable to keep his eyes open any longer,

Constantine Ambroise drifted into a light sleep, waking every few minutes but unable to open his eyes. He could hear the ship's paddle wheels, and smell coffee as well as smoke from Swain's cigar. Occasionally Ambroise caught bits of conversation between the pilot and steersman. They had passed Captain Thornton Jacobs's *Dixie*, tied up at Jeter's Landing for the night, her boiler fires out. Clouds still obscured the moon. The decks of the *Mittie Stephens* looked deserted. As best as Swain figured, they were less than three miles from Swanson's Landing.

Swanson's Landing — they would be in Texas — and, after brief stops at Port Caddo and Benton, would reach Jefferson.

Silence resumed, and Ambroise felt himself falling into that welcome void.

"You smell something burning?" Lodwick asked.

"Me ceegar," Swain said with a dry chuckle.

"I'm serious, William." The door swung open. Ambroise fought to remain awake.

"See anything, Joe?" Swain asked seriously.

"No . . . wait!"

Ambroise made his eyelids lift. He sat up groggily, started to stretch as Lodwick

319

slammed the door, and pointed out the window. "Smoke, William! Smoke's coming up from underneath that tarpaulin. Larboard side!"

Swain leaned forward, removing his cigar, straining to see in the dim light. Ambroise stood, stamping his feet to get the blood in circulation, and moved between the two men.

Ambroise spotted smoke billowing into the light from the torches and the metal fire baskets. Swain must have seen it at the same time because he began spinning the wheel furiously. "We're puttin' to shore. I need full power." A bell rang. "Wake up the captain, Joe!"

The door opened, and didn't shut as Lodwick raced outside. Ambroise clenched his fingers, staring at the smoke, while looking for the shadows of land. To his right, Swain concentrated on his task, and recited "The Lord's Prayer". The steamboat moved between cypress trees, picking up speed. "Come on!" Swain interrupted his prayer. "There! Land."

All Ambroise could make out was a vague tree line, but it had to be shore — fifty feet or less. Ambroise made out the distance. Forty — thirty — twenty — and the *Mittie Stephens* came to a jarring stop that flung Ambroise against the glass and Swain against the wheel. Ambroise heard the crunching of wood and grinding of gears as the momentum stopped, and he fell backward, onto the floor, rolling over and almost out the door.

Swain had stopped praying and starting cursing, screaming into a horn-shaped tube, begging for power. "All right!" Swain yelled. "Then reverse engines! We're in the shallows! We're. . . ." Swain looked out the glass, and dropped the tube, his face pale.

Ambroise pulled himself to his feet, and staggered to Swain, looked outside. The bow had lifted a few feet out of the water, and the impact had ignited the bales of dry hay, sent sparks everywhere, starting other fires all over the deck. Already the flames shot skyward, spreading across the bow like burning oil.

"Oh, my God," Ambroise said.

One moment Jules Honoré was whispering to Sidney Paige, and the next moment both were hurled against the chest of drawers. Randow crashed to the floor, Laura on top of him, and watched Apolline bounce off the wall, and slide down. The lantern on the wall flickered, and Tennyson groaned. Randow was on top of him.

Randow's shoulder ached, and he must have bitten his tongue for he tasted blood in his mouth, but still he came up with the .22 Sharps in his hand. Honoré, clawing at the chest of drawers with one hand and clinging to the Henry with his right, saw him. The killer swung around, keeping his feet, levering a shell into the rifle.

Randow pulled the trigger repeatedly, heard four quick pops, tossed the empty gun aside, and dived for the rifle that Paige had dropped. As Randow's fingers slid into the Henry's lever, he rolled over, jacking a shell into the chamber, lifting the barrel. Honoré hadn't moved until then, still standing, scarcely hurt, it seemed, by four little bullets in his belly. Honoré fired, but somehow missed despite the close range. Acrid smoke had filled the room from the gunfire, obscuring Randow's view. Randow shot anyway, slid into a seated position, cocked the Henry again, fired a second time.

Gunsmoke stung his eyes, and Randow stood, working the lever, trying to find a target, Honoré or Paige. Like a phantom, Jules Honoré stepped out of the smoke, still clutching his rifle, blood streaming from his mouth, at last feeling the effects from the Sharps bullets and a .44 slug that

322

had caught him in the throat. Randow pulled the trigger, but nothing happened except a metallic *click*. Randow knew the rifle was fully loaded, guessed the rim-fire cartridge had misfired, so he brought down the lever, and tried to bring it up again, but the mechanism jammed. Cursing, Randow hurled the weapon at Honoré, catching Honoré's rifle as the murderer brought it level. The blow knocked Honoré astride, his gun booming at the same time another shot sounded, almost like an echo, and Honoré dropped the rifle, and crashed through the door and onto the passageway, screaming as he fell over the railing.

Only Honoré hadn't been screaming, Randow realized, not with a bullet in his throat. Honoré had only grunted as another slug — fired by Laura? . . . Apolline? . . . maybe Tennyson, perhaps even Paige by mistake — propelled him outside. And more than one person had screamed. In fact, it sounded like half the passengers on board were yelling, begging, praying.

Paige! His mind working, Randow looked for the other man, saw him in the corner, standing, bringing up a pocket revolver. Paige's trembling finger tightened against the trigger, and Randow grimaced, braced for a bullet, but felt only a whizzing past his right ear as the gun bucked in Paige's hand. Randow started to charge before the embezzler thumbed back the hammer, but Paige's face suddenly disappeared in an explosion of blood and smoke, and Randow tripped over Slade's cane, and sprawled on the floor.

Randow rolled over, blinking repeatedly, his eyes tearing from the smoke. He had landed on top of Paige, whose face had been blown away.

"Laura!" Randow yelled.

"I'm . . . all right." Randow found Laura, holding a Derringer in a trembling hand. Randow saw Apolline Rainier, too, the New Orleans boot pistol hanging at her side. One of them had shot Honoré; the other, probably Apolline, had killed Paige. Tennyson still writhed on the floor.

Randow tried to swallow, couldn't, and picked up the rifle Honoré had dropped. His ears were ringing now, but he made out the clanging of bells, the screams and cries of people. His brain, his memories, kept working, though, and Randow scrambled to his feet, stepping outside, where he was almost trampled by panicking women, children, men — even crew members.

Randow smelled smoke, a lot of smoke. "You two get to the yawls," he told Laura and Apolline. "Get off this ship. Get to shore."

Randow knew he should go with them, but he couldn't. He had to find Nicholas Sloan, stop him, kill him.

"Bobby!" Laura screamed, but Randow bolted out of the stateroom.

Stunned, confused, Laura glanced at the Derringer in her right hand, dropping it as if it were on fire. She started after Randow, but the ghastly sight of Sidney Paige stopped her. Paige's feet blocked the doorway. Laura's eyes fell on Apolline Rainier.

"I'm sorry, Laura," said Apolline, dropping the smoking boot pistol beside Paige. "I'm sorry for everything." Her old friend stepped over Paige's legs and out into the darkness.

Screaming. Crying. Conversations that made no sense. Laura crept around Paige's legs, and leaned out the door. She looked toward the stern, saw only blackness, then found women, men, and children — some in nightshirts, some wearing only pants, all without boots or shoes — standing by the yawl. On the other side of the wheelhouse, a brilliant glow reminded her of sunset until flames leaped into the black air, reflected off the dark water below.

Many passengers had begun to climb ropes and throw themselves into the boat despite protests from helpless crew men. Paddle wheels slapped the water violently, and a black-bearded mate appeared at Laura's side, leading four young girls toward the yawl. "Don't panic," he told the children in an Irish brogue. "Just follow Mister O'Donnell."

Laura reached for him. "Where is the ship's safe?"

"Forget your valuables, lady!" the crew man snapped as he hurried on past. "And get your bloody arse off this boat!"

Turning back into the room, Laura saw Roy Tennyson trying to get to his feet. "Help me," Tennyson pleaded. Laura looked back outside, then ran toward the stern stairs, shouting Bobby Randow's name.

"We're stuck, Capt'n!" Swain shouted. "Twenty feet from shore!"

Ambroise's mind still hadn't cleared as Homer Kellogg stared out the window at the rapidly spreading fire.

"All right," Kellogg said. "Have the engine room keep the wheels moving forward at full speed. Maybe we'll get lucky." The flames began creeping up the derricks. Wood popped from the heat, showering the night with sparks.

"Mister Lodwick," Kellogg said, "take command of the starboard side, sir. While lowering the yawl, have the crew throw anything overboard that will float. Furniture, anything. Women and children on the yawl, Mister Lodwick. Tell the men to jump overboard. Mister Swain, take the port side. We're abandoning ship."

"The *Dixie*, sir!" Lodwick said. "Maybe she can help us."

"You said her boiler fires were out," Kellogg said, "and she's too far away. No time. You have your orders, gentlemen. May God help us all."

Swain and Lodwick leaped outside, and Kellogg put a strong hand on Ambroise's shoulder, steering him out of the pilot house. "I'm going to help Mister Swain, Constantine. I desire you to assist Mister Lodwick at the starboard yawl."

Ambroise's head nodded dully, and Kellogg patted his shoulder before leaving him on the texas deck.

"What are you still doing here?"

327

Obadiah Denton shouted at his wife. Zoë sat crouched in a corner, hugging her two sons, her face masked in terror. "I told you to get off the ship. Get to the yawl!"

"You . . . ," Zoë began, and hugged her sons tighter. "You . . . left us."

"I'm a crew man. I was with Erskine." Denton couldn't explain any more. He hadn't the time, and he realized Zoë, overcome by panic, had lost her reason. Denton knew how fear could paralyze a person. If he had known Zoë would have been in this condition, he wouldn't have gone to his post. He would have seen to his family. It was a miracle he had found them. Thomas had sent him checking the decks, making sure all passengers had gotten off the lower deck. Most of them had — except his own family.

Denton took a deep breath, and pulled his wife to her feet. He tried to give his sons a brave smile. "It'll be all right," he reassured them. "Let's find Erskine."

A woman screamed, a baby cried, and the jackstaff collapsed into the Caddo's dark waters, which, from the fiery reflection, appeared to be ablaze itself.

Constantine Ambroise fell to his knees, pushed back his hat, and started shaking

328

his head, reliving the carnage of the *Princess* disaster. "Not again," he said, sobbing uncontrollably as his head collapsed into his hands. "Not again. Dear Lord in heaven, not again."

Chapter Twenty-Four

Brutal, intense flames drove Obadiah Denton, his family, and Robert Erskine Thomas away from the bow. When they had realized the ship was lost and heard that Captain Kellogg had given the order to abandon ship, Thomas practically dragged the two boys toward the unholy fire itself, yelling at Denton that the water was shallower up front, closer to shore. Denton and Zoë had trusted him, followed him, for one good reason: nobody in the Denton family knew how to swim. Only now the blaze made them retreat, burying their faces into the crook of their elbows, coughing from the brutal smoke, and Denton wished he had gotten off at Mooringsport, instead of cowering to Zoë.

Now it was too late.

"My boys can't swim!" Zoë screamed, as if Thomas hadn't heard her the first dozen times. Denton looked over the railing. The water, shimmering from the fire, appeared to be boiling, but somehow he realized the heat wasn't causing this, but the paddle wheels. Denton understood now that the ship was pointed up after running aground on a sandbar, just enough to lift the wheelhouse partly above the water's surface.

"No good!" Thomas shouted to him, reading his mind. "Wheels'll crush us to death, pull us under." Thomas pointed up. "The yawl!"

Denton shook his head. "She's already in the water. Over yonder."

Thomas believed him, because he didn't chance a look. "The starboard side then," Thomas said, and kicked open a door. Running again, fighting smoke.

"My boys!" Zoë cried.

"I've got them!" Thomas shouted. "Follow me!"

Thomas busted through another door, and they were on the opposite passageway, still on the main deck, but the fire felt closer. Denton prayed Thomas didn't lead them to a horrible death. They reached the staircase, and Denton ran, following his wife, Thomas, and Denton's sons. Cut off again by a wall of fire, they stopped halfway up, turned, hurried back to the main deck, heading for the bow, for deeper water, but halted before reaching the wheelhouse. Thomas had decided on another plan. "Come on," he told Denton. "We'll throw some stuff overboard, stuff that'll float."

Zoë swept the boys into her arms. "I want that boat up yonder!" she yelled.

"No good!" Thomas thundered. "Can't get to it! I said come on, Obadiah!"

Dizzy from heat and smoke, Denton didn't want to follow Thomas. He wanted to leap overboard, yet he couldn't run, couldn't leave his family. Thomas stood beside him, tossing a chair into the lake. Denton stared at the waters, blacker than a bottomless pit, but also orange, horrible, reeking — like staring into the depths of hell.

Thomas had thrown something else overboard. The splash made Denton blink. Suddenly Thomas swore. "My god," Thomas said. "The gunpowder. It'll blow us all to kingdom come. Come on, Obadiah. Hurry!"

By the time Denton had turned, black smoke had swallowed Thomas. The fool was running back into the inferno. Denton couldn't move, not that way, and spun toward his family. Roaring fire raced over their heads on the upper decks, chasing crew and passengers toward the violent wheels and dark stern.

"Daddy!" Matthew yelled. "Daddy!" The boy was crying, and Denton blinked again. He shook away his fear, and lifted Matthew into his arms.

"I'm gonna lower you over the side, Matthew." Denton discovered his voice to be surprisingly calm. "I want you to take hold of that chair Mister Erskine tossed overboard, and don't let go. Just kick, kick your legs as hard as you can. Make that way, for land."

"For God's sake, Obadiah!" Zoë barked. "He can't swim!"

He didn't listen. Gently but urgently Denton lowered his youngest son into the lake, watching, praying as the boy gripped the chair back, sank once, then pulled himself up, above the water, floating with the wooden chair. With a silent prayer, Denton let go.

"Kick, boy, kick! Get away from here! Don't let go!"

Zoë wailed, and Denton started to lift his other son, but Matthew's cry stopped him. "Mister Erskine, Daddy! Where's Mister Erskine?"

"Kick, boy!" Denton yelled at Matthew. "Kick for shore." A window popped from the intense heat above him, and he cringed as hot glass rained down on him. As he straightened, a thought made him shudder.

Gunpowder!

His hand gripped Emanuel's shoulder. "You got to help your mama, Emanuel. Got to be a man. All right?" His son's lips mouthed a yes, sir. "Do what I did, the both of you. Help your mama. Ease over the edge, grab anything that'll float." Denton tried to block out the sounds of the burning, the drowning all around him. He looked up at his wife, and swore loudly. "Don't sass me, Zoë! You get in that water. You listen to Emanuel! Grab a box, furniture, anything. You hear me!"

She had fallen quiet, and nodded slightly.

"What about you, Daddy?" Emanuel asked.

"I got to help Erskine, Son. Or we'll all be dead."

Denton wasn't thinking about himself any more, wasn't thinking about anything really, just the fact that he had to find the ship's hold, find Thomas, and throw those kegs of gunpowder overboard.

Constantine Ambroise hadn't moved.
He sat on the texas, choking from

wretched fumes, scalded by a blaze rapidly approaching him. He didn't see anything, though, at least not on the *Mittie Stephens.* All he saw was the awful wreck of the *Princess*, the dead, disfigured, and dying on the Mississippi River near Baton Rouge in 1859. He saw himself, ten years ago, only he wasn't running from deck to deck now, wasn't saving lives. He wanted to, but his legs would not co-operate.

So he sat, and sobbed.

"Constantine!" The voice sounded far away, then came an urgent tug on his shoulder. "For the love of God, son, move."

Ambroise wanted to, but couldn't, couldn't choke down a paralyzing fear. He felt himself being lifted up, saw the face of Captain Homer Kellogg, enraged, face blackened and streaked by sweat, resembling a demon's. Almost instantly Kellogg's features softened.

"It's all right, lad. It's all right."

Moving. Only Ambroise wasn't running. He was being carried, draped over Kellogg's shoulder like a potato sack, retreating past the pounding paddle wheels. He had no sense of time, felt himself being lowered to the floor.

"We've no way down, lad, but by

jumping. Hang on to me."

He didn't understand the words, stared into the flames, then looked into the darkness, seeing nothing but orange, red, and yellow spots and circles. Blinded. Ambroise didn't even realize they were falling, dropping like an anchor, until the frigid water took his breath away.

Bobby Randow couldn't go any farther. He only had a vague idea where the ship's safe was, and, if Sergeant Sloan remained on the *Mittie Stephens*, he was likely dead. The fire scared Randow, but so did the fear of losing his memory again. Over and over, he kept one thought running through his mind: *Keep remembering. Keep remembering. Please God, don't let it happen to me again.*

A gunshot made him stop. Or was it a shot? An explosion caused by the heat, fire? Randow had no way of telling, but knew he had to forget this pursuit. Sloan had to be dead, or in Caddo Lake. *Jump overboard. No, find Laura!* He shouldn't have left her.

An instant later, the door on his right burst open, and a man slammed into him, knocking him against the cabin deck's balustrade. Two Henrys rifles bounced over the railing, and splashed into the water.

Two rifles!

Randow had been wrong about Sloan. The Yankee turncoat remained on board, right in front of Randow.

Sloan tried to get to his feet, his face masked by panic. The plan was a disaster. Sloan should have listened to Roy Tennyson, only he hadn't fathomed how rapidly the *Mittie Stephens* would burn. Sloan had probably killed George Remer a moment ago, then started to run for his life.

Before Randow could react, Sloan kicked at Randow's face, missed, and Randow realized the soldier's right sleeve was ablaze. Randow grabbed Sloan's ankle, twisted it, heard the big man cry out as he crashed back to the groaning deck.

Randow rose to his knees, swung at Sloan's face, caught a glancing blow, but Sloan buried his right fist into Randow's stomach. Although Randow had braced for the punch, he still went down, and Sloan was on top of him, punching hard, his burning arm singeing Randow's hair. Desperately Randow clawed the brass buckle around Sloan's waist, arched his back, kicked out, tossed Sloan over his head.

"Bobby!"

Her voice sounded so close. Randow

wanted to tell Laura to run, to jump over the side, save herself, but Sloan must be on his feet by now. Only Randow couldn't find him.

Randow's own shirt was smoldering, and he pounded at it with his hands, desperately trying to find Sloan through the suffocating smoke, the blinding light surrounded by darkness. He never saw Sloan, just felt the blow, the overpowering weight as the leviathan wrapped strong arms around Randow's back, crushing the air out of his chest. The railing stopped them, but only for a second, then the timbers creaked, snapped, and both men fell for an eternity. Through it all, he heard the furiously churning paddles, understood that they were near the wheelhouse, that they would be crushed to death or drowned.

They slammed into the water, and Randow's world turned black.

Laura screamed as Sloan and Randow disappeared over the side. She ran toward the fire, stopped by the wheelhouse, leaned against the railing still intact, and stared at the relentlessly foaming water.

"Bobby!" she cried again, and coughed. Her clothes began to smoke as she fought for breath, crying out his name whenever she could, dropping to her knees, waiting for him to emerge from the water. She felt weak, alone, light-headed, choking for air. Her eyes teared, and she was face down on the deck.

This must be how it feels to die.

She knew she should move, crawl away from the smoke, the flames, but lacked any strength. She closed her eyes and coughed violently.

They worked like a bucket brigade, Obadiah Denton taking a keg from Thomas, staggering to the port side of the burning wreck, and heaving the keg overboard, then darting through the flames back to the hold as Thomas emerged with another keg. Sergeant Street used to joke that soaking wet, wearing a greatcoat, holding a Spencer carbine, and carrying a haversack loaded with a week's rations, Trooper Denton weighed maybe one hundred and ten pounds. Never a strong man, Denton had no idea how he managed to carry those gunpowder kegs to the side of the ship. But he did.

Even before the keg splashed, Denton whirled, but the flames had surrounded him, cut him off from the hold and

Thomas. Shielding his eyes and choking on smoke, Denton kept taking tentative steps, but couldn't go any farther. A devil bolted from the hell, and Denton almost screamed. He heard another splash, then a familiar voice.

"That's the last of them," Thomas said, after throwing the last keg over the side.

Denton started to say something, but Thomas shoved him over the railing, and Denton sank into the lake, came up spitting water as Thomas dived overboard. Now Denton screamed, afraid of drowning, but somehow kicked away from the nightmare, hearing Thomas shout: "This way, Obadiah! This way!"

I can't swim, Denton thought. Yet he did, driven by the image of his wife, his sons, praying they were safe. Denton reached forward and pulled, knew he was moving, until, exhausted, he found it all hopeless.

"This way, Obadiah! This way!"

"I can't!" he cried out weakly, exhausted, sinking, feeling his knees in the mud.

Mud!

Amazed, Denton lifted his head. He wasn't under Caddo Lake, but in water three feet deep, with another foot of mud. Denton stood, sloshed through the murky water and bogs, ran straight into a cypress tree, and hugged it, kissed it, and churned forward, guided by Thomas's voice. "This way, Obadiah! We're in the shallows!"

"I'm comin', Erskine!" Denton started bawling. "I'm coming, Zoë. I'm comin'."

"For the love of God. . . ."

Constantine Ambroise came to at the sound of the stranger's voice. At first, Ambroise didn't know where he was, then he smelled the smoke, felt the heat, and heard the screams. Wearily leaning back in a skiff, Ambroise looked around. He didn't know anyone in the boat except Captain Kellogg, had no idea how he had got there. He found his bearings, and stared at the horrible image.

Flames had reached the back of the wheelhouse, where the starboard lifeboat, filled with people, still hung, only a few feet below the cabin deck. Ambroise had heard of this happening before. An over-crowded yawl being lowered, but the weight causing the mechanism to fail. He had never seen this, though: passengers re-mained inside the lifeboat, hanging from the ropes, screaming, praying.

"Jump!" someone in the skiff shouted. "For God's sake, jump!"

Yet they didn't, and, although he

wanted to, Ambroise couldn't look away from the sickening sight as the fire burned through the ropes, and the yawl crashed into the water, overturned, spilling its passengers, most of whom sank without another word.

Kellogg realized Ambroise had come to. "Don't look, lad. Don't look." Yet the captain turned back himself, his shoulders sagging, leaning against the edge of the skiff as it made its way closer to the capsized *Mittie Stephens'* yawl.

"You're on the *Dixie's* skiff, son," a Greek voice told Ambroise. "Capt'n Thornton saw the fire, he did, knew we'd never get our boilers fired in time, so he ordered us to come help you. But. . . ."

The Greek lifted Ambroise's head. Ambroise tasted ouzo, most of which burned his tongue and rolled down his chin. He coughed, shook his head, and pulled himself up straighter, looking again at the *Mittie Stephens,* wanting to close his eyes, to shake away the images like a nightmare.

Women, clinging to their children and each other, huddled together on the cabin deck, backed against the stern, near the calliope. The fire had consumed the rest of the ship. So fast. So awful.

"Jump, ladies!" a mate on the skiff pleaded. "Jump!"

But they only stood there, helpless, crying, scared to move until they collapsed from the smoke, and the flames overcame them.

Silence fell over the *Dixie* skiff. Some hung their heads. The Greek began a prayer. Others made the sign of the cross or simply stared at the horrible sight.

"Help me! Help me!"

Ambroise's head shot up. It was a girl's voice, and Ambroise saw her as she went under near the capsized yawl.

"There!" Ambroise yelled. "Row, men, row!"

Hot air filled her lungs, and she coughed, gagged, and vomited. Laura Kelley felt herself being dragged away. She didn't know how far, or even that they had stopped until strong hands pulled her to a sitting position.

"You'll be all right." She was lifted into the arms of a man she knew.

"Bobby?" She scarcely recognized her own voice. They were moving, staggering, weaving down the deck's passageway. She was being carried away from the fire, then they tripped, tumbling down the stairs.

We'll both die here. Her wrists hurt. Blood trickled from a busted lip. She heard only the faraway screams, flames licking wood, glass shattering, paddles seething. Laura lifted her head, but didn't see Randow. He had probably left her. Or was dead on the staircase from a broken neck. She tried to stand, but a wave of nausea sent her back to the deck with a thud, then someone was gripping her ankles, dragging her off the boat, into water so cold she blacked out.

When she awoke seconds later, she felt herself drifting away from the burning hull.

"We're almost to shore," the fatigued voice said.

Bobby. . . . Her heart raced, but a dull knowledge chilled her. It wasn't Bobby Randow.

It was Roy Tennyson.

Chapter Twenty-Five

Laura woke up, shivering in the gray light of dawn, blinking, trying to understand why a steamboat was moored in front of her. Maybe it had been a dream, she hoped, but if so, why was she wet, cold, and sleeping on the shores of Caddo Lake?

She found her feet, and saw the bold letters emblazoned on the wheelhouse: *Dixie*. Beyond the steamboat, smoke and a few small fires rose from the smoldering ruins of what once had been the *Mittie Stephens*, maybe twenty feet from shore. A memory shocked her, and she turned suddenly, but Roy Tennyson was gone, and she soon forgot about him, haunted by fearful voices she now heard, calling out all around her.

"Mama?" — "Randall? Randall!" — "Emily! Emily! I've got to find Emily!" — "Where's Grandma, Papa?" — "Hush, child, hush." — "Have you seen my wife? Amelia Jordan Lyon? We called her Meal.

Meal? Meal! Meal!" — " 'Blessed are the merciful, for they shall obtain mercy. Blessed are the pure in heart, for they shall see God. Blessed. . . .' " — "Dorothy! Dear Lord, where's Dorothy?"

She took up her own cry as she wandered along the thick-wooded lakefront, weaving among people, their clothes wet, people she did not recognize but whose faces — some smeared with soot, others burned — resembled ashen masks, blank, eyes wide, mouths agape.

"Bobby!" Laura choked out. "Bobby!" Another image flashed through her mind, and she yelled: "Apolline! Has anyone seen Apolline Rainier or Bobby Randow? Please."

She almost tripped over a wiry, black man, showering two boys and a large woman with kisses, hugging them, lifting his head, and thanking the Almighty. Laura felt jealous of them, and slightly ashamed of it, but touched the Negro's shoulder, recognizing him as the ship's musician.

"Have you seen Bobby Randow?" Her voice sounded like a dream. "Or my friend Apolline?"

Friend? Well, Apolline had been a friend, once. A good friend. Apolline had let Randow keep that hideaway pistol, and had shot

346

Sidney Paige dead to stop him from killing Randow.

Sadly the Negro shook his head.

"Bobby had blue eyes, like a baby's. He. . . ."

"I know Mister Randow, ma'am. He . . . he's. . . ."

Dead.

But the word never came. Instead, the musician's wife, her voice trembling from shock, said: "Child, that fellow is back in Shreveport. In jail." She addressed her husband in a whisper: "Poor thing's out of her mind."

"No!" Laura snapped. "Bobby's. . . ." Laura shook her head, not wanting to explain. "Apolline. A redhead. Beautiful. About my size. . . ."

Another voice behind her called out softly: "Miss Wilson."

Laura spun to find young Lieutenant Ambroise. A little girl clung to his neck, a blanket wrapped over her delicate body, wet red curls plastered to her burned cheeks and neck.

"I'm looking for Apolline Rainier and . . . ," Laura began, but the lieutenant dropped his gaze, and she stopped. Her chest ached. "Please . . . you met her. Redhead, like. . . ." She pointed at the frightened girl, who hugged the lieutenant tighter, and looked away from Laura. "She was wearing. . . ." Laura had to think, bit her lip. "A green and white dress. She's. . . ."

"She's dead, Miss Wilson."

Laura didn't remember falling, but when her eyes focused, she knew she was on her knees. Still holding the girl, Lieutenant Ambroise had dropped beside Laura, reaching out with his free hand, trying to comfort her.

"I'm sorry," Ambroise said.

"Are you sure?" someone asked. Hours later, Laura would understand that she had asked that question.

"This child was drowning," Ambroise said. "Would have drowned, too. We couldn't pull her in time into our skiff. Miss Rainier came out of nowhere, grabbed this little girl, here, held her up until we got close. When we pulled alongside, I hauled the girl into the boat. I could see plain as day from the fire, the torches, could see that long red hair floating on the surface. And then it was gone. I reached for her. So did the men from the *Dixie*, and Captain Kellogg, but she was gone. Disappeared. And there was another man begging for help, about to drown. We couldn't

348

wait there, couldn't look for Miss Rainier. She was gone. Like that." Ambroise glanced at the girl he held. "She hasn't said a word since we pulled her onto the skiff. I don't even know her name. Here, ma'am, let me help you."

Instead, Laura climbed to her feet, and ran from Ambroise, from his words, trying not to believe that Apolline was dead, that she had drowned saving the life of a girl she didn't even know. That was so unlike the Apolline Rainier of Baton Rouge. Maybe the Apolline she had known back in Alexandria. Maybe. . . .

"Bobby!" Laura began the cry again. "Bob . . . !"

She slid to a stop, staring at the rows of bodies, some draped with blankets, others merely dumped on the muddy ground. "Bobby . . . ," she gasped, and turned away, running back into the forest in a panic, unable to stop herself until she found herself wrapping her arms around a pine.

A hand gripped her shoulder. "Laura?" a haunting voice whispered.

She let out an agonizing moan, and confronted Roy Tennyson, his face pale, clothes covered in mud and soot. She wanted to tell him that this was all his fault, but she couldn't do anything but groan and sob.

"I didn't want it to happen this way, Laura. You know that." Tennyson had to grab a low branch on a nearby tree for support. His other hand pressed against his abdomen. Blood seeped through his fingers.

"Don't know what happened to that clerk, if he's alive or dead. If he's alive. . . ." Tennyson shook his head. "If they learn what started that fire, I . . . I don't want to hang."

Laura's mouth hung open, but she couldn't curse him, or say anything.

"Come with me, Laura. The horses. The ones for our escape. The horses are still there." Tennyson pointed deeper into the forest.

She found her voice. "No."

"But I love you, Laura."

Her stomach turned. She looked past him, through the trees and brush, at the *Mittie Stephens*.

Tennyson swore now, and his fingers dug into her shoulder. "Bobby's dead, Laura. He and Sloan both. You can't bring him back. Come with me." He weaved, released his grip, almost collapsed. "I need help, Laura." He tried to smile, to regain his charm. "I could use a nurse. Come. . . ."

She pulled away from him. "Get to your horses . . . whatever your name is. Ride away, but you best ride far, because, if ever I see you again, I'll kill you."

"I could have let you die on that ship!" Tennyson snapped.

"I wish you had."

He mouthed her name, reached for her, and she slapped him, staggered him. Her fingers and palm ached from the blow, and she pushed past him, running back to the shore, screaming Randow's name, blinded by tears until she stopped, exhausted, heard a gentle voice, and looked into the weary eyes of Captain Homer Kellogg.

"It'll be all right, Miss Wilson," Kellogg said. She knew otherwise, however. Kellogg looked so frail. Laura wanted to bury her head against his shoulder. She wanted to cry some more, but a sudden strength came to her, a realization, a need to help.

"I'm a nurse, Captain."

She moved busily along the main deck of the *Dixie*, from survivor to survivor, giving them water from a jug or a slug of brandy, helping a surgeon bandage the badly burned, placing salve over the cuts and

. . . those less seriously injured.

. . . *a nurse,* Laura kept telling herself. . . . tried to block out her sorrow, busied . . . erself in the work. She came to the little girl she had seen Lieutenant Ambroise carrying, and gave the child a weak smile. "I'm going to put this on your face, honey," Laura said. So fragile. So young. The girl looked a lot like Apolline Rainier had as a child. Laura dipped her fingers in the jar and tentatively reached for the little redhead.

The girl shied away from her, but not too far. "Will it burn?"

Laura's smile returned, stronger, and she shook her head. The girl hadn't been rendered mute by the fire. "No. It's cool. It'll feel good."

Exhaustion forced Laura to sit underneath the jackstaff. Behind her, she heard Captain Kellogg talking to the *Dixie*'s master, Thornton Jacobs.

"How many?" Jacobs asked.

"Forty-two, so far."

Forty-two dead or missing. Laura shook her head sadly. All because of greed. Confederate greed. A week ago, she had thought only Yankees and carpetbaggers possessed that foible, but men of the South had wrought this tragedy. Forty-two dead.

The next words made her moan.

"Sixty . . . maybe seventy. Dead. May God have mercy on us."

She had misunderstood. Forty-two survivors. Out of more than 100 passengers and crew. Laura pulled herself up, staring at the rows of bodies in front of the tree line.

"George Remer, my clerk, is missing," Kellogg was saying, "likely dead. Remer wasn't even supposed to be on this trip. He got on at Shreveport because Mister Hayes was sick. Do you believe in fate, providence, or luck, Thornton?"

"I don't know what I believe in. Not after today. I don't know anything."

A baby started crying, and Laura made herself return to her task.

"My daddy was a hero," Matthew Denton told the *Dixie*'s first officer. "He and Mister Erskine tossed gunpowder kegs overboard. He was a hero before, too. Fought Injuns in Texas. They give him a medal."

Obadiah Denton leaned against a cypress, listening to his sons brag while he sipped coffee supplied by his wife, busy helping in the *Dixie* galley.

"How'd you know I was a deserter?" Denton finally asked Thomas.

"Capt'n Kellogg says you told him you was discharged after two years, or so." Thomas tossed the dregs at his feet. "Enlistment's for five years. So that got me suspicioning you a little bit, and, well, your wife and me both could see you was troubled by something bad. Now you could have been honorably discharged for some ailment or the likes, but, well, I wasn't convinced. You ain't much of a poker player, Obadiah Denton."

"Ain't no hero, neither." Denton sighed wearily. "Not like my boys think."

"Weren't for you, Obadiah, I never would have gotten them kegs off that boat. Powder would have blowed us all up. Being a hero is a funny business, I reckon. Anyway, you're in Texas, or close to it. Pretty soon you'll be settling down in that freedman's town in Colorado."

Denton handed Thomas his empty cup. Lieutenant Ambroise, one of the first passengers he had met on the *Mittie Stephens*, stood a few yards away, staring at the smoking carnage, his boots submerged in shallow water.

"Reckon I won't be goin' to Colorado for a while," Denton said.

"What you mean?" asked Thomas.

"Mean I ain't runnin' no more, Erskine."

"You can't turn yourself in, Obadiah," Thomas said. "You practically free. What about your wife? Think about your boys."

"That's what I'm doin'." Denton took a deep breath, and slowly exhaled. "First, I gotta do some explainin' to Matthew and Emanuel." He held out his hand. "You been a good friend, Robert Erskine Thomas."

Thomas gripped Denton's hand warmly, tightly, then pulled Denton into an embrace. Denton couldn't be sure, but he thought the old mate was bawling like a lamb.

The Army personnel who had been aboard the *Dixie*, along with privates Emmerich and Silvia, worked on the safe, removing the gold then streaming from the wreckage to the Army camp being set up in a nearby clearing. Constantine Ambroise hadn't seen Sergeant Sloan, and knew the big man, his friend, was dead. Probably died a hero. Ambroise vowed to fight to make sure the late Nicholas Sloan received a medal for his bravery. *Bravery. Hero.* The words made Ambroise close his eyes, remembering his own cowardice last night.

"Lieutenant?"

Slowly Ambroise turned toward the ship's musician and carpenter, who stared at him, hands folded at his waist. "I need to speak to you, sir."

Ambroise nodded without interest, and listened to Denton's confession, the words slow to register, the story hard to understand. When the deserter had finished, he stood at attention and announced he was turning himself in. To Ambroise.

"Where are your sons?" Ambroise asked.

"On the *Dixie*. Helpin' their mama."

"Go to them, Mister Denton."

"But. . . ."

"That's an order, mister!" Ambroise's voice carried a sharp edge to it.

"I run," the musician wailed. "I done told my boys what I did. I run away. I'm a deserter, a coward, and I'm ready to take my punishment, face that court-martial, be sent to prison."

Ambroise shook his head. Denton didn't understand. If the fool surrendered, especially being black, he wouldn't only face a court-martial for desertion. Not in this man's army. No, in all likelihood, Obadiah Denton would be accused of cowardice in battle and would be executed by firing squad. And Constantine Ambroise had seen enough people die needlessly.

"You tell your boys that you were a man, and men get scared," Ambroise said. "Sometimes. I was petrified last night. Ten years ago, the Baton Rouge newspapers wrote that Odysseus's blood pumped through my heart. Last night. . . ." Denton stared at him with little comprehension, and Ambroise shook off a headache. "When it counted, Mister Denton, you saved many lives last night, including your family's. I've given you orders, mister. Go to your wife and sons. Forget the Army. Forget San Saba. As far as I care, as far as the Army cares, everyone on that scout died at San Saba. Now get out of here before I change my mind!"

Conversations echoed around Laura. "God have mercy. Half of them must have drowned not knowing how close to land they were." — "Any idea what started it?" — "Pilot said he saw smoke from the hay bales. Some fool with a cigarette, or sparks from the fireboxes or torches." — "Yeah, and, when they hit that sandbar, it sent flames everywhere. Old bucket was a tinderbox."

Laura smelled pipe smoke, and felt slightly comforted, knowing Captain Kellogg stood beside her again. "We'll be shoving off, Miss Wilson," Kellogg told her when she opened her eyes. "There's a berth for you and the children. I'll escort you upstairs, and I thank you for your help today."

Shaking her head at his praise, Laura stared at the shore. The Army had set up tents, had a campfire going, and would guard the dead until another steamboat came to carry the corpses, and the federal payroll, to Jefferson. The *Dixie* would have the honor of bringing in the survivors. Only forty-two.

"Why?" she asked weakly.

"I don't know, ma'am," Kellogg said. "All I know is that I'm quitting the river for good. Twice in my lifetime I've seen this. That's far too much for my old heart."

When Kellogg removed his pipe, Laura kissed his cheek, and let him lead her up the main stairway. They had reached the cabin deck when she heard a shout from the Army camp.

"We've found another survivor!"

She pulled away from Kellogg, and bounded down the stairs, half blinded by tears, by anxiety. She felt numb. *Bobby was a good swimmer,* she told herself. *He could have made it. Maybe his memory plagued him again. A good swimmer. But could anyone have survived the paddle wheels?*

Laura hurried across the deck, bounced off one stunned crew man, raced down the plank. "Where?" she demanded. A shocked private stared at her. "Where is *he?*" She wouldn't even let herself think that the survivor was a woman or child.

"In camp. Captain Andersen's with him."

She cut through the woods to avoid the bodies. Briars scratched her face and hands as she clawed through brambles to the clearing where the Army had set up camp. She smelled wood smoke, boiling coffee, and saw tents, the American flag she had despised for years flapping from a sapling pole.

When she saw him, she slid to a stop at the sight of a man warming his hands over the campfire. Graying black hair — mustache and beard already white — barrel chest — huge arms.

"No!" Laura yelled in rage, thinking: *Nicholas Sloan! Not Nicholas Sloan! Why him? Why not Bobby?*

The man looked up, removed a corncob pipe from his mouth, and Laura blinked. It wasn't Sloan. Only a man who looked like him.

"Aye," the sergeant said, pointing a pipe

stem toward a far tent, "you'd be looking for the Reb."

Laura couldn't move. The tent flap opened, and a figure emerged. Her heart raced, but it wasn't Randow, either, just a portly captain. The officer staggered forward, pushed aside by someone behind him, and Laura's heart fluttered.

Leaning against a thick walking stick for support, Bobby Randow stepped into the afternoon sun, his eyes scanning the camp, white bandage wrapped around his forehead. He coughed slightly, and his eyes locked on her, but his face remained confused.

His memory? Could he have forgotten? Tears started cascading, and Laura held her breath.

Randow straightened in recognition. "Laura!" he shouted, and took a tentative step for her, grimaced, and fell against the Yankee officer for support.

Laura lifted her skirt hems, and ran. The captain righted Randow, let him lean on his shoulder, and started saying something, something about Randow being tougher than a cob, that they had found him a half mile down the shore.

She didn't care about that. Didn't care about anything. She felt surprisingly giddy,

360

thinking about those rich old ladies back in Alexandria, how they would turn up their noses and talk about that crazy, spoiled, unlady-like Laura Parker Kelley. *Running to a man!* Laura didn't care about that, either. All she cared about was Bobby Randow. She wrapped her arms around his neck, and pulled him from the grinning Yankee. She kissed him, told him she loved him, hugged him tighter, kissed him harder.

"Easy," she heard him say. "I'm all stove up, Laura."

She didn't listen, kissed him again, overjoyed, crying, and suddenly he was returning her kisses.

Author's Note

I first discovered the *Mittie Stephens* by accident. In early 1998, I was an assistant sports editor at the *Fort Worth Star-Telegram* working on an outdoors article about Caddo Lake in East Texas. I went to the newspaper morgue to double check outdoor editor Bob Hood's spelling of an Indian tribe, which I found — Bob had it correct, by the way — in the library's *The Handbook of Texas*. Curious, I kept reading and found a brief passage about the 1869 steamboat disaster.

Overly excited, I returned to my desk and informed colleague Mike Bambach of my discovery. Ever the true friend, Mike pretended to be interested, said it sounded like a great story, would make a fine novel, and went back to work.

That ignited what eventually permeated into borderline obsession. The more I researched the *Mittie Stephens*, the more fascinated I became. After pitching a non-fiction article to *True West* magazine, I took my wife on an impromptu weekend vacation to Caddo Lake and Jefferson, where the Jefferson Historical Society Museum allowed me access into the archives. I wrote various libraries and bribed Laura Struck, a good friend in Baton Rouge, to check out the newspapers and city directories in the Louisiana state archives. My article, "Disaster on Caddo Lake: The Burning of the *Mittie Stephens*", appeared in the August 1999 edition of *True West*.

Still, I wasn't satisfied.

So I wrote this novel.

Homer Kellogg was the *Mittie Stephens'* captain, and he did vow to "quit the river for good" after the tragic accident. Pilot William Swain, steersman Joe Lodwick, and clerks Cal Hayes and George Remer were actual people. Hayes was replaced by Remer, who did not survive the disaster. The rest of the characters, however, are purely fictitious, including Robert Erskine Thomas and Obadiah Denton. The real ship's carpenter was named Phillip Hill, and it was he who threw the kegs of gunpowder overboard during the blaze.

The death toll has been estimated from

fifty-six to seventy, but sixty-two is the common figure cited. The gold — reported at anywhere between $40,000 and $100,000 — was transferred to the *Dixie*, captained by Thornton Jacobs, although rumors surfaced that the fortune remained somewhere in Caddo Lake for years.

What caused the fire has never been proved, and the plot to rob the Army payroll is a figment of my imagination. Human carelessness could have been the culprit, or a cinder from the ship's torches or fireboxes. *The Caddo Gazette*, however, reported the true villain was "the passion of the American people for rapid transit, reckless of life and limb. . . . And without wishing to cast unnecessary censure upon the captain of the *Mittie Stephens*, it is certainly true that this disaster was the American system worked out to its terrible accomplishment."

I am grateful to my friend Charlie Powell of Dallas for sharing his unfortunate, first-hand insight into Transient Global Amnesia, or TGA, the modern terminology for the affliction suffered by this novel's Bobby Randow. TGA typically strikes people older than fifty, after a period of high stress or swimming in cold water, constipation, or even sex. Symptoms alleviate usually in less than twenty-four hours, although some recent memory lapses — such as the one in Randow's case — may last longer.

In addition to 1869 newspaper accounts, other primary sources include Louis C. Hunter's *Steamboats on the Western Rivers: An Economic and Technological History*; Fred Dahmer's *Caddo Was . . . : A Short History of Caddo Lake*; Fred Tarpley's *Jefferson: Riverport to the Southwest*; and the pictorial essay "Red River Steamboats" by Eric Brock and Gary Joiner. I found a good starting point in Mark Twain's *Life on the Mississippi*, while *Danger Rides the River*, a novel by Les Savage, Jr., provided more information on steamboats than any riverboat pilot could, and, like Twain's masterpiece, is a fabulous read.

Many thanks to the aforementioned Laura Struck for her research help, and the staffs at the Dallas, New Orleans, Santa Fe, and Shreveport public libraries; the National Archives; the State Library of Louisiana; Louisiana State University–Shreveport Archives and Special Collections; University of Wisconsin–La Crosse Murphy Library–Special Collections; Howard Steamboat Museum in Jefferson,

Indiana; Caddo Lake State Park; and the Jefferson Historical Society Museum; as well as the friendly Texans of Jefferson and Uncertain.

Johnny D. Boggs
Santa Fe, New Mexico

About the Author

In addition to writing Western novels, Johnny D. Boggs covered all aspects of the American West for newspapers and magazines on topics ranging from travel to book and movie reviews, to celebrity and historical profiles, to the apparel industry and environmental issues.

Born in South Carolina in 1962, he published his first Western short story in 1983 in the University of South Carolina student literary magazine. Since then, he has had more than twenty short stories published in magazines and anthologies, including *Louis L'Amour Western Magazine*. After graduating from the University of South Carolina College of Journalism in 1984, Boggs moved to Texas to begin a newspaper career. He started as a sportswriter for the *Dallas Times Herald* in 1984 and was assistant sports editor when the newspaper folded in 1991. From 1992 to

1998, he worked for the *Fort Worth Star-Telegram*, leaving the newspaper as assistant sports editor to become a full-time writer and photographer. His photos often accompany his newspaper and magazine articles.

He won a Spur Award from Western Writers of America for his short story, "A Piano at Dead Man's Crossing" in 2002. He won the Western Heritage Award from the Cowboy Hall of Fame for his novel, *Spark on the Prairie*, published in 2003. He lives in Sante Fe, New Mexico, with his wife, Lisa Smith, and their son, Jack.